*This book is dedicated to the Peacock family
and my husband, Ken.*

Parading fanned feathers,

Sapphire eyes open,

The Peacock carries its burden of vanity

Vigilant, ready to scream.

INTRODUCTION

This is a story loosely based on the Peacock family, a family as old as Chicago. Born in 1837, the city and family grew side by side, undergoing tremendous physical and cultural changes. Even before Elijah Peacock arrived at the tip of Lake Michigan, the region was subject to radical change. In less than 30 years, it passed from French to British and then to American control. When Illinois became a state in 1818, it was noted for its fur trade, but fourteen years later, the game had all been killed off and that trade ended. Settlers moved in to take advantage of the flat farmland only to find that its soil drained poorly. The thick layer of clay that the retreating glaciers had deposited in the last Ice Age was practically impermeable.

Early Chicagoans coped with swampy conditions by building wooden sidewalks and covering their streets with planks. The high water table led city dwellers to take the drastic measure of raising buildings, some as high as fourteen feet off the ground. Sewage disposal was another unanticipated problem. Dumping waste into the Chicago River was hardly a solution. The river's "lazy" flow rate couldn't dissipate the putrid odors fast enough. Local Indians recognized this problem head-on and named the city Chicago, meaning "skunk, smelly place." Recently, some have suggested the name was a corruption of "shitago."

In chapter one, Safi doesn't ask why Elijah Peacock emigrated from England, but rather why he chose to settle in Chicago. Upon arriving on the Atlantic coast, he could have overheard soldiers returning east from the Black Hawk War. Yet why would their promise of cheap land

and adventure on the southern shores of Lake Michigan tempt a third-generation jeweler and watch repairman to choose a destination that required an arduous journey overland? Or did Elijah go to Chicago by water? By 1825, the Erie Canal linked the Hudson River to the Great Lakes, allowing a continuous water passage from New York Harbor to Chicago. If he had arrived by water, he would not have done so in the winter when ice stopped all shipping on Lake Michigan.

However it came about, the general timing of Elijah's arrival was fortuitous. 1837 was the year that Chicago was incorporated as a city. A prior speculation bubble had just burst. Land sold for 5% of its value in the previous year. Elijah was nineteen-years old, eager to go into business.

Like other immigrants, he took advantage of the new balloon-frame construction methods, circular steam saw, and machine-cut nails. He built a two-story building in ten days. His living quarters were on the top level above his shop—*The House of Peacock*. Sometime within that first year his wife, Rebecca, arrived from England with their newborn son, Charles Daniel Peacock, later known simply as CD.

It took the city twelve years to construct the Illinois and Michigan Canal. Once completed in 1848, Lake Michigan was connected to the Mississippi River. Cattle yards and steam-powered grain elevators became part of the landscape. The new steel plows helped homesteaders on the prairie grow wheat and corn. Chicago soon became the largest lumber, grain, and pork market in the world. The creation of new jobs attracted immigrants. Chicago's population more than tripled in just six years.

Two more Peacock children were born before Rebecca died of consumption in 1850. At that time, trains already had begun to supersede the Illinois and Michigan Canal. Railroads coming from the northeast were required to go around Lake Michigan's southern tip. Chicago was the obvious nexus for commerce and passengers, linking eastern markets with western resources. No matter from which direction a train came, Chicago was the final terminal. Passengers going beyond the city would have to change to another rail company. By 1857, almost 100 trains entered and left Chicago each day. Rail travel brought even more immigrants.

It appears that Elijah recovered quickly from the loss of his first wife. Two years later he married an 18-year-old German girl, Mary Kolze. Ten years later still, Mary had given birth to four more Peacock children.

This story is about the Peacock family as it was in the mid-twentieth century, when it started to let go of its former power and prestige and awakened to the contributions from all its members. Like families everywhere, its current form can only be truly understood when its past secrets and ordeals are revealed.

CHAPTER 1

LATE SUMMER, 1950

Safi ran to catch her bus, giving her the perfect excuse to avoid talking to Officer Murphy, who was running after her. As soon as she jumped on board, the door shut and the bus took off.

"You're too young to be in that kind of trouble. What'd you do, steal a lollypop?" The bus driver chuckled.

"Thank you," said Safi flashing him her bus pass before collapsing into the nearest seat, too out of breath to say more. She placed her book bag on the floor between her feet and glanced at her watch. She had enough time to get to her class. Out of habit, she tracked the progress of the bus in getting across town. In this area there were 3- and 4-story apartment buildings, each smack up against the other. No yards separated the sidewalk from the buildings. She suspected an alley ran flush with their back side as well. As unattractive as they were, their structures appeared more substantial than the buildings on Maxwell and Halsted Streets where she grew up. Now that she thought of it, Mrs. M's apartment building was also unattractive. It was red brick without recesses or bay windows. Not even trim around the windows softened its flat façade.

For close to four years now, Safi had been living with Letitia Peacock Mercer, or Mrs. M, as she had come to think of her. Back when they were first introduced, her guardian had explained that the Peacock family "was one of the founding families of Chicago with a reputation for integrity." At this recollection, a snorting laugh involuntarily erupted from Safi and caused the woman sitting next to her to shift away. The family might be refined, she thought, but one of its members was a murderer!

What rotten luck to have Patrick Murphy see her coming out of the police station. Of course he will want to know what she was up to, being a policeman. Unfortunately, he was also a friend of Mrs. M's, and Safi knew it was best not to let Mrs. M know of her suspicions. She needed more time to gather information. How did her involvement with the Peacocks get so messy? Her mind drifted back to when it began.

SEPTEMBER, 1946

One rainy Saturday morning, Safi stayed in bed later than usual. Her roommates left the room quietly for their early shifts so Safi could continue to sleep. Once she heard the door finally close, she quickly rose, put her sweater on over her PJs, and made her bed. A minute later she was curled up in the chair with her book.

The room held four cots and a chair. There was no space for a dresser, so each woman kept a box for her personal belongings under her cot. That suited Safi fine. At eighteen she had few belongings but boundless energy. She relished having time to sit in the chair, not to rest but to read, and sometimes to draw. Even those nights when she found it difficult to sleep, she could catch the moonlight on her sketch pad if seated in the chair. Positioned at an angle to the window, she could also easily keep tabs on the bustling street activity below.

Hull House, located on Halsted Street, the center of Chicago's Near West Side, was both Safi's home and place of work. It was conceived in 1889 by Jane Addams to offer neighborhood immigrants social and educational opportunities. It was not a house for orphans. But the current director, who had been a "comrade-in-arms" of Safi's parents before they died, made an exception and allowed her to live in the settlement house, at least until she finished high school.

When Hull House was founded, the Near West Side was filled with German immigrants. Years later, they were replaced by Irish immigrants, who later moved still further west to the "greener pastures" of

Englewood. Now Poles, Lithuanians, and Negroes dominated the area. Safi, however, was a descendant of one of the original German families.

Gazing out the window, she noticed a taxi come to a stop in front of the building's entrance. How unusual, she thought. People in this neighborhood never use taxis. The windshield wipers continued to sweep away the rain while an elderly woman with white wavy hair stepped out. She wore a brown raincoat. Safi thought she had very white skin and rather full lips, but it was difficult to see clearly through the rain. After paying the cab driver, the lady went right in to Hull House without hesitation.

Safi read another chapter of her book before her attention was drawn again to the window. By now it had stopped raining. Another taxi pulled up. It waited in front of the building with the motor running. Nothing happened, so Safi went back to reading her book. Then she heard voices at the entrance. Christi Kochs, the director of Hull House, helped the woman in the brown raincoat to the taxi. Her coat was no longer buttoned up. Safi caught a glimpse of a pearl necklace on a dark dress. The two women smiled at each other, seemingly pleased with their meeting. With the window closed, Safi couldn't hear their conversation.

Later in the day, Christi asked her to step into her office. "I don't want you to think that we want to get rid of you, Safi, but an opportunity has opened up that you may be interested in." It was then that Safi first learned of Mrs. Mercer. "She's a widow who lives on the Near North Side, right near Clark Street. She has a small apartment and an extra bedroom off the kitchen. You do cook, don't you Safi?"

"Yes, I know how to cook several things, not everything, but my mom and I used to share the cooking."

"Good. Well, I know you can clean. You certainly do a fine job here cleaning."

"Thank you."

"Mrs. Mercer will give you free room and board if you clean, cook, and type for her. She's writing a book."

"Really?"

"There's something else, something I think you will like." Safi's ears perked up. "She will pay for two college courses a semester."

"That's wonderful!" Safi had always wanted to get a college education, but with her parents gone now, she didn't know how that would ever be possible.

"Before you get too excited, we had better go interview Mrs. Mercer. She may not be to your liking. We need to look over her place. I know that area is not very safe."

"Yes, I have heard about Clark Street," Safi said.

"By the way, Mrs. Mercer's full name is Letitia Peacock Mercer. That may not mean anything to you, but the Peacocks are a well-established family who have been in the jewelry business here for generations."

Two mornings later, Safi and the director emerged from the subway at Clark and Division, and started walking north on Clark Street. Both were silent but alert. When they turned at the corner of Schiller, their pace relaxed. Still, they had to pass a broken whiskey bottle and dodge spit, but Schiller at least had two trees. Mrs. Mercer's building was the second one in from the corner. It bordered an alley that bisected the block.

"There's a small bedroom off the kitchen for Safi," Mrs. Mercer said apologetically. Safi suppressed a smile so she wouldn't appear too eager. It had a real bed, a bedside table with a lamp, a dresser, and a small closet—more room and privacy than she had known since her father died. In the bathroom and kitchen, Safi looked for but saw no signs of cockroaches. The furniture in Mrs. Mercer's bedroom and the living room was ornate and delicate. At one point they were asked to sit down. Safi chose the couch. It was so tightly upholstered all she could do was perch. "Empire," Mrs. Mercer explained, in what Safi thought might be a French accent.

Safi returned to Hull House briefly to say goodbye and gather her belongings. She assured her friend Mel and the others that she would try to return each Sunday afternoon so she could continue tutoring children. It was sad leaving her old neighborhood. Hull House had been more than her home for the last three years. Both of her parents had been deeply involved in its activities when they were alive. Her mother had been their typist for at least 15 years. As a community and union organizer, her father held most of his meetings at the settlement home.

During the first few months after she moved in, Safi began to refer to Mrs. Mercer as Mrs. M, and shortened her first name, Letitia, to Letty, in her thoughts. As different as they were, they actually got on quite well together. They both could work side-by-side at the kitchen table without one disturbing the other. Safi noticed that Letty was most productive in the morning. Then, around eleven, she started sipping sherry. At times later in the day, she sat quietly for a half-hour or so in the wing-back chair, legs crossed at the knee, covered from neck to toes in her elegant but worn bathrobe, lost in thought, with a bemused smile on her face. At such moments Safi hoped she was at least enjoying a happy memory. Safi made several secret sketches of Letty in the winged-back chair.

In winter the apartment was cold in the early morning. Only after 6:00 A.M. did the radiators start clanging, trying to heat the place. Safi often got up early so she could work for a few hours before Mrs. M rose. Sometimes she pulled the blanket from her bed and wrapped herself in it until the apartment warmed up. She and her mom had also been cold during the winter in their little apartment. In those days, it was her mom who got up early and Safi who awoke to the tapping of typewriter keys. Her mom typed students' theses, in addition to her regular job at Hull House. Safi could remember her joking that she moonlighted best at sunrise ... a thought that threatened to send her day into a sad spiral. There was some irony in all this, though. Now she was the early rising typist and an old woman, not her mother, was sleeping in. Safi shut the kitchen door so her typing didn't awaken Mrs. M, but she could do nothing about the radiators' irregular thumps....

She started typing the third chapter of Mrs. M's book. The title page said: *One's Family (A Family Journal)* by Letitia Peacock Mercer. Safi speculated that Mrs. M would have copies of the book bound—but not with the thick binding used for theses. She wondered how many copies she would have printed. The book should be less than 300 pages when finished, she thought. Mrs. M had already been working on it for three years. "Doing research took up at least two years," she commented to someone on the phone. Once it was written, what would Mrs. M do? Maybe she would no longer need her help.

After five months, Safi felt comfortable living with Mrs. M, in spite of her drinking. It was easy to clean for someone who spent her days writing and reading. The typing went well. She thought Letitia was an engaging writer, witty and amusing, but at times, the content of the book troubled her. Sometimes Mrs. M wanted Safi's opinion about a particular passage. That was awkward. Safi wanted to be supportive, but what can you say that is tactful about exaggerated claims and outright boasting? Why did she want to aggrandize her family? When she described Elijah Peacock's first born son, Charles Daniel Peacock (usually called CD), Mrs. M wrote: "He was an upright citizen and astute businessman who 'set the standard for honesty and integrity in the Chicago business world.'" When one of her relatives died, Mrs. M said the family received "personal notes from several of the royalty of Europe, including a long letter from Queen Victoria." Safi typed it, but she simply couldn't believe such nonsense was true.

Also troubling were some glaring omissions. "In 1837, at the age of 19, Elijah Peacock left Huntingdon, England, to make a new life for himself in Chicago." Why did Elijah come to Chicago? The city had only 4,000 people in 1837. What attracted him to what in those days was a stinky, muddy frontier town? Perhaps Mrs. M didn't know the answer. Nonetheless, she should have posed the question. She devoted six paragraphs to Elijah's pedigree before she plainly stated: "As a third generation jeweler and watch repairer, Elijah opened up his store at 155½ Lake Street—The House of Peacock."

By now Safi knew some of Letitia's stories by heart. She liked the one about the gambler:

> *Quite early in the days of Elijah's business, he sold a five-hundred-dollar diamond to a gambler who had the stone made up into a ring. The gambler never paid Elijah for the stone, although pressed to do so several times. One day in a cloud of dust, the gambler stopped short in front of Elijah's little shop, dismounted from his horse, and hurriedly entered the store.*
>
> *'Peacock, Peacock,' he bellowed, 'I have to leave town in a hurry. No time to lose! Have no money and I have lost the stone. Want to do what I can, but I have little left—practically nothing! Here's the deed to some property that I bought. Take it. It's not worth much, but I will see what I can do later.'*
>
> *The gambler was out of the store almost as soon as he came in, off in another cloud of dust. Great-grandfather put away the deed, but never heard from the gambler again.*
>
> *Years later, Elijah realized that it had some value. It was a large tract of land around 37th Street and Shields Avenue. Eventually Elijah built his farm on one corner. The Pennsylvania Railroad leased part of the land for their switches and switch-tracks and the rest became the factory sites of two large Chicago companies. The rentals and leases brought in a steady income for Elijah for many years.*

A fun story, Safi thought, but she didn't believe Elijah would have given the gambler the stone without getting paid for it. Typing Mrs. M's manuscript, Safi had no doubt that Letitia hoped to establish that the family had "superior" lineage, but her unequal treatment of various members was suspicious. She would spend pages discussing the aristocratic roots of some distant relative while neglecting to give the name of someone closely linked but of a lower social status. Safi wanted to know about Elijah's second wife and their children. Mrs. M only referred to them as the "second family."

of "quiet elegance," but Safi wasn't fooled. Shoppers had to pay heavily for the privilege of seeing this "quiet elegance." Nothing cheap here, she thought.

"I'm so glad to see you Walter, before Safi and I have to go home."

"Hello Safi. You two can't go home without having lunch with me."

"Oh, do you have time? Could we take you to lunch?"

"No, no, you two must be my guests. I'd like to take you to the Palmer House Café."

"Well, that's very nice. If you insist, that would be lovely."

"Meet me here in…," he paused to check his watch, and then checked it with the standing clock beside the elevator. Walter prided himself on being the expert on timepieces at CD Peacock's. "Meet me here in one hour, around 12:17, and we'll walk through together."

Through? That's a funny way of putting it, Safi thought. Then she remembered that there was another set of peacock doors at the other end of the store that led directly into the Palmer House. From *One's Family* she seemed to remember that Potter Palmer, when building his new luxury hotel, invited CD to relocate Peacock's, offering him the State and Monroe corner of the Palmer House.

Mrs. M directed Safi toward a display of men's jewelry. Standing behind it was her first cousin Blair Davis. He had blondish-gray hair, a welcoming smile, and wore a silver lapel pin of a rearing horse. Good heavens, is living with Mrs. M making me pay attention to jewelry? Safi asked herself.

The three of them talked about the weather, but when the conversation turned to Letty's Aunt Bertha (Mr. Davis' mother), Safi lost interest. Next she vaguely heard them talk about another relative, Bernard Peacock—something to do with ice fishing in Wisconsin. Safi moved away slightly and gazed at the items in the case. There was quite a display of men's gold necklaces and numerous items with rearing stallions on them, even a silver belt buckle where the tongue looked like it was an extension of the horse's—oh my God! She started to laugh but saw Mr. Davis watching her so she quickly looked away. She walked slowly over to look at another case. Maybe if you're a Peacock you can get away with that, she thought. If Letitia knew, it certainly wouldn't appear in *One's Family*. Personally, "faygeles" didn't bother her at all. She remembered Mrs. M telling her that her cousin Blair was the buyer for the jewelry store. Safi wondered whether Walter Peacock "realized."

Minutes passed before Safi became aware that a man was standing quite near, looking at her. Letitia turned from Mr. Davis and walked over to Safi, introducing her to the man. William Thatcher was in his early forties with a pencil mustache and rimless glasses. He could have been an accountant. Safi suddenly remembered who he was and without thinking blurted out: "Oh Mr. Thatcher, you are the treasurer." Immediately, Safi realized that she should have just remained quiet.

"No, that's my father, but I am good with figures." Safi noticed Blair roll his eyes and Mrs. M looked annoyed.

"Yes, William, this is Safi Winter, who lives with me," Letty said. Turning to Safi, she added: "William's wife, Cornelia, is my relative. She also works in the store, in the gift department on the second floor. Is she here today, William?"

"Yes, let me show you where she is," he suggested while keeping his eyes on Safi.

"And where is Charles?" Letitia asked.

"Out having a bit of sport with mommy-in-law at Arlington Park, I believe. She just went for the third race today. 'Blue Lightning is a sure win,' she said, or something of the sort. Anyway, they should be back at three." He seemed to avoid looking directly at Mrs. M even though she was questioning him, and he ignored Blair completely. "Let's go up and see Cornie." He proceeded to the elevator. They followed after him, although Safi noticed a degree of hesitancy on Letty's part.

In the elevator, William again stood uncomfortably close to Safi. "You both must be terribly hot in your coats. You could leave them in the staff room up where we're going, if you would like." Safi welcomed the suggestion and started loosening her scarf and unbuttoning her coat until she noticed William watching her hands. *Oy!* On Maxwell

Street we have a name for this type: *schürzenjager!*

Cornelia turned out to be in quite a state at the moment they encountered her. A pretty woman with soft blond hair and deep brown eyes, she was frantic, having just been told that one of her and William's five children had become ill at school and needed to be taken home as soon as possible. She turned to William and asked his help in solving the problem. He was very obliging, Safi was glad to see.

"...and then drop the two of us at home? I'll just have to miss another half-day of work, but there is nothing that can be done about it."

"Certainly. I'll go tell Walter and meet you at the Monroe Street entrance."

Mrs. M wanted to stay on the 2nd floor until Cornelia and William were out of the building, "so we don't delay their departure." She said the gift department was where women came to select stem- and flatware, china, and stationary. "Cornelia deals mainly with stationery. She has good taste and an eye for design, but it's difficult for her to work more than a few days a week." Safi guessed that the store was flexible about her work schedule because she was a Peacock. This would never happen on Maxwell Street. She could hear her father bemoan the firing of factory workers if they missed just a few hours to care for a sick child. The family employees of CD Peacock's didn't have to unionize.

Back on the first floor, Mrs. M placed an order with Blair for some silver cufflinks that looked like ice skates. She wanted them sent to Bernard Peacock, and turning to Safi she said: "Bernard's my first cousin, once removed." Safi's family had never used such terms. Aunts, uncles, cousins, and grandparents were all they ever talked about. To Mrs. M it was important to delineate connections precisely. Safi asked her why silver skates?

"You remember that Elijah Peacock won the Silver Skates Contest?'

"Yes. Let's see, soon after he arrived from England, wasn't it?"

"It was in 1840. Well, our Bernard is also an excellent skater—the talent has skipped three generations."

CHAPTER 2

Like last year, after his father died, Bernard planned to spend the final part of his Christmas break up at Dartford Lake, Wisconsin, where the Peacocks had a summer home called Sugar Loaf. It was a 40-acre property, mostly woods, comprising a large hill on a peninsula into Dartford Lake. From across the lake, everyone thought it looked like a big lump: hence the name Sugar Loaf. His three great-aunts, Mamie, Boots, and Ella, owned the place and paid all the expenses. In September, the aunts repaired to the Pearson Hotel in Chicago and the main house was closed for the winter. The aunts always returned to Sugar Loaf in late May.

Their caretakers, Freddy and Marjorie Faber, lived on the property year-round and always welcomed Bernard to stay in their small home. Their house was so cluttered with knickknacks, mementos, photos, and sewing projects that when he arrived, Bernard left his skates and cross-country skis on the back porch. It never occurred to the Fabers that there might not be room for Bernard. At night they sat close together by the wood-burning stove. They each took turns cracking open hickory nuts with a handmade device that Freddy had fashioned. The grounds of Sugar Loaf were covered in hickory trees. Marjorie started collecting the nuts in late summer.

By the end of December, most of the lake was topped by four inches of ice. The day after Christmas, people started arriving, asking Freddy if they could park their cars at Sugar Loaf so they could ice fish. Freddy would only give permission if he thought the ice was thick enough. Once given, some friends dragged small shanties on sleds out onto the lake. Most fishermen, however, did not bother with a shanty.

By 4:00 P.M., they would have had enough of sitting on the ice and were looking forward to a hot cooked meal in a warm home and a decent bed to sleep in.

Dartford Lake is deepest and the third largest lake in Wisconsin. To get to the town of Dartford on the other side from Sugar Loaf took 25 minutes driving on the road, but only 10 minutes over the ice. In January and February, cars could be seen crossing one way or the other.

Ice fishing was a social activity, enabling the fishermen to maintain the holiday spirit until March. There was a fair amount of drinking. Stories were told and retold. A few men kept it simple and carried onto the ice only a jig, line, pole, small stool, bait, and a drill and saw for cutting a hole. Some, usually of Scandinavian descent, didn't socialize at all, but enjoyed the sport for the solitary contemplation it afforded.

For Bernard, the pleasure came from the camaraderie more than the fishing. When the men let him, he used their holes to collect samples of lake water. For as long as anyone could remember, Sugar Loaf got its water from the lake. A pipe went out 75 yards or so into the deep. A pump on shore extracted water from the lake and stored it in a holding tank. For three years, Bernard took his water-testing kit with him so he could measure the hardness, pH, and purity of the lake. He now had adequate proof, he thought, that the lake water was not good enough to drink and was getting worse. In the summer, he hoped to convince Boots (Aunt Bertha) of the need to convert to well water. Boots was the tough one. She had a forceful personality. Once she was convinced, Bernard figured, the others would go along with the plan. Aunt Bertha ruled.

On the cold New Year's Eve morning of 1947, Bernard sat on a stool in front of an ice hole dangling a line. If truth be known, he had little interest in catching a fish. There was no one nearby with whom he might strike up a conversation. The morning was not only cold but windless. The sole distraction Bernard could find was his breathing. With each exhalation he noticed more moisture was expelled than the air at that temperature could hold. His breath could probably be spotted fifty feet away, he figured. Soon he felt some degree of pain in his throat when he inhaled. This happened to him often when he skated in Lincoln Park. He knew what to do, and adjusted the wrapping of his scarf so that it covered his mouth and nose, as well as his neck.

Now that he was more comfortable, Bernard felt able to tackle his problem with Uncle Walter and his extended family of Peacocks. Aunt Mamie was married to Uncle Ed, who could barely hear. They had no children. Aunt Ella had married Ed's brother, Uncle Toby. Uncle Toby had been a "lamb pot" (an affectionate term among the Peacocks). He looked like Bing Crosby and he loved children, which was sad, because he and Ella never had any. No one knew whether it was the sisters or the brothers who were sterile. Chances are that it was the brothers, Bernard thought, because the third sister, Aunt Bertha, did have a child: Blair. Boots' husband was Brode Davis. Bernard remembered Aunt Letitia's description of Brode. Like most of Aunt Letty's descriptions, it was suspiciously generous: "He was a sharp, brilliant, and fine lawyer, and was considered at one time to be one of the West's most silver-tongued orators." Both great-uncles, Brode and Toby, were now dead—only Uncle Ed was left. Of the six children born to CD Peacock, three men and three women, only the great-aunties were still living and they were all in their seventies.

Uncle Walter was concerned that Bernard was the only male Peacock of the fourth generation to carry on the Peacock name. His uncle constantly suggested that Bernard work in the store so there would be more of a Peacock presence there. For a long time Bernard thought his uncle was saying this out of pity, trying to make him feel part of the larger family, now that both his parents were dead.

Was Uncle Walter right that he was the last Peacock? Bernard opened his lab book and turned to the last page. He normally didn't approve of writing extraneous items in a lab book. It should only be used for recording data, but he was out on the ice, sitting on a stool. To go back to the house just for a sheet of paper was more trouble than it was worth. So keeping his mittens on, he sketched an abbreviated family tree as best he could. He found himself using the eraser of his pencil as much as the lead. Finally, he thought he had gotten it right:

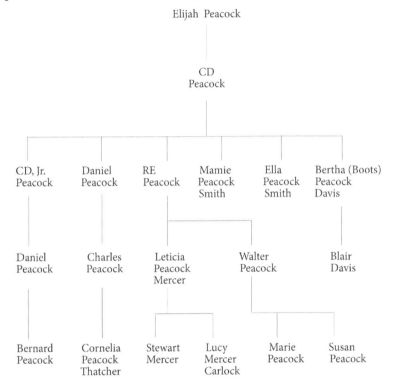

Yes, he *was* the last man with a Peacock surname. His cousin Stewart, Aunt Letty's son, was a Mercer. This made Bernard aware that the custom of women adopting their husbands' surnames upon marriage caused many difficulties.

What Bernard liked about the jewelry business was not the sort of thing his Uncle Walter would want him to pursue. The study of crystals, rocks, and minerals fascinated him. He thought about accommodating his uncle by becoming a gemologist, but identifying different types of gemstones and their imitations would capture his interest only for awhile. He would enjoy learning how to differentiate between natural gems and ones that had been treated to enhance color or clarity. Examining optical, surface, and internal characteristics could be intriguing, but for a lifetime? No. He didn't care about the value of gems. Designing and making jewelry held no interest for him, and as for selling it, absolutely not!

The person who claimed to be a gemologist was William, Cornelia's husband. But as far as Bernard could tell, William didn't do much other than walk around the store's main floor. William could change his surname to Peacock. So could Blair or Stewart. It just doesn't need to depend only on me, he thought.

Bernard's father had also decided not to get involved in the jewelry business. He followed his interests and became a librarian. Bernard could just hear the family's reaction to that decision. LIBRARIAN! Aunt Letty was the only one who understood. She loved doing research in libraries. Too bad she didn't research anything important. Why she thought the Peacocks deserved so much of her time he would never know. At least writing *One's Family* gave her something to focus on.

Bernard just couldn't please his uncle. In the fall of 1945, the year his father died, he had started teaching chemistry at the Chicago Latin School. He liked teenagers, and he loved having summers free for travel, camping in the wilderness, and bird watching. He liked living in the city and being close to his work. As a housing activist, he could use Chicago's excellent public transportation system to get to meetings and protests easily no matter where they were held, and only use his car when absolutely necessary. He had no desire to live in the suburbs. Some friends suggested that he pursue a career in research, but he enjoyed people too much to be shut up in a lab, wearing a lab coat, and watching liquids bubble. Bernard was pleased with his decisions. What he had chosen to do was well-suited to his personality and interests.

CHAPTER 3

1947

Letty was glad Safi had chosen to go to Loyola, although she had hoped to send her to a college with more prestige, like Northwestern or the University of Chicago. She quickly discovered the tuitions at such universities were much more than she could afford. Loyola had additional advantages. Safi only had to walk four short blocks to catch the #23 bus on Lake Shore Drive. With good timing, she could be in the lecture hall a half hour after leaving home. Another benefit that Letty hadn't thought of until Safi pointed it out was that most of the students at Loyola had either full- or part-time jobs, so Safi felt she fit in better.

Before Safi came to live with her, Letty used to call up a local market that would deliver groceries. Her sherry could be ordered at the same time. Now Safi did the shopping and saved the bills for Letty's inspection. There was no question about it, Safi saved Letty money, but she flat-out refused to buy her sherry. "It's too heavy for me to carry and it's not good for you," she said. Letty's way around this hitch was to order several bottles from her old expensive market and have them delivered when Safi was in school. She hid them under her bed. Of course Safi knew about her stash within days. She was far too thorough a cleaner not to notice. Neither of them mentioned it.

Safi was a decent cook. They enjoyed eating dinner together at the kitchen table, chatting about the day's goings-on. Over the first two semesters, Letty learned she could trust Safi. She was unusually mature for her age, perhaps too serious. Letty had been much more frivolous at Safi's age, although just as keen about learning. Safi worked hard at her studies. Unquestionably, she valued the education she was getting.

When summertime came, Letty wanted to spend as much time as

possible at Sugar Loaf. This was her chance to be in the country, catch up with the relatives, and frankly, live at the expense of her aunts. She planned to go up there before Safi finished summer school, leaving Safi by herself for a couple of months. "You could have a small vacation before your classes start in the fall by coming up to Sugar Loaf. Would you like that?"

"Oh, yes," was Safi's immediate reply.

Letty suggested that she take the train up to Princeton, Wisconsin, where she could be picked up and driven to Sugar Loaf. She reminded Safi that her grandfather, CD, had bought the place in 1882, as a summer home for the entire Peacock family. "Only three of Grandfather's six children are still living: Mamie, Ella, and Boots. My father was one of CD's three sons. Sadly, all the sons have died." Letty had already told Safi several stories about her aunts and the house.

"There are two piers: visitors by boat land at the one in front of the house and that's where the mail is delivered."

"Mail is delivered there?" Safi questioned.

"Yes, you'll see the mailbox at the end of the pier."

"The other pier, on the south side of the house, gets more sun. As kids we called that one 'freckly pier.'"

Safi immediately asked about swimming. She had only gone swimming twice in her life—both times in Lake Michigan, once with her mother and once with a group of friends from Hull House. "I'm a little bit afraid of the waves," she admitted.

"Dartford Lake is calmer and there is no beach. At Sugar Loaf, the shoreline is rocky and the rocks are slimy. Most everybody gets in the water by jumping off the pier."

"Is it over your head?"

"Yes, but you can come right out by climbing up the steps."

"I'll need to buy a swimsuit. When should I come?"

"As soon as you want after your exams."

"Who will be there?"

"The three aunts, of course, and Uncle Ed, Mamie's husband,

Bernard will already have returned to Chicago, but I think the Thatchers will still be there. They have five children."

"Oh yes, I remember William," Safi moaned.

"Don't worry, everybody is wary of William."

"Can I bring my books?"

All she does is think about her studies, she really needs to have more fun in her life, thought Letty, remembering all the parties and gaiety she had experienced when she was Safi's age.

"Of course. All the aunts are eager to have you come."

In truth Aunt Ella was eager to have Safi come, but Letty had not consulted the others.

"That's a lot of people to be in their house all at once. How will they manage?"

"The main house has eight bedrooms and five baths," she replied. "Each bedroom has at least two beds in it. It's big but not fancy. The house has just simple country furniture."

Now was not the time to tell Safi about the jewel hunt that Aunt Mamie was planning. How would Safi react to it? Letty continued to worry about Safi. Her background is so very different, she thought. From some of the things Safi had said over the last several months, Letty concluded that Safi was a socialist. She hoped that William wouldn't catch wind of that. He could be ruthless. Only the defense of capitalism could distract William from his usual womanizing pursuits. Oh well, no point in worrying about such things now, Letty told herself. Nothing may happen.

"How old are the aunts?"

"They're in their seventies," Letty answered.

"Oh, close to your age then."

Letty bristled but tried not to show it. She considered herself a generation younger than the aunts. Letty was only 55, for heaven's sake! As soon as Safi left the room, Letty went to her mirror to check her wrinkles.

The previous fall at the annual Thanksgiving gathering of the

Peacocks, Aunt Mamie had made the startling announcement that she intended to sponsor jewel hunts at Dartford Lake. There would be one hunt per summer for each of the next five years. The specific day set aside for the hunt would be announced in April so anyone interested in participating could arrange their summer vacations accordingly. Mamie would hide a jewel somewhere on Sugar Loaf: either inside the main house or on the grounds. Once someone found a gem, they could not be the winner of another hunt and they were expected to sell the gem before the following summer.

This summer marked the first hunt. Letty was not surprised at which relatives showed up. Cornelia and William Thatcher were always pressed for money because they had five children. Also, because of the five children, they had a decided advantage—seven pairs of eyes to help find the gem. Cornelia's mother, Aunt Gertrude, stayed home. Her favorite activity was betting on the horses at Arlington Park Race Track, which put Cornelia's father, Charles, under considerable financial strain. Charles showed up. Letty's nephew Bernard stayed home. He had already spent a few weeks at Sugar Loaf and was ready for the adventures of backcountry camping. Bernard wasn't interested in money. He had plenty of it and spent little. Walter, Letty's brother and president of CD Peacock's, showed up, not because he needed money, but because he wanted to stay on top of things and know what the family was up to. Blair Davis, Boots' son, came with his old friend Tom Hartley, who could only be a witness, as only a Peacock relative could win. Letty, of course, made sure she was there. She needed money.

The jewel for the first hunt—the hunt of the summer of 1947—was an alexandrite. Letty was not familiar with this stone, so she looked it up in the library before she left Chicago. Evidently the color of an alexandrite changes, depending on light. In daylight it will appear green/blue, but in artificial light it will seem red/orange. She read that the gem was discovered relatively recently, in the 1830s in Russia, and was named in honor of Alexander II. Aunt Mamie said that the alexandrite that she would hide was 5.2 carats. Of course, Letty knew that the weight of a gemstone is measured in carats, but how heavy is a carat? she asked herself. Ah, here it is, "exactly one-fifth of a gram." She read on: " 'Carat' is a corruption of 'carob.' For over a thousand years, carob seeds were sold in all the bazaars of the Middle East. Since they were both light and uniform, they became ideal for weighing jewels."

The day of the hunt, Letty gathered with the rest of the family in the dining room. At 9:00 A.M. sharp, Aunt Mamie carried in a tray and placed it in the middle of the table. On the tray were slips of paper. Written on each slip in a wobbly handwriting was the same clue:

CD waited without alarm

"Just four words!" someone complained.

"It doesn't make sense!"

"I don't know where to start!"

Family members milled around. After a few minutes they dispersed to other parts of the house. Several went outdoors. All were deep in thought.

Walter, however, was on another bent. When he arrived at the Loaf this summer, the grandfather clock in the living room was keeping the same time as his watch, up until this morning, that is. Walter was in the dining room precisely at 9:00, when the clues had been placed on the tray. He picked up a clue, read it, and then the grandfather clock in the living room chimed. Hmm, three minutes late, he said to himself.

Forgetting the hunt altogether he went to the clock. He turned the nut to the right to push the bob up, so the clock would speed up. Then he asked himself: how could the pendulum all of the sudden become too heavy? He felt the back side of the bob's disk and found the alexandrite taped to it

So the first gem to be hidden was found by Letty's brother Walter, who needed another jewel as much as a beach needs a grain of sand. Yet the others were pleased to see Walter more excited than he had been in years. By dinner time, he had retold the story of his discovery at least five times.

Letty overheard Mamie complain to Boots: "I don't regret that Walter found the gem, or that he found the gem so quickly, but he did so without using my clue."

"Not only that," Boots commented, "but Letty had to explain to him, that 'waited' meant 'weighted' and that 'CD' referred to the 'grandfather' clock."

When Safi arrived at Sugar Loaf, only Letty, the aunts, and Uncle Ed were still there. She was given the bedroom next to Letty's on the second floor. Letty heard Safi mumble: "Imagine, a house with two sets of stairs."

For the rest of that day and the next, Letty watched Safi wander around when she wasn't reading on the porch or in the living room. It occurred to Letty that Safi hadn't had much experience with leisure. There was no one her age to talk with. Uncle Ed must have also noticed, because by the second afternoon he asked Safi if she would mind going on a walk with him. "Mamie doesn't want me to walk alone anymore," he shouted. "Walking's my favorite thing to do. I'd love you to come with me. We can walk on the road through the woods, past the other two farms until we get to the road that leads into town. It'll be about 6 miles by the time we get back."

It amused everybody that Ed had never learned that he didn't need to shout. It was only the rest of them who had to shout to be heard by him. Ella explained it once, saying that Ed also wanted to hear what he was saying.

"Oh, yes, I would love to," Safi answered quickly, then she repeated herself at higher decibels.

"You needn't worry. I don't talk when I walk. I learned years ago that my talking drives away the animals."

Perhaps it was on account of these walks, but in any case, by the fourth day, Letty noticed that Safi had much more confidence in herself. At the luncheon table on the fifth day, Safi and Boots got into a a tussle. It all started with Ella's comment to Safi about her father. She spoke loud enough so that Ed could hear.

"Your father must have been a brave man," Ella said.

"Yes, he was," Safi answered.

"Brave?" shouted Uncle Ed. "How so?"

Ella continued: "He traveled to Nazi Germany from Chicago in 1939 to try to save four of his Jewish relatives."

For sure, Ed heard this. "Jesus!" he said.

"Please, Edward, that language isn't necessary," Mamie admonished.

Letty noticed that Boots flashed a frown when she heard the word "Jewish."

"Yes, he was brave. He had never been to Germany before, but he spoke German," Safi explained.

"Was he a recent immigrant?" Boots asked.

"Unfortunately, I don't know the names of my ancestors but I know they first arrived in Chicago from Germany in 1836—a year before Elijah," Safi answered. Letty noticed Boots stiffen again, so she came to Safi's rescue:

"Safi, of course knows a great deal about our family, Boots, because she is typing my book for me."

"And what did your ancestors do when they came to Chicago?" Boots asked.

"I don't know, but I think they were peddlers. Mrs. M is going to help me trace my genealogy. I hope to find out by the next time I come here."

"Presumptuous!" Boots said, not quietly enough. Safi's face discernibly reddened.

Ella quickly asked if Safi's father knew the relatives he was trying to save. Again she spoke loud enough so Ed could be included in the conversation.

"No," Safi answered, "he knew only their names and where they lived."

Mamie commented in a strong voice: "He risked his life for four people he didn't know?"

"Yes," Safi replied, "because they were trying to kill all Jews. 'You couldn't just do nothing,' my mom said."

Letty was taken aback. "How did you know they intended to kill the Jews when the rest of us here were so ignorant, especially at the beginning of the war?"

"It's happened before many times, but not on that scale. Fear of pogroms probably drove my ancestors to emigrate in 1836."

"It's horrible, the number of lives lost in wars," Boots commented. "Ed," she shouted, "how many American soldiers died in the war to keep us free?" The family always deferred to Ed for facts, because he was so well read.

"Six million," he answered.

"No!" everyone echoed.

"Yes," Ed replied defiantly, "Six million Jews were killed in the war."

The pause was deafening. Finally Boots corrected him and said: "I'm asking how many of *our* soldiers were killed?"

"Oh, I'm sorry, more than 400,000. And most were drafted."

Boots seemed annoyed, "Of course they were drafted."

Mamie asked Safi to finish the story. "What happened to your father and his four relatives?"

Safi looked down at her plate, but she raised her voice to say: "Dad was able to get them out of Germany and to Holland. He booked them on a ship to New York and sent Mom a telegram. But the ship hit a mine. Dad and his relatives were among the 87 people who drowned."

Uncle Ed was the only one who could speak, and when he did so, he whispered, looking directly at Safi, "I hear you loud and clear. Thanks."

That night, Letty had trouble going to sleep. The waves lapping the shore didn't perform their usual magic. She went over the discussion at the lunch table. Maybe she should have defended Safi more, but she had needs herself. She had to keep in the aunts' good graces, so she could spend the summer months at Sugar Loaf, enjoying their generosity. She needed a change of scenery each year and a chance to enjoy the outdoors, which she couldn't otherwise afford. But she was mortified that Boots felt so superior to Safi that she was openly rude to her.

Just before falling asleep, Letty noticed light coming in below the door to Safi's room. The next day, a drawing was found on the dining room table—a less than flattering depiction of Boots. Several people saw it before Letty was told. She quickly removed it and took it to Safi. Safi took it back from her but didn't apologize.

Later, Ella said to Letty, "After all, she's only eighteen." Mentally, Letty made the correction, "nineteen."

CHAPTER 4

Living with Mrs. M had made Safi realize that there was a lot that she didn't know about her own family. She knew her mother's maiden name was Rose. She became Iris Winter when she married her father, Neil Winter. Her grandparents on her mother's side were Miriam and Leonard Rose, but she didn't know what that grandmother's maiden name had been. She realized she was catching the genealogy bug from Mrs. M. What was it Mrs. M said? "A woman is a lady if she knows the maiden names of her four great-grandmothers." Safi didn't aspire to be a lady, but now, with her parents dead, she wanted to know more about her ancestors.

Tomorrow, Monday, she planned to go to Newberry Library with Mrs. M. Safi had bought a special spiral-bound notebook just for taking notes about her own relatives. Tomorrow her genealogy search would begin. For the heck of it, she thought she would also look up the Silver Skates Contest that Mrs. M wrote about in *One's Family*, the one that Elijah Peacock won. That would be her second task.

But today was Sunday and like all Sundays, Safi would go to Hull House to tutor children from that neighborhood. Once there, she had the opportunity to reminisce with the other helpers, some of whom had known her parents. It was like going home for Sunday dinner. Hull House was the same, but the district was different now. When her grandparents were alive, the neighborhood was largely Jewish. Now the majority were Negroes who had moved up from the South.

Before leaving home she remembered that Hull House had a library. Perhaps she could find out something about her family there. Mrs. M had also taught her the value of writing things down. She should be prepared. Even today she might find out something important about her family, so she took her new notebook with her.

Safi knew her parents were of German descent. As expected, she found books in Hull House's library that gave information about the immigrants of the Near West Side of Chicago. There were many waves of immigrants that came there to live. She read that by 1850, Germans were the largest ethnic group in the city. "By 1900, one out of every four Chicagoans (470,000) had either been born in Germany or had a parent born there. It was believed that by 1920, fewer Germans emigrated, but this was not certain because after World War I, many changed their names to hide their German heritage."

The first large wave of German immigrants arrived in the 1850s. "They brought with them radical ideas that had originated in the years preceding the thwarted revolutions of 1848." Safi knew nothing about those revolutions. "They also brought practical organizational experience, which translated into their forming Chicago's first unions."

As Safi read on, she swelled with pride in being German, until she reminded herself of what German Nazis did to German Jews. Her father was one of their victims. She could still remember what her dad looked like. It was from him that she got her bushy hair. His grew so fast that her mom had to cut it every three weeks. He would sit on a stool so his head would be at the right height for her. He was tall with a sallow complexion. He didn't look Jewish. His friends said if any Jew could get into Germany in 1939, it would be him. His surname could also pass. "Winter" could be either Jewish or Gentile.

Her father was Jewish by culture only. It wasn't just that he didn't go to Temple. He actually felt that Judaism, the religion, held Jewish people back. Her mother explained it to her a few years after he died. "He would never have become a Christian either. No one would call him a 'circumcised Jew.' Your dad was like other Communists. He felt that religion kept people from working for political change. He and his activist friends purposely scheduled important meetings on Saturday." Safi remembered that these meetings embarrassed her mother who, though equally not religious, felt some respect for traditions. She thought that by scheduling meetings on the Sabbath they were thumbing their noses at other Jews.

Early in 1939, her dad started to raise money to get relatives out of Germany. Although he spurned religion, he admitted his gratitude to the Makom Shalom Synagogue. Most of the money for his trip was donated by people from that congregation. Safi hadn't told the Peacocks the whole story. She couldn't help but go over it again and again in her mind. Once her dad had located the four German relatives, three of whom were Winters and one a Rose, he bribed officials to get them safely out of Germany to the Netherlands. Then he bought passage on the *Simon Bolivar* to New York City. The night before they sailed, he telegraphed Iris, Safi's mom: "Sail with JW, ZW, AW, and IR tomorrow, 11/18, on the Simon Bolivar."

Safi could imagine the relief they must have felt as they sailed out of Rotterdam Harbor. How many hours of peace did they have onboard ship before the *Simon Bolivar* struck the mine? Did the mine kill her dad or did he drown? Had he been walking on deck, chatting with his newly found relatives, or was he fast asleep, curled up in a blanket when the disaster occurred? The official letter addressed to her mom said clearly that Jacob Winter, Zillah Winter, Aaron Winter, Neil Winter, and Ira Rose were among the 87 who perished.

Her mom had known his chances for success were slim. She said over and over again: "We had to do what we could." She was never the same after losing him. She continued to work as the typist for Hull House, but took on additional assignments that could be done at home so she would have enough money to raise Safi. The best paying assignments were from graduate students at the nearby Universities of Chicago (U of C) and Illinois (U of I). They were difficult typing jobs because no mistakes were tolerated. The hardest of all were science theses. There was one in particular, a chemistry thesis for a Master's degree that caused Yiddish swearwords to fill the apartment. Her mother moaned: "Subscripts, superscripts, capital, lowercase letters, and weird mathematical symbols." None of those meant anything to her. Unlike other writers, the author of this thesis came to their two-room apartment to pick up the finished product. Safi was in school at the time, but her mom said he arrived with a fancy dark blue cardboard box with a gold rim around the lid. He put the thesis in it so he wouldn't damage it on his way to have it bound. The student paid her so well that when Safi got home from school that day, her mother was preparing a gefilte fish casserole. Iris had invited her friend Moriah over for dinner to celebrate. After dinner they even drank schnapps.

During those years, Safi learned to type. Sometimes she helped her mother finish some of the easier assignments. Although Safi's mom kept busy and took good care of her, Iris had lost her spirit. She occasionally told Safi stories about ancestors, but nothing was written down. It was good that Mrs. M did this for her two children. Safi could only recall some of her mother's stories. She was not entirely sure who did what, when, or where. She knew the names of the four relatives who had drowned with her father only because the Hebrew Benevolent Society gave her mother a plaque with an inscription honoring them and her father:

To Neil Winter

And to his brethren:

Jacob Winter

Zillah Winter

Aaron Winter

Ira Rose

Whose lives he courageously tried to save,
May you all rest quietly.
An ocean of hatred will never extinguish your light.

The plaque now belonged to Safi. It was better than a gravestone, she thought, because it could always be with her. Now it hung on the wall, above her bed. To the left, Safi had put up a picture of her mother and father on the day they were married. They both wore suits and hats. To the right, she had pinned up a somewhat blurred photo of her mother and herself riding their tandem bicycle a year before her mother died.

Perhaps, she thought, if she chose her term paper topic carefully, she could do research both on her family and the Labor movement. She read on: "German Social Democrats, expelled by Bismarck's anti-Socialist laws, supported the nascent Socialist Labor party and were well-represented in Chicago industry. They concentrated on organizing unions." Safi was comforted reading this description of what she was sure were her parents' roots.

Chapter 5

Letty had lived two years alone before Safi moved in. During that time she was dreadfully lonely. Her children didn't understand how difficult she was finding her change in circumstances. They rarely contacted her. She did see her nephew, Bernard, fairly frequently. He always cheered her up. The first time he visited her, he gave her his father's old binoculars. They were heavy but she could hold them up by leaning her elbows on the window sill. Bernard loved bird watching. He had a special new pair for himself.

"Thank you, Bernard, but how can I bird watch from a city apartment?"

"I think you'll find many things to keep tabs on, Aunt Letty. Even pigeons are interesting. Maybe you'll be able to spot their hatchlings."

That was when it all started. Letitia was not interested in pigeons at all, but she soon had gotten in the habit of checking on neighbors during the day, learning their routines: when they got up or came home from work and who smoked. She took notes. The man who lived on the third floor of the Poinsettia smoked and had a dog, which he walked at 7:00 A.M. each weekday morning. On Saturdays and Sundays the dog was walked at 8:00 A.M. When the man came back from the walk, he stopped to buy a newspaper from the corner store. The Poinsettia was the apartment building on the other side of Schiller Street. It ran parallel to Letty's building. Both buildings bordered the alley and ran east of Clark Street. The alley was the dividing line between the respectable neighborhood, with buildings that could be entered from Dearborn Parkway, and the ones that bordered on the slum. Clark Street was crime-infested and run-down.

During the previous two years, Letty had seen a few incidents which she reported to the police. Once she saw a woman's purse snatched on the other side of the street. She always reported screams that she heard in the alley. She made her calls anonymously. But recently, two weeks ago in fact, the buzzer rang and an Officer Murphy wanted to come up to ask her a few questions about one of her calls. He turned out to be quite young (or was it just a young-looking face?) with freckles, reddish-blond hair, blue eyes, and a muscular body.

"How did you know who I was?" she asked.

"We had your number traced. We wanted to thank you for your reports. We wish more people would be so alert. We were going to contact you several months ago to thank you for your service, but your phone was disconnected. So we are glad you are calling us again."

Letty noticed his eyes shift toward the window where her binoculars were. She was about to show him her notebook when they heard Safi's key opening the front door. Letty observed Officer Murphy's reaction. He seemed a little out of breath, waiting patiently to meet her. Letty read his thoughts and said to herself: Yes, she is very pretty. She introduced the two of them and explained that Safi was a student at Loyola.

"I used to take some classes there myself. Let's see, to get there from here you must have to take the bus on Lake Shore Drive."

"Yes, that's right."

"I hope you don't walk that at night."

"Not often, my classes are in the daytime."

"Good."

Actually, Safi had commented to Letty several times about how much she enjoyed her walks to Lake Shore Drive. From Dearborn Parkway on, the streets were lined with elms, oaks, and maples.

"Why are you here, if you don't mind my asking?"

When Officer Murphy explained, Letty noticed Safi trying to smother a smile. She knew Safi was aware of her studies of the neighborhood, but so far the two of them had avoided talking about it.

Chapter 6

When Safi returned from Hull House, the afternoon turned gray and the wind picked up, thrashing both of the trees on Schiller that she could see from the window. Scraps of paper were airborne. She was pleased that she had made it home before the weather turned, but she was somewhat disappointed that her research, though interesting, had turned up no specifics about her family. Such musings stopped when she heard Letty speaking to her: "Newberry Library is famous for its genealogy records. Weather permitting, I'd still like to go there tomorrow morning to look up some information on Harold's relatives." Safi had to think who Harold was. Oh yes, she thought, he was Mrs. M's deceased husband.

Safi only knew about Newberry Library for its adjacent park, politely known as Washington Square, where on several warm summer evenings, she had gone with her parents to listen to soapbox orators talk about community or progressive issues. Early on, Chicago conservatives referred to the park as Bughouse Square. Their intent to ridicule backfired, as free speech intellectuals and everyone else adopted the name with endearment. Letty planned to take a taxi home at noon, but Safi wanted to spend the whole day at the library. For lunch, she would eat her sandwich in Bughouse Square.

Her college education had made Safi more experienced with using library facilities, but not for genealogy purposes. So that morning, she decided to first look into the easy topic: the Silver Skates contest. There was little to be found concerning Elijah Peacock's award back in 1840, but what she did discover was that there was another contest in 1870, and it was won by a man named Leo Glitz. The name Glitz rang a bell. She thought she remembered her parents talking about someone named Glitz, but before she went on to look him up, she happened on an article about the contest in the *Chicago Tribune*. It mentioned—oh my goodness—both Leo Glitz and CD Peacock. The article read:

Silver Skates Winner Snubbed

Skaters from all over the city came to Lincoln Park this morning to enter the Silver Skates Contest sponsored by CD Peacock's. Among the many prominent customers who frequent this elegant jewelry store on 221 Randolph Street Avenue is President Lincoln's wife, Mary Todd Lincoln.

To enter the contest, a skater had to sign in and was given a number to wear on his lapel. When the gun was fired, each had to skate around the large rink three times before doing the fourth and last lap backwards. After the first round, Leo Glitz was clearly ahead. On the second lap he appeared to have been tripped by a fellow skater. Mr. Glitz got up and resumed his lead by the end of the third lap. Spectators agreed that what was truly thrilling was the speed at which Mr. Glitz could skate backwards. At the end of the race, both spectators and fellow contestants applauded for a magnificent performance.

Taking a minute to catch his breath Mr. Glitz made his way to the platform where CD Peacock awaited to give him his prize—a set of sterling silver cufflinks in the shape of ice skates. Mr. Glitz surprised everybody by taking hold of the megaphone to say how pleased he was that the Glitz and Peacock families were now linked together in yet another way. The statement obviously took Mr. Peacock by surprise. He abruptly ended the ceremony by removing the megaphone from Mr. Glitz's hand and replacing it with the small box of cufflinks. Without a word of congratulations or even a handshake, Mr. Peacock walked off the platform.

The morning temperature of 10° was like a balmy day in

Florida compared to the reception given Mr. Glitz by CD Peacock. Was Mr. Peacock embarrassed at the suggestion that his store was in the same league as Glitz's Jewelry which, five years ago was merely a pawnshop on Maxwell Street; or was Mr. Peacock embarrassed that his half-sister, Emily Peacock, had recently become engaged to be married to Glitz himself? Spectators were of mixed opinions: Some, like Aaron Rose sided with Mr. Glitz. He quoted an old Jewish proverb: 'Pride is the mask we make of our own faults.' Others, like Jonathan Cobb, III felt Mr. Glitz's behavior presumptuous. He said, 'Lack of breeding will out.'

Spectator "Aaron Rose?" Safi wondered if he was a relative. Leo Glitz must have married into the "second family" of the Peacocks. What would Letitia have to say about this? Before questioning her, Safi wanted to look up Leo Glitz.

It was easy to find Leo's date of birth. He was born in 1848. Perhaps because he was arrested during the Haymarket Riot, she was also able to discover that he was a socialist activist as well as a journalist by profession. She found two accounts of his death: one said that he was murdered in Bughouse Square in 1893. The other said that he was burned to death in a fire at the World Columbian Exposition on the same day. Safi had to know about the Haymarket Riot for both of her courses, so she let go of the topic of Leo Glitz and started reading about the Haymarket Riot of 1886:

Exhausted by 12–14 hour work days, six days a week, Chicago workers sponsored a general strike in 1867. Using direct rather than legislative action, the Eight-hour Movement united skilled and unskilled workers of all nationalities. Through much of the 1870s and 1880s, Chicago was a leading center of labor activism and radical thought. Early in 1886, union activists again called a one-day general strike in Chicago and on May 1, Chicago workers struck for shorter hours. Speakers appealed to the crowd from a wagon which was used for a makeshift stage. While the police were dispersing the crowd, a bomb exploded. Eight policemen died.

The following day, under the direction of the State's Attorney, police began a fierce roundup of radicals, agitators, and labor leaders, seizing records and closing socialist and labor press offices. Eight men were finally brought to trial for conspiracy.

Although the bomb thrower was never identified, and none of the eight could be connected with the crime, a judge imposed the death sentence on seven of them and the eighth was given fifteen years in prison. The court held that the 'inflammatory speeches and publications' of these eight incited the actions of the mob. The Illinois and U.S. Supreme Courts later upheld the verdict.

On November 11, 1887, four men were hanged. One man committed suicide in prison awaiting his death sentence. The sentences of two others were commuted from death to imprisonment for life. On June 26, 1893, the governor pardoned the three who were in the penitentiary.

Worldwide appeals for clemency for the condemned Haymarket martyrs led to the establishment of May 1st as an International Workers' Day. Though May Day is now commemorated as a labor holiday in many countries, it has never been adopted in the United States.

Leo Glitz must have been released from jail soon after being arrested, Safi surmised, because he wasn't mentioned in any other article about the riot. For most of his career Glitz wrote articles for German socialist newspapers such as the *Chicagoer Arbeiter-Zeitung*. His topics were political, mostly about worker rights and labor conditions in the workplace. Safi could excuse herself for spending time on this because it somewhat had to do with a term paper she was working on.

CHAPTER 7

In the early winter of 1947, Bernard Peacock read an article in the *Chicago Tribune* about some innovative research by the Linde Air Products Company in Indiana. They had successfully synthesized star sapphires. The thought occurred to him that perhaps he could dabble in this research over the summer. He wrote to the company asking if he could work as an intern in their sapphire synthesis lab. He knew he would be turned down if he didn't somehow impress them, so he added that he had worked as a lab assistant on the Manhattan Project at the University of Chicago from 1943–44, under Professor David Oxtoby. This was a stretch of the truth, but he felt Professor Oxtoby would give him a good recommendation. Oxtoby had been Bernard's mentor for his Master's thesis in chemistry.

By spring of 1948, Bernard heard that he had been accepted for the internship. Prior to this, he hadn't thought of how it would look for a Peacock to be involved in gem synthesis. Somehow he would have to keep this summer activity from his Uncle Walter and the rest of the family. When relatives asked him what he planned to do for the summer, he simply told them that he was planning to visit the Indiana Dunes.

The director of the research was Dr. Steven Colton, who synthesized the first star sapphire. Colton directed Bernard and four other assistants. Bernard's first task was to purify ammonium alum, $NH_4Al(SO_4)_2$, by the process called recrystallization. Fortunately, this chemical was not very expensive, because by the time Bernard had his sample sufficiently pure, he had lost 90% of the original amount. (It needed to be at least 99.9995% pure, as traces of sodium would cause the crystal to be cloudy.) He had overheard the director say to a colleague that giving a lab assistant a recrystallization job was a good indicator of his promise as a researcher. Bernard was glad he had his teaching job to fall back on.

After three weeks, Bernard was allowed to go on to the second stage. He put his sample in a Verneuil furnace which he sketched in his lab book:

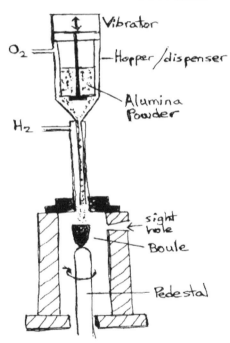

Flame - fusion synthesis of Saphire
Verneuil Furnace

High temperatures were attained by feeding oxygen and hydrogen gases to a flame. The furnace was really just a blow pipe, Bernard realized. The heat drove off ammonia (NH_3), sulfur dioxide (SO_2), and water as gases, leaving alumina, which is also called aluminum oxide (Al_2O_3). He wrote the chemical reaction in his lab book:

$$2NH_4Al(SO_4)_2(s) + 6H_2(g) + O_2(g) \xrightarrow{heat} 2NH_3(g) + 4SO_2(g) + 7H_2O(g) + Al_2O_3(s)$$

Bernard learned that if small amounts of chromium oxide were added to the alumina, a red ruby crystal could be synthesized. If an ordinary sapphire was desired—ferric oxide was substituted for chromium oxide. The Linde Company had discovered that if 2% titanium dioxide was mixed with the alumina, along with the ferric oxide, and if the boule were reheated, the titanium dioxide would precipitate out as needles along the three lateral axes of the crystal.

Bernard spent the rest of the summer of 1948 trying to create star sapphires. He got pretty good at it. When it was time for him to return to Chicago, he asked if he could take one of his creations home. By this time, the company had realized Bernard's connection to the CD Peacock's jewelry store. It hoped to convince jewelers that synthetic stones could be just as beautiful as the natural ones. The company gave Bernard a star sapphire that was grayish-blue in color. He took it back to Chicago and had it cut with a smooth, curved surface known as a cabochon, the most common cut for a star sapphire.

As much as he wanted to, he couldn't brag to his family of his accomplishments that summer. Instead, he just mailed home postcards showing scenes of the Indiana Dunes to various aunts, uncles, and cousins. They were convinced he spent his days identifying prairie grasses and looking for Solitary Sandpipers.

Once he got home in Chicago at the end of the summer, Bernard wanted to see his Aunt Letty. She lived within walking distance of his apartment. He was tempted to tell her about the sapphire, but then he thought better of it. She probably wouldn't be able to resist telling others in the family.

For the first few years after Aunt Letty had moved into her apartment, he tried to see her once a month. He had felt sorry for her, knowing she was lonely without Uncle Harry and forced to live on little money in a rough neighborhood. Bernard, like all the relatives, was relieved when the girl moved in with her. After that, although he had always intended monthly visits, in actuality, he had seen Letty only four times in the last year. Telephone calls often took the place of visits.

One fine day that fall, he called to say he would pick her up and bring her to his apartment for lunch, so she could have a change in scenery. "I'll be over around 11:00 A.M. Is that OK?" Once off the phone, he realized that it would be silly to drive his car such a short distance only to not be able to find a parking place, so he walked over to her building. He would hail a cab to take them back to his place.

This time, Letty wasn't ready to leave when he buzzed her apartment, so she asked him to come up and wait for her. Bernard saw this as something positive, because a year or so ago, he felt she would have been reluctant to have him see her apartment. As soon as he walked in, he recognized a change. Everything was neat and clean. He noticed that the empire couch was gone. Thank God, he thought. He remembered how uncomfortable it had been. Hadn't there been two Louis XVI side chairs? Yes, oh my God—they were so delicate, you were afraid to sit in them. Somebody was not only picking up after his aunt, but had gotten some comfortable furniture in the place. It was obviously second-hand, but who cares?

He asked about the girl. "Oh yes, Safi moved in a year ago. She's at school right now." Bernard flagged a cab to take Letty back to his apartment. He served her a salad, some roasted chicken, and fruit. It was a very good meal, Bernard thought, but Letty was definitely uneasy. It finally occurred to him that she was having withdrawal symptoms. He had no sherry to offer her. What would he do if he did have some? He decided that he wouldn't offer any. He tried, as best he could, to distract her. "Tell me about Sugar Loaf. Did anything special happen there this summer while I was gone?"

Aunt Letty started telling him about the summer's events. "It's too bad you missed the jewel hunt," she began, "but it did sound like you had an interesting time at the dunes, judging from your post cards." Letty went on, commenting about how Aunt Gertrude, Uncle Charles' wife, who rarely came to Sugar Loaf, had arrived this summer in good spirits the night before the hunt. "I think unraveling the clue to find a gem gives her the same kind of thrill as betting on the horses. She likes to challenge her analytical skills. The morning of the hunt, Gertrude was bathed, dressed, breakfasted, and in the dining room precisely at 9:00 A.M., when the tray of clues was placed on the table. Walter could not win again according to Mamie's rules, but this didn't stop him from running around for the next five hours trying to figure out for himself where the emerald was hidden. Gertrude, of course, found it behind *The Grapes of Wrath* in the bookcase. The clue was just three words:

not sour grapes

"You should have seen the grape arbor by the end of that day. Boots had a fit. People were all over it looking for a green emerald among its leaves."

"Did Aunt Mamie say anything about why she is having these hunts every year?"

"No, and I find that very peculiar. I think she said that when the last stone is found, she will give us all an explanation." After a pause, Letty went on to say, "Isn't it a shame that Gertrude found it this year? I mean the money from selling the emerald will just be used to bet on horses. Poor Uncle Charles, he can never stay out of debt."

"Were Cornelia and William there?"

"Oooh yes, they assigned each of their little ones a section of the grape arbor."

Bernard laughed. All of Cornie's children had names beginning with T. One was Tommy, another Tammie, and so on. Bernard referred to them as T_1, T_2, T_3, T_4, and T_5. He could never keep them straight.

"In fact, it somewhat saddened me," Letty went on to say, "to see Gertrude so oblivious to her grandchildren. Every one of her gray cells was concentrated on finding the jewel."

"What about the well?" Bernard asked.

"Oh yes, yes, I should have said. It was operating before the aunts arrived this year. Everybody agreed that the water looked and tasted better. They all thanked you and were sorry you couldn't be there."

"Good. Well, I'm glad that the water is better."

"Did Sophie go with you to Sugar Loaf?"

"You mean Safi?"

"Sorry, yes, Safi. I've never met her."

"Oh you haven't, have you? She's such a dear, and she refuses to let Boots intimidate her."

"What do you mean?"

Letty then went into a long dramatic recitation of various dinner "conversations" that had occurred at the Loaf that summer. "First of all, Uncle Ed loves Safi. They often sat together in rockers on the front porch reading. When not doing that, they would be walking in the woods.

"Safi's interested in Chicago history. At lunch she asked what they liked best about the World Columbian Exposition. Aunt Mamie said it was the Wild West Show."

"What was that?" Bernard asked.

"You know, Buffalo Bill's show."

"Oh yeah."

"Ella said the electric lights and moving sidewalks. Both Boots and Ed liked the Ferris wheel best.

"When she asked if Peacock's did anything special for the event, I told her about the medallion." Bernard raised his eybrows. "You know, you must have seen it, with reliefs of Elijah and CD on the front side and the peacock doors on the back side. The store sold millions of them."

Bernard was beginning to wish that his aunt would just stop talking. He tried to feign interest by saying: "Oh yes. Peacock's must have had a booming business that year…1893, wasn't it?"

"Yes, something like 27 million people visited the fair during the six months it was open. Then for some reason Ed blurted out: 'Except that Samuel almost put an end to CD Peacock's.' As soon as he said that, all the aunts glared at him. I even think one of them kicked him under the table, because Ed suddenly jerked."

"Samuel? Who's Samuel?" Bernard asked.

"That's what Safi asked. Samuel was Elijah's other son, my great uncle, a brother to CD, seven years younger. Ella told me once that Samuel absolutely worshipped CD. He was a bit strange, but very smart. He was an amateur carpenter and scientist. All I know is the family never talks about him. I think that's why Ed was kicked. Boots forcibly changed the subject. For once she spoke loud enough for Ed to hear. Safi, who had just finished a course in Chicago history and was so eager to discuss it—even she knew to keep quiet after that. During the rest of the meal we discussed roses, lilies of the valley, and grape jam."

"Did Aunt Mamie say what jewel will be hidden next summer?" Bernard asked.

"No. I think she'll tell us in April when she announces the day the hunt will take place.... Oh wait a minute, she did say that the gem would be a star sapphire."

"Hmm."

CHAPTER 8

A year prior, Letty had a spell of financial difficulty. Actually she had had several such spells in the past, but this one was particularly serious because the electricity had been turned off. She tried to imply to Safi that she had just been careless and forgot to pay the bill, but after a month of no lights, Safi knew the truth. She politely accepted the situation without complaint. Letty always had a difficult time making her money stretch through to the end of the month, but that September, she hadn't anticipated the added expense of Safi's tuition for the fall semester. She should have cut something else out of her monthly budget—not that she had a monthly budget!

What made Letty feel worse was that Safi loved to study. Her grades showed her to be quite a capable student. During the "blackout," Letty knew Safi found it difficult to read. They kept running out of candles. At times, Safi asked if she could spend the night at a friend's apartment. Letty noticed that those requests coincided with the nights before a test or when a paper was due.

So that September in 1947 when they had no electricity, Letty had the excuse to expand her binocular activities to nighttime. When Safi was home, she studied at the small kitchen table with a candle, leaving Letty alone in the dark of the living room. On those few nights that Safi spent at a friend's, Letty actually had fun. She learned that the couple on the fourth floor overlooking the alley frequently shouted at each other. Windows were kept open on these warm September nights. Letty even recorded what she heard them say when it was decipherable.

Six months later—on an icy day in March, after Safi had gone to bed, Letty sat in the dark looking out the window facing the Poinsettia.

She hoped to see a glimmer of the waning moon, but it was still early and it had not yet risen. No streetlight lit the middle of this short block. At the alley's entrance was just where one was needed. All sorts of nefarious things went on in the alley. The closest lamp was at the end of the block, where Schiller intersected Clark Street. Letty only had to say "Clark Street" to her friends to sense them shudder.

At first nothing much was happening. In fact, it had been a dull week so far, but that's all right, she thought. She enjoyed the peace when nothing happened. It made her feel more secure and gave her the chance to plan her research for the following day or to fantasize about the people's lives in the Poinsettia. *One's Family* was more than half-finished. She had sent a few of the relatives a copy of the first three chapters. She had called her children, Stewart and Lucy, to ensure they had received their copies in the mail. That was three weeks ago and still she hadn't heard if they liked it. Bernard, Walter, and two of the aunts responded. Bernard suggested she give a copy to the Chicago Historical Society when it was finished.

"It's an important document of Chicago history," he said.

Suddenly Letty's daydreams were interrupted. Oh my, what's that? A man ran down the street, looking over his shoulder, the alley curb almost tripping him. He recovered his footing and dashed into the entranceway to the Poinsettia. Letty picked up the binoculars to study the doorway. She saw that the man had not tried to go into the building. She waited. Still the door had not opened. She thought he was probably hiding behind the partition where the mailman left packages when buzzing the owner's apartment brought no response.

What's this? A police car cruised down Schiller from the Dearborn Parkway end. It was quiet, stealth-like, no siren or pulsing lights. It stopped to shine a spotlight both ways down the alley. Satisfied, it moved on to the entranceway of Letty's building and then to that of the Poinsettia. The police car continued down Schiller until it turned left onto Clark Street. They probably figured the man was headed to the subway station at the corner of Clark and Division.

Letty looked at her watch and tried to recall details of the man's appearance while dialing the police station. Once she had reported the incident, she quickly returned to her perch at the window. The man could have left his hiding place while she had made the call, but Letty thought not. If he was smart, he would stay put, as he was relatively safe in that recess. After all, the patrol car could just go around the block and come back again. Fifteen minutes passed before three police cars drove down Schiller. The first one went to the corner of Schiller and Clark and waited. The second one stopped in front of the Poinsettia and the last one stopped at the alley.

The police soon ferreted the man out and had him in handcuffs. Letty thought she saw one policeman look up at her window. What a satisfying night. It was 12:15 A.M., past time for bed.

Early in December, 1948, Letty took Safi on another visit to the store. Relentless sleet made walking through slush inevitable. Letty condescended to wear the plastic boots that Safi had bought for her. They fit over her heels and were fastened with an elastic loop over a button. Of course they were ugly, but they had the advantage of being able to be removed quickly. Safi had said she would carry them for her in a bag once they were indoors.

After their lunch with Walter, Letty suggested that they walk to Marshall Field's. This department store was only one block from CD Peacock's. Before they left the shelter of the peacock doors, Safi took out of her purse a plastic scarf and suggested Letty wear it to protect her wig. Letty realized no one could recognize anybody in such weather conditions so she might as well do as Safi suggested and stay dry.

Letty was in a good mood. It was the beginning of December and she had money to buy some presents. She enjoyed exposing Safi to Chicago's fine stores. "You know Marshall Field's is the largest department store in the world. It takes up an entire city block. The service there is excellent. They've thought of everything to help the shopper. There are little tea rooms and even places to rest on every floor."

Safi was impressed with the store's size, but said that it was not as elegant as CD Peacock's.

"What I really want to buy is your Christmas present," Letty told her. "I don't know how to do it without letting you know what it is because you have to try them on." Letty went to a floor manager and asked where she could buy ice skates. The manager walked them to the department himself.

On the way Safi said, "But I've never skated."

"You can learn."

Letty was finding it difficult to keep up with the manager. When he realized, he slowed down to match Letty's pace.

"But I don't even know where an ice rink is."

"There's one in Lincoln Park, near the zoo. It's a pond, really, South Pond. I skated there as a young girl. You could even walk there from our apartment."

"Thank you, but…"

"No 'buts' about it. Remember I took a chance and got rid of my empire couch on your advice. Now you can pay me back and try ice skating. It won't kill you."

"Well, OK, thanks…. You do like the couch don't you? It's much more comfortable, isn't it?"

"Yes, yes, but remember, don't tell anyone that it's used."

"Mum's the word."

For a brief moment, Letty thought Safi had said: "Mom." A feeling of warm contentment spread through her.

CHAPTER 9

Bernard indulged in a leisurely breakfast on Saturday mornings. He warmed half of a Sara Lee coffee cake in the oven, fried four strips of bacon, and scrambled some eggs. Then he spent an hour slowly eating while reading the paper. Why was he still subscribing to the conservative *Chicago Tribune*? He should switch to the *Chicago Sun-Times*. After a second cup of coffee, he still had no incentive to start correcting his students' papers. He decided to go skating.

Wearing his navy blue peacoat, a brown stocking hat, and fur-lined gloves, he swung his skates over his shoulder and took the elevator down from his seventh-floor apartment. He greeted Henry, the doorman, who said there was a visitor waiting to see him. This took Bernard by surprise because he lived alone and had few guests. As he proceeded through the first set of doors, he saw that his visitor was the same dog that had followed him home from Lincoln Park the previous Saturday. He was a shabby, black and white, medium-sized dog with a tail too long for the length of his body.

"I be gonna get into trouble if I's keep helpin' this dog. Mr. Sivwright on three tol' me not to let it in the buildin' again."

"OK, Henry, let me see if I can find a home for him. You don't happen to have any spare leashes in the basement?"

"No, but I think there's a collar or two."

It was too risky to leave the mutt unattended in the entrance way, so Bernard picked it up and followed Henry into a back corridor. They made their way down a dark stairway to the basement, walked past the incinerator, the boiler, and into the small room where Henry could sit down during his breaks. Bernard shut the door so he could put the dog down, while Henry rummaged through drawers and looked on shelves.

He remembered Henry telling him the last time they spoke that he didn't want to retire, even though he wasn't as agile as some of the tenants wanted him to be. "They's expects me to carry up heavy bags, change light bulbs at a moment's notice. Some's wants me to be a janitor as well as a doorman. They'll complain if I ain't at the door to greet 'em, evens though I'm off doin' some errand for another tenant. You's can't win for tryin'."

Fifteen minutes later, Bernard walked briskly north on Lake Shore Drive clutching a rope that served as a leash attached to "Alley's" collar. What he was going to do once he got to South Pond he didn't know. Maybe while he skated, Alley would run off and never come back. An hour later, however, Bernard had skated around the pond several times with Alley chasing after him. The dog never seemed to tire. He followed Bernard into the clubhouse, which was a large one-room structure with a wood-burning fireplace at one end, around which skaters gathered. There were benches in the middle of the room to sit on while putting on or taking off skates. At the other end, a park attendant sold hot cocoa. Alley got himself as close as possible to the fire, curled up, and went to sleep.

It was then that Bernard noticed a girl entering the clubhouse holding a box. She sat down on one of the benches and looked around. Bernard thought she was rather pretty. She had a long thin nose, large dark eyes, and bushy black hair, with shiny ringlets that extended below her shoulders. He wondered why she was alone. He noticed that she didn't seem to know what to do. She watched others put on socks and skates, and continued to watch as they laced them up. She picked up a hook lying on the bench near her and examined it, then put it down. Finally, she opened her box and took out a brand-new pair of skates. Bernard tried not to stare, but he checked on her progress regularly before going back outside. He skated around the pond at top speed before noticing that she had emerged from the clubhouse and was trying to keep from falling down by holding onto a railing. He considered going over to see if he could help her, when she gingerly reversed her direction and made her way back inside. He skated some more, then curiosity got the better of him and he decided to go back inside to see what she was up to.

He found her sitting on a chair by the fire, leaning over Alley and stroking his scruffy coat. Alley's tail beat the floor in appreciation. He'll never run away now, Bernard thought. The girl took out of her coat pocket what must have been a sandwich wrapped in wax paper. She offered Alley half, which he gobbled down without hardly chewing. Bernard walked up and said: "Thank you for feeding him. I'm afraid he's ..." The girl glanced up at him and in that split second, before Bernard could finish his sentence, Alley snatched the other half of the sandwich from the girl's hand. "Oh, oh ... I'm so sorry. Oh dear!"

"So this is your dog?" She asked looking him straight in the eye.

Why did she ask that? Then he realized that she hadn't seen him walk in with Alley.... Oh I get it. She thinks I'm neglectful of my dog. "He's a stray," he protested. "The door ... Henry, a friend, turned him over to me less than an hour ago. He hung around me last weekend too when I was here. He actually followed me home, then." She smiled, looking down at Alley, scratching him behind his ears. Her smile intrigued him. It was a little crooked.

"This is the best type of dog to have," she said looking up at him again, "resourceful, wiry, intelligent." She looked at him longer than necessary, as though she was making an important point.

Seconds of silence passed, then Bernard felt her stare softening, or was he just more used to its intensity? He pulled up a chair, held out his hand, and introduced himself: "Hi, I'm Bernard, and this is Alley."

"Alley," she repeated raising her eyebrows. Her head swung slightly to turn toward the dog, looking at Alley fondly. The crooked smile reappeared. Bernard took note that her thick, dark hair seemed to compete with her scarf to keep her head and neck covered.

"What's your name?" he asked simply, now that he was eye level with her.

"Sapphira," she answered.

"Really?" Bernard couldn't contain his amazement.

"Yes, it's unusual, but I like it." Looking down at Alley, she added: "It's a Hebrew name." After a pause, she gazed back at Bernard. "What's your name again?"

"Bern … Bernie", he said nervously.

"Bern or Bernie?" she asked, smiling again.

"Bernie," he said positively, realizing how ridiculous it was to appear so uncertain about his own name. To make amends, he asked decisively: "Could I take you out for a sandwich, now that you have fed Alley with yours?" She made no response. "Please let me do that, but first maybe we should skate some more because it's a little early to eat."

She still didn't respond to his invitation, but said, "I'm not really skating. I can't even stand up on the ice." She laughed. "I don't mind looking ridiculous, if I could just make some progress." She got up and proceeded to the door to try the ice once again.

Bernard held open the door for her. Then he picked up one of the clubhouse's chairs and carried it outdoors. "Here, try holding on to this. Let me get it on the ice for you." He put it next to the railing so she could easily transfer her grasp to the chair.

"Really? Like this? They don't mind if we take a chair outside?"

"No, not at all, that's how most people learn to keep their balance." He wondered if she had ever been to a skating rink before. Why was she alone? Girls usually came with someone. "See how it goes with the chair." He left her on her own while he made several tours of the pond. He knew he was showing off but couldn't help himself. He turned around and was skating backward as fast as the wind when out from the clubhouse burst Alley. The dog was barreling toward Bernard. In response, Bernard put his knees together and did a quick half turn so he could come to an abrupt stop. He didn't want Alley to start chasing him around the pond. Alley, however, wasn't as skilled as Bernard at stopping on ice. He ran smack into Bernard at full speed, knocking him off-balance so that he fell and landed on his elbow. The collision caused Bernard's stocking cap to become airborne. Alley pounced on the cap and ran off, trailing a sling of saliva. Bernard got himself up and proceeded to chase the dog, who darted about, dodging his grasp.

When Alley got near Safi, she stuck her hand in her pocket and brought out the wax paper. This made Alley stop dead, probably thinking Safi had another morsel to offer him. Instead, she let go of the chair and lunged for his collar, holding on to it even while she fell. Bernard was there in a flash, picked up the mutt and took him into the clubhouse, securing one end of the rope to his collar and the other to a bench. Then he returned to tend to Safi, who had managed to get up and was pulling herself into the clubhouse by groping the railing again.

An hour later, Bernard and Safi were heading towards Antoine's, a small French restaurant that Bernard loved. Bernard remembered that there was a veterinarian on Clark Street along the way. "If I'm to bring Alley home," he explained to Sapphira, "I should have him checked over by a vet first." Bernard could tell she doubted his sincerity when she asked if she could go with him when he returned to the vet after lunch. He tried to reassure her that he wasn't going to have Alley put down. "Sure, you certainly may," he said, glad to have an excuse to extend their time together. She seemed so concerned for Alley that he felt he should ask her if she wanted to keep the dog for herself.

"No ... well yes, I would like that, but it would be impossible. I live with someone else as a servant. I know my employer wouldn't like to have a dog around." As they approached Antoine's, she asked him what kind of work he did.

"I teach chemistry in a high school nearby." They were shown to a small table for two in front of the marble fireplace. The fire was blazing hot, so they hung their coats on hooks along the wall. She took off her scarf as well. It was so long it had to be folded in three so it wouldn't touch the floor once it was hung on the hook. Bernard continued: "I feel like I'm a servant too—to my students, that is. I'm forever correcting papers, making up lab experiments—I'm really only free a couple of nights a week and the equivalent of one day a weekend. I like my students though." She responded that she had never heard of the Chicago Latin School.

"It's a small private school. Did you go to school around here?"

She burst out laughing. "Nooo." She explained how she grew up on the Near West Side. "Have you ever been there?"

He was concentrating on the shapeliness of her figure and almost missed the question. "Yes, I once went to a meeting at Hull House."

Sapphira smiled again. She looked like she wanted to explore that line of conversation further, but they were interrupted by the presence of a waiter wanting to take their order. When he left, their conversation jumped all around. There was so much they didn't know about each other. At one point Sapphira said: "I have a good situation because the woman I live with is very studious herself, so I have a lot of time to study. She even pays for the two courses I take each semester."

"That sounds wonderful. What are you taking?"

"The history of Chicago, for one, and the history of the Labor Movement in the United States. I love history," she laughed. "I thought about taking Yiddish Language and Culture. Imagine Loyola College offering such a course! I'm not especially interested in the religion, but I would like to keep in touch with my cultural heritage."

"That must please your parents."

"I think it would, but they're both dead."

He was so stunned that he couldn't speak for a moment. His thoughts were jumbled. All he could do was look at her. Finally a few words stumbled out, "Oh no, I'm sorry. Mine are, too. Mine are dead, too.... How did yours die?"

She put the menu down and looked up at him. "I'm sorry, too." After several seconds, she sighed, "How did that happen?"

"I asked first," he said.

Once they placed their order, Sapphira started to tell her story. By the time she had finished, they were sipping coffee. "That's the short and simple of it. Now it's your turn. Please tell me what happened to your parents."

She listened carefully as Bernard started talking, but ten minutes into his narrative, the Napoleonic carriage clock on the mantle struck two o'clock. Sapphira suddenly looked at her watch and said, "Oh my goodness, I should have been home an hour ago. I'm sorry, I have completely lost track of the time. I have to go, and I want so much to hear the rest of your story." She had stood up and was putting on her coat. "Will you be skating next Saturday morning?"

"Yes, I believe so."

With a flurry of thanks and goodbyes she buttoned up her coat—a coat that had definitely seen better days. "I don't have time to go with you to the vet, I'm afraid. Will you be bringing Alley with you next Saturday morning?"

"I think so. A lot depends on what the vet says.... Yes, I'll probably be at South Pond ... with Alley," he added.

"Thank you so much for a delicious lunch."

She held out her hand. He shook her cold fingers, giving them a gentle squeeze before she put on her mittens. After leaving the restaurant, she turned to look for him through the window and waved goodbye again. He sat back down, smiling, savoring the memory before he called the waiter over to pay the bill.

CHAPTER 10

The following Saturday morning was particularly cold. It had snowed for a few days and the sidewalks had not been cleared yet. Safi decided to take a bus so she wouldn't become exhausted, trudging through snow just getting to South Pond. She planned to arrive there around ten. She kept looking out the bus window hoping to see Bernie and Alley making their way to the park. After she was at the pond for more than a half-hour, she spotted them and watched them approach. Alley had been cleaned up, coat brushed, and he had a proper leash, but he was still the same dog, ready to bolt at the slightest provocation. Without thinking, Safi waved vigorously at them from the ice. That was all Alley needed to make a lunge for freedom. Bernie was prepared, however, with a firm grip on the leash. They were both breathless by the time they reached Safi. She gave Alley a big hug. Bernie still held on tightly to the leash.

"Sapphira, would you come into the clubhouse with us so I can calm Alley down? If you're out here, he won't want to go inside."

"Oh, sure."

"I hope you don't have a sandwich in your pocket. If so, hang on to it. I've never seen an animal eat so much," he laughed.

"He's probably been starved for years. What did the vet say last week?"

"He thinks Alley is about four years old. He wanted to do some dental work because the dog has been eating any old thing and his teeth are showing signs of deterioration. Otherwise, he couldn't find much wrong with him. I had him bathed and trimmed up a bit. Can you tell?"

"Oh yes, he looks beautiful … well, he looks a lot better."

"No, Alley will never be beautiful," he laughed. "But I've gotten rather fond of him. The other thing the vet recommended was that I have a kennel for him at home."

"Oh, no, not a kennel!"

"Well, it seems to work. The door's left open when I'm at home and he's free to roam around. At night he goes in willingly. It's plenty big enough. The vet said that it actually makes a dog feel secure and gives him his own space. Oh, there was something else. The vet recommended having him neutered."

"You must have had to spend a lot of money to have all that done."

They talked and skated—at least Bernie skated, Safi hung on, took a few glides, then hung on again. With the excuse of keeping Alley company, they went into the clubhouse and talked some more. He took her out to lunch again.

"I've been thinking about your name. Where does Sapphira come from?"

"Sapphira is a Hebrew girl's name. I think it is pretty, but a lot of Jews don't like it because I guess Sapphira was a woman who supposedly was executed by God for lying."

"That's rather grim."

"I think my parents gave me the name to show that they weren't superstitious." Safi went on to explain her parents' attitude toward religion. Then Bernie told her about his summer experience, learning how to synthesize sapphires. She listened carefully, impressed with his pursuing something so complicated. She could tell he really liked to eat. Both times they had had lunch together she noticed that he ate everything put before him. He probably relished having another person cook for him, what with his living alone. He told her about ice fishing.

"Please continue telling me about your parents," she requested. Last week, Bernie had told her that his father had died of a heart attack about five years previously. There had been no warning. Now she learned that his mother had died after a prolonged struggle with what sounded to Safi like breast cancer. She died two years before his father.

"I don't mind living alone, but of course I miss them dreadfully," Bernie said, finishing the story.

Alley was getting restless, so they had to bring the lunch and conversation to an end. He asked her for her phone number. They definitely planned to see each other next Saturday. She was touched that he politely stayed with her at the bus stop until her bus came. Once alone on the bus, she realized she was developing a crush on him. It felt good. She wished she could tell Mrs. M, but she had better not. Just thinking about Bernie's long eyelashes and drooping eyelids could make her swoon.

Later that afternoon, she thought again about the other Silver Skates Contest—the one that Mrs. M did not mention in her book, the one sponsored by CD Peacock's in 1870. Maybe Mrs. M didn't include it because it did not reflect well on CD. Mrs. M would not like to say anything critical about CD. Of course there was also the possibility that Mrs. M didn't know about the second Silver Skates Contest.

Safi could only think of one story that was somewhat critical of CD in *One's Family*. It was an incident concerning CD's youngest child, Ella, Safi's favorite "aunt" at Sugar Loaf. Evidently, CD hated opals and refused to have any in the store. The next time Safi was in a library she decided to look up opals. She wondered if there was anything about the gem that would make CD afraid of them.

She learned that opals, unlike other precious stones, are amorphous, meaning that they have no definite crystal structure. They can be found in nature filling cavities, like those in geodes and wood. She read that "Opals both fluoresce and phosphoresce. Basically opals are like glass, silicon dioxide (SiO_2), with varying amounts of water, from 5–10%." She wrote this down so she could remember it correctly when she talked to Bernie. Maybe he could tell her what the difference between fluorescence and phosphorescence was? "Some parts of the gemstone will be more organized than others. Each of these organized regions can diffract light at various wavelengths, creating colors. The multicolored flashes of light are what make opals beautiful." Safi speculated that CD might have disliked opals because they could so easily lose their splendor. Supposedly, if they are heated, they can lose their water of hydration and become a dull white. She also read that in the past, opals had the reputation of being bad luck. Surely CD wasn't superstitious?

The story, as Letty told it in *One's Family*, was about Ella when she was ten years old. Like all Letty's stories, Safi wondered just how much of it was true. Evidently, Ella stopped a woman she saw on the street to ask her about her necklace. In particular, Ella wanted to know the type of stones in her necklace. Ella said that she had never seen such stones before. The woman took off her necklace and gave it to Ella, explaining that they were opals. Ella was so pleased to have the necklace, and so overwhelmed by her good fortune to have met such a generous woman, that she proudly wore the necklace the next day when she visited her father's store. Upon seeing Ella, CD immediately told her to walk out of the store, take off the necklace, and throw it away. After obeying her father, Ella came back into the store crying. Reportedly CD then quizzed Ella as to the details of the "generous" woman and where she had met her. In her book, Letitia commented that the witnesses of this incident were most bemused and asked each other how such an astute businessman as CD could be so terrified of little milky stones.

That night the telephone rang and Letty answered it. Then she hung up. "That's funny," she said. "The person just hung up." A minute or so later the telephone rang again and Safi heard Letty say: "Hello.... Hello.... Oh for goodness sakes, say something!..." Then she hung up again.

Safi was working on her term paper at the kitchen table. All the lights were off in the rest of the apartment. Letty said something about saving electricity, but Safi knew she had a second motive. She wanted the lights off so she could see out the window better.

Safi was finding it difficult to keep focused on her work. She recalled the time a few days ago when she got home from Loyola, Officer Murphy was in the apartment, as had happened a few times in the last six months. She suspected that Letty was trying to get them together. Surely Mrs. M isn't that much of a help to the police to warrant these visits. He is nice, good looking even, Safi thought, but it was Bernie she couldn't stop thinking about, and she still didn't know his last name.

Bernie wasn't that good looking. In fact he was slightly pudgy. His drooping eyelids gave him a languid look and contradicted the energy and power he displayed when skating. Safi noticed he chose his words carefully, but he obviously paid little attention to the way he looked—another contradiction. That lock of hair that bounced on his forehead was somehow alluring. Would she ever be able to ask an intelligent question about chemistry? The only science course she had taken was biology. Safi was still thinking about Bernie when she fell asleep that night.

Late in the afternoon of the following day, Safi was home in the kitchen cooking dinner. She looked forward to skating the next day in Lincoln Park and seeing Bernie again, but wondered why he hadn't called. She thought for sure he would have by now. She must remember to ask him what his last name was. Her thoughts were interrupted by Mrs. M saying something in the living room about the windows being particularly dirty, complaining that it hadn't rained recently. "Why, I think that *is* Bernard!" She called Safi into the room. "The other day, I saw this man who looked like Bernard walking a dreadful-looking dog up and down the street. The funny thing is, I had never seen him before until a couple of days ago, but now I've seen him twice today. But Bernard doesn't have a dog. Maybe he's walking someone else's dog for them. Bernard would do that, but why here?"

Safi's heart was beating fast but she tried to appear calm on the exterior. Joining Letty at the window, she confirmed silently that it was

Bernie and Alley. Oh my God, Bernie is Bernard!

There was no time to consider the implications of her discovery. He must want my attention. Why doesn't he just ring the buzzer? No sooner had that thought entered her mind than they saw Bernard, with Alley in the lead, cross the street and walk to the door of their building. They couldn't actually see the entrance without sticking their heads out the window, which they were not going to do on this cold February evening. The buzzer rang. "I'll answer that," Safi said quickly.

A man's voice through the speaker said: "Package for Apartment 19 that requires a signature."

"I'll buzz you in."

"Sorry, Ma'am, against regulations, someone needs to come down to sign for it."

Safi noticed Letty watching her with a little smirk on her face. Safi started laughing. She was sure she was blushing. "All right, I'll be right down." She couldn't look at Letty. She got her keys, shut the door, and quickly descended the two flights. She hoped she looked alright, but she couldn't check in a mirror with Letty standing right there. The building had a small foyer with its twenty mail boxes and buzzers. The three of them filled the space.

"I've been trying to call you, but Aunt Letty keeps answering the phone," said Bernard in a rush. "I was shocked the first time it happened—I thought I had misdialed the number. I never imagined that the woman you worked for would turn out to be my aunt!" Alley started jumping on Safi, who was already cold, because she didn't have her coat on. "Down, Alley!" Bernard quickly took off his peacoat and wrapped it around her. "I just wanted to tell you that I can't go skating as usual tomorrow, but I was wondering if you would like to go out at night, maybe dinner and a movie, without Alley? Down, Alley!"

"Oh, I would love to. I have a lot to tell you. Mrs. M knows it is you."

"You're joking."

"No, really, she's watching for you now at the window."

"Are you comfortable with her knowing?"

"Are you?"

"Absolutely, she's a good sort. She has her quirks but basically she's ... how do you explain Aunt Letty? We'll have to talk about it tomorrow night. Is six o'clock all right?"

"Yes, fine."

"Tell, Aunt Letty that I wanted to come up, but couldn't because of Alley."

"All right." Safi knew, however, that Mrs. M would see through that. She couldn't keep herself from looking in his eyes. It seemed they pulled her in. A big shiver brought her attention back. "Uh ... here's your coat. Thank you. I'd better get back up or she'll wonder what's going on." As Bernard put on his coat, Alley was free to jump up, this time pushing Safi right into him. He held on to her. She looked again into his eyes. He bent down and kissed her. She gently pushed herself free.

"You see, I'm training Alley well," he said tenderly.

By May, Safi and Bernard were dating steadily, even walking Alley three times a week together. Bernard took Safi to museums, some of which she had never even heard of. She discovered that Bernard loved architecture. On their walks he often pointed out features of construction and design that opened up a new world to her. And Safi took him to Hull House, introducing him as Bernie. She taught him how to shop at the Halsted Street Market, where he bought her the ingredients to cook some special meals for him and Letty. On Sundays they joined the crowds of people shopping and browsing on Maxwell Street, hearing the Black musicians and barkers urging passersby to get knives sharpened or buy goods, which were laid out on card tables or blankets. She explained that for decades Jews had taken advantage of the Christian Sabbath. Sundays, when the rest of the city had shut down, were Maxwell Street's busiest days.

Sharing interests served to broaden their appreciation of the city. Both became concerned when they heard about the changes the city planned for the Near West Side. Parts of these old neighborhoods were to be sacrificed for freeways. The plan was to house the displaced families in high-rises. Once again, people in powerful positions considered the homes and micro-businesses of the poor as expendable. They could foresee that in another ten years, the communities of the Near West Side would be forever changed.

Toward the end of May, Letty commented that she was long overdue to visit the graves of her relatives. She hadn't been there since Safi came to live with her. They planned to go at the end of the week. Safi recalled from *One's Family* that Rebecca, Elijah's first wife, had originally been buried in Lincoln Park, but for some reason the city ordered those graves to be moved elsewhere, so Elijah bought the family 60 grave sites in another cemetery, giving half to Rebecca's side of the family and half to that of his second wife, Mary Kolze.

This could be interesting, Safi thought—a little macabre maybe, but interesting. As they rode in a taxi to Oak Woods Cemetery, Letty said that she would first stop off at her late husband's grave on one side of the park and then drive over to the Peacock sites on the other side.

"Park? I thought we were going to a cemetery," Safi exclaimed.

"We are." Letty smiled. "Oh I see … cemeteries are often referred to as memorial parks."

Twenty minutes later, when they drove into Oak Woods, Safi did feel she was in a well-manicured park. Why do people put such effort into convincing themselves that their dead relatives are being carefully looked after? Lawns were regularly mowed and gravesites were evenly spaced. Artificial hills and ponds had been constructed to make the setting appear natural, and possibly to break up the line of sight. What good does all this do? A slab of stone can't replace the vibrant presence of a living person.

Safi was interested in relationships—the connections within the Peacock family. She had brought pencil and paper with her to record names and dates. She finally got up the nerve to ask Letty the question that had long bothered her: "Why didn't you mention Mary Kolze's name in your book?"

"My dear, they were really not family."

Safi didn't respond but she thought to herself: They are family, in fact they're Peacocks!

Letty directed the cab to her husband Harold's grave site. She got out, placed some flowers next to his headstone, and stood quietly for a minute. Then she got back into the cab and directed the driver to the Peacock site. Safi saw the memorial obelisk first thing. It looked to be about twenty feet high. Mrs. M asked the driver to come back in a half-hour.

When Safi got out of the car she realized that the shaft was not in the center of the entire site, but was surrounded by the graves of descendants of Rebecca. Hmm, did that run contrary to Elijah's wishes? However, she wanted to show respect for Mrs. M, so she put that thought out of her mind and concentrated on reading the gravestones of Letty's immediate relatives. After a few minutes Safi walked over to the other side and began surreptitiously to write down names and dates. She started with "Mary Kolze Peacock (1828–1907)." There were four markers for children: two were named Frank. That's odd, thought Safi, but both children barely lived beyond infancy. Then there was a Susan who must have been fourteen when she died. However, Mary and Elijah's first child lived a full life. She was Emily Peacock Glitz (1853–1920). Next to Emily's gravestone was one presumably for her husband, whom Safi knew was Leopold Glitz. The tombstone was erected, but nothing was engraved on it. Safi continued to write everything down. She wanted to have as much as possible recorded before the taxi came back to pick them up.

Next to the gravestones for Leo and Emily were two others, doubtless for their children. One was engraved: Gordon Glitz (1873–1942), but the other was blank. Why was it blank? Safi asked herself. She couldn't take the time to contemplate the ramifications of the moment, as there were so many other gravestones with inscriptions that she wanted to copy. She looked over at Mrs. M and saw she was deep in thought, so Safi went on. The rest of the tombstones were engraved with names like Fitzgerald, O'Riley, Mulligan, all Irish. There were no more Jewish names. Safi counted the number of gravesites on this side. There were 30. That meant they all had been taken. Maybe that's why the blank tombstone was placed before the person died, to make sure a place was saved for him.

This caught Safi off balance. Is there a Peacock/Glitz living that no one is aware of? This brought tears to Safi's eyes. She realized how much she missed her own parents. She kept an eye on Mrs. M to make sure she wouldn't notice her crying. Fortunately, the mower running nearby drowned out her sobs. Finally Safi quieted herself down, dried her tears, and became composed enough to walk over to Letty's side of the lot, where there were several unoccupied sites.

Going to where Rebecca, Elijah's first wife, was laid to rest, Safi looked for the headstones of her three children. CD's was very impressive, with two large peacocks on either side of the inscription. Next to his was a much smaller grave marker for the "beloved wife of CD: Mary Ann." Then there were two other tombstones for the younger children of Elijah and Rebecca: Caroline Peacock (1842–1857) and Samuel Peacock (1844–1901). Caroline died at age 15. She never married. There was no stone for a wife of Samuel, even though he lived to the age of 57, so perhaps he never married.

Back home Safi looked into her copy of *One's Family*. She wanted to recall just what Mrs. M had said about the burials on the Kolze side of the Peacock site. She remembered Letty writing that the first family was suspicious that the second family had given permission for their friends to be buried there. "Not always are the names on their headstones such that we are thrilled to have them mingled with our names. Their ancestry and genealogy do not seem to be in accord with our English-Scottish-American line and background."

Safi couldn't imagine how Letty became so snobbish about such things. It was disappointing. What caused her attitude? Was she anti-Semitic, anti-immigrant? She couldn't figure it out. Safi wasn't comfortable having bad thoughts about Mrs. M. She has been so kind to me, she thought. A sudden wave of loneliness came over her. She missed her parents more than ever, but knew that the only comfort their love could give her now were memories. Could she share these feelings with Bernard? Yes, she thought she could because he had suffered a similar loss, but perhaps their relationship needed to develop more before she disclosed her disgust for his aunt's snobbery.

Early in the next week, Safi took an afternoon off from studying.

She wanted to go to the public library to try to find out more about Leo Glitz. She had already read articles he had written for various newspapers, but had found nothing about the man, himself, except for the article about the 1870 Silver Skates Contest, his arrest in the Haymarket Riots, and the conflicting reports of his death in 1893. Maybe the public library would have more information. She decided to begin her search in 1893, the year of his death, when the World's Columbian Exposition was held in Chicago. She thought she might learn something interesting about the city's history during that eventful year, even if she was not able to find out anything more about Leo. While reading about the July 10th fire that destroyed the Cold Storage building at the fair, however, she was excited to find a "missing person" report involving him:

Leo Glitz, journalist and volunteer fireman, was reported missing by his wife, Emily Peacock Glitz, after the Cold Storage fire yesterday. She reported he had left her and their two children, Gordon and Miriam, to go ice skating there earlier in the day, and another fireman claims to have seen Glitz trying to put out the fire with him. His body was not among those recovered after the fire, however, and there was a conflicting report that he was seen in Bughouse Square later, where he has been known to give speeches. Police are investigating his disappearance.

Was there more news about this to be found? She scanned through articles for the next few weeks but could find no further mention of Leo Glitz. However, she did notice another report of a rather strange event on the same day as the fire:

Samaritan Killed in Bughouse Square

Last night, an unknown man tried to catch an escaped horse for a carter who was guarding his load of produce from thieves. The Samaritan slipped and was trampled by the horse. When the police came, the carter was gone and the man was dead. He was decently dressed, but no wallet or identification was found in his pockets.

Was this the source of the conflicting reports of Leo's death she had read from later years, Safi wondered? She was pleased with her discoveries so far. Now she knew the names of both of Leo and Emily's children. She realized that it was possible that Leo's tombstone was not engraved because the family didn't have a body to put in the grave, if he had just disappeared. But why was there no engraving on their daughter's tombstone? It was blank, whereas that for their son, Gordon, was marked. Oh my goodness! She had it all wrong. It's not the parents who erect the tombstone for their children, but the other way around. The children of Miriam Glitz did not bother to engrave the tombstone for their mother. Maybe she never had any children? Or never married?

Safi asked the librarian how she could search for Miriam Glitz in the Record of Marriages. Let's see, Safi thought, if she was born in 1875…. A half-hour later, Safi squealed: "Here it is."

The librarian put her finger to her lips: "Shush!" She smiled and walked over to Safi.

"I'm sorry," Safi whispered, overcome with emotion and starting to cry. "But I think Miriam Glitz became Miriam Glitz Rose because she married my grandfather, Leonard Rose."

"If they were your grandparents, then there may be a record of their child. Would that child be your mother or father?"

"My mother—she was Iris Rose Winter." Safi recalled her dad joking about his good fortune to have flowers in winter. For their anniversary he always bought her a mixed bouquet of irises and roses.

The librarian put her hand on Safi's shoulder. "How lovely for you to discover this … but … let's look further and see what we can find."

Twenty minutes later Safi had the proof—the record of her mother's and then her own birth in a continuous chain from Leo Glitz.

"Sapphira, what an unusual name," the librarian said. "Is it Hebrew?"

"Yes."

CHAPTER 12

SUMMER 1949

Safi couldn't make up her mind about going to Dartford Lake this summer. Now that she knew she was connected to Bernard's family she felt the affront of their snobbery even more. Two weeks before Bernard was planning to drive Letty and Alley up there, she still hadn't made up her mind. She knew Bernard was worried that her feelings for him had cooled. They hadn't, but she had started to feel somewhat more uncertain about the idea of becoming so deeply involved with him. She also dreaded being insulted by Aunt Bertha again.

When the time came to leave for Dartford Lake, Bernard was very disappointed that Safi was not coming. Worse still, he was just beginning to think he was in love with her, and now she was showing signs that she did not like him as much as she used to. He didn't know what he had done wrong. He planned to talk with Aunt Letty on the drive up north.

He still hadn't told anybody that he had a synthetic star sapphire. He had a vague plan in mind to swap it for the real one during the jewel hunt to see if anyone could tell the difference, if he was lucky enough to find it first, and the real gem was close enough in size and cut to the one he had made. Now he was inconsolable about losing Safi. Even planning this prank didn't brighten his spirit.

When he drove over to pick up Aunt Let, Safi wasn't there to say goodbye to them. That hurt. He tried to put on a happy face for Letty's sake. He waited until he had driven well beyond the city before he said anything about it. Finally he sensed that she was relaxed. Alley had been fast asleep in the back seat for almost an hour, so he asked her about Safi. "Do you know what has happened?" he asked his aunt.

"No, but I have sensed her cooling towards me. She has been aloof ever since we went to the cemetery together. I think she doesn't like the fact that I didn't name Mary Kolze in my book."

"Why didn't you?"

"Oh dear, here we go again … as I told her, she wasn't really family."

"Her and Elijah's descendents are as much Peacocks as we are." Bernard paused so as to allow Letty to absorb that point. "Tell me," he went on, "what did you both do at the cemetery?" Letty said, "Safi spent a good deal of time examining the tombstones on the other side."

"'The other side?' What do you mean by that?" Bernard asked.

Letty explained about Elijah leaving 60 grave sites.…

"What's the other side look like?" he asked.

"I haven't looked at it in years, partially because it has been completely full for years. Irish names are on most of the markers. They weren't relatives. I think they were just friends." She paused. "But you know, Safi was even more disgruntled after she spent the afternoon at the public library. It wasn't like her, but she was a bit snippy with me after that. She went to the library a few days after we went to the cemetery."

"Did she go with someone, I mean, to the library, or did she meet someone there?"

"Not that I know of.… No! Bernard, I know she likes you. I can tell by how excited she gets before the two of you go out."

Bernard wanted to turn the car around and drive to Oak Park Cemetery. What did Safi see there? If I call her, will she tell me? he wondered.

At dinner that night, Aunt Mamie and Aunt Ella said how sorry they were that Safi couldn't come. Bernard found it hard to smile and excused himself during dessert. He went to the trunk room, shut the door, and called Safi.

"Safi, what happened at the cemetery? Please tell me what's wrong. Have I done anything you don't like?"

"No, you have always been wonderful, Bernard," she answered. "It's just that I found out that I'm a Peacock too, but I guess the wrong kind of Peacock."

"Safi, I love you."

"That's the trouble, I think I feel the same way, but it would never work out.… So it's best if it just ends, I'm afraid. I'm going to hang up now, Bernard." The phone went dead.

Three miserable days went by. He had so looked forward to having Safi with him this summer. Tomorrow was the sapphire hunt. Bernard hardly cared about it anymore. That night he couldn't sleep, just tossed and turned in his bed. Finally he told himself he had to get out of his unhappy state. Let's see, maybe I can figure out where the sapphire is hidden before anyone else. He tried to anticipate where Aunt Mamie would hide it. He thought of the eye in the peacock weather vane on top of the roof, but how would his aunt get up there? Aunt Mamie was the smallest of the great-aunts, she would hide it fairly close to the ground. He could think of no obvious place, so he would have to wait for the clue and hope that he could figure it out before anyone else.

Bernard, like most of the others in the household, was in the dining room at 9:00 A.M. sharp to pick up a copy of the clue on the tray at the center of the table. The clue turned out to be an anagram:

Arrange in three words: abefggops

Bernard put his analytical skills to work. There were only three vowels: a, e, and o. Each of the three words must have only one vowel. Nine letters total, so there were only three possibilities:

Two 4-letter and one 1-letter word: _ _ _ _   _ _ _ _   _. Then the one-letter word would have to be "a," but the only four-letter word he could think of with the remaining letters was "pegs" or "begs." So he rejected this possibility.

Three 3-letter words: _ _ _   _ _ _   _ _ _ (bag, peg, and gag). He stopped there and went on to the third possibility.

A 4-, a 3-, and a 2-letter word _ _ _ _   _ _ _   _ _. The two-letter word had to be "of," because "so" didn't leave any other words that made sense, giving: bags of peg or *bag of pegs!*

Bernard didn't immediately remember that the word "peg" could also mean "clothespin," but he started walking around the grounds to see if any ideas came to him. He saw the clothesline between the main house and that of Marjorie and Freddy. There was a bag hanging from it. Of course! He looked around. Nobody else was nearby. He walked casually up to the bag, turning a full circle, making sure there was no one watching. Inside he found the star sapphire. He took it out and quickly compared it to the one in his pocket he had made the previous summer and brought with him. They were very close in size and almost the same color. He switched the synthetic gem for the real one, hung the bag back up, and slowly walked away, checking again for any potential witnesses. The coast was clear.

By late afternoon, Cornelia and William had figured out the anagram. They were elated to find the jewel. Bernard said nothing.

CHAPTER 13

At Sugar Loaf that summer, Letty had taken to sitting in an Adirondack chair that was at the back of the main house where the aunts never went. She sat under a hickory tree that kept her from being visible to those at Marjorie and Freddy's. Today, a warm breeze rustled through the trees and smothered distant conversations. She could even sip her glass of sherry unnoticed and contemplate without interruption.

Letty was grateful to the aunts for giving her a "home-away-from-home" in such a beautiful setting, where she could sit and reminisce with relatives, a place where she could come each summer. When Harold was still alive, Mercer Farms, their apple orchards in Pepin County, Wisconsin, had been her getaway for the summer. She had wonderful memories of their children, Stewart and Lucy, at the farm. Fire blight and the banks took all that away and then Harold died. She was left with only her small apartment and two children, who rarely called or visited.

Letty missed Safi and wondered how she was doing alone in her apartment. She had begun to think of Safi as her child, a grown-up child, a very mature child, but, like a child, she needed love, and Letty did love her.

Her thoughts went to Bernard. He was miserable. Even his damn dog was dejected. It didn't run madly around the house like it had, but stuck close to Bernard. She had heard that dogs can sense the moods of their masters, but this was Letty's first chance to witness it.

At dinner, William basked in his glory for having found the star sapphire. "Isn't it a beauty!? If Cornie and I didn't need the money so much, we wouldn't sell it," he said.

Letty glanced at Bernard. She noticed he was not listening to conversations. That was not good. Had she caused this unhappiness? It was then that she resolved to help bring Safi and Bernard back together. On the drive back to Chicago she asked Bernard if he would like to take a look at the gravesites of the second family.

"Yes." He laughed. "You read my mind, Aunt Let. I intended to go by myself as soon as we got back, but it would be much easier if you were with me. Would you mind if we went there first, before I drive you home?"

"No, I want to look at them myself," Letty responded.

"I didn't tell you, but Safi said she looked up her relatives at the library and we are related, through the other side of the family," Bernard said.

"No! Really?" Letty ramained speechless for some time before continuing, "Oh dear ... I see why she's upset."

After visiting the cemetery, Bernard drove to Schiller and double-parked outside of Letty's apartment so he could quickly carry her suitcase up for her. She heard him comment on how light the suitcase was this time. She was glad she had had the foresight to leave one of her bottles of sherry at home so she had something to drink now that she had returned.

Safi wasn't there to greet them. She must have purposely gone off so she wouldn't risk seeing Bernard. How sad! Once Letty saw that Safi was not at home, she said, "Bernard would you consider going with me to the public library sometime so we can find out how Safi is related?" He smiled at her. It was good to see him smile again.

"I was going to go myself as soon as I dropped off Alley."

"Oh dear, I think I am too tired to go right now—could we go together another time?" Letty asked. She noticed that Bernard's eyes narrowed.

He looked away from her but then looked back to say: "How about tomorrow?"

"Tomorrow's fine."

CHAPTER 14

Two months later, the Peacock family shattered. Evidently, William, the so-called gemologist, had tried to sell the sapphire as a natural gem to the brokerage firm Smiths and Parker, a Chicago company of the highest reputation. CD Peacock's had done business with Smiths and Parker for more than 30 years. The firm took William Thatcher at his word, knowing he represented the store, and gave him $32,000 for the sapphire. Only two weeks later, a young technician working for the brokerage firm scrutinized the gem. Shining a light on it, he noticed that the star didn't move. He said that supposedly was a sure sign that the star sapphire was synthetic. He told his boss, who had an expert in the firm look at the lines of growth using a jeweler's loupe. Again the conclusion was that the stone was man-made. Before they accused Thatcher of fraud, the company sent the stone to a gem laboratory for an identification report. The conclusion was definite.

It was a Saturday morning when that fateful doorbell rang. Walter was sitting in his breakfast nook sipping his morning coffee. At ten he would get up and work in the yard. Today he'd rake leaves. He could afford to hire someone to do the work, but he enjoyed being outside even though the weather in early November was getting nippy. On Saturdays he didn't want to read *The Wall Street Journal*. He barely glanced at the *Tribune*. He needed to clear his mind of business concerns, have a change of pace. He was looking forward to checking on the squirrel nest. Last Saturday, he caught a glimpse of one of the babies. By this time they could be weaned. Maybe they have left the nest altogether.

Walter signed for the letter, which was hand delivered. Hmm, from Smiths and Parker. What could be so important? he asked himself. Oh God.... For God's sake why didn't William know it was synthetic?

Useless skirt chaser! What in hell is Mamie up to? He picked up the phone and called the Pearson Hotel. "Room 713, please...."

Mamie was as shocked as he was that the stone was synthetic. She said she had owned the stone herself for many decades. Questioning her further was of no use. She absolutely refused to tell him why she was conducting the gem hunts. "I'll tell everybody in due course," she reiterated, "meanwhile, Walter, not a word about the hunts to the public. Do I make myself clear? This incident is minor compared to what could happen if news of them leaked out."

Walter was usually a placid man, soft spoken, but he couldn't help himself: "Jesus Christ!" He walked back into the breakfast nook but kept on going, touring the downstairs of his house two or three times. "Jesus Christ. What is going on?" After five minutes of pacing and ranting, he set on a plan of action. To do so in just five minutes was amazing for Walter. He showered and quickly dressed as though he were going to work. Indeed he *was* going to work. He found out where the president of Smiths and Parker, Mr. Patterson, lived and drove there with a check for $32,000 in hand.

Next Walter called William and asked for his explanation. William was shocked as well. Walter was furious and said if he valued his job as store gemologist he would turn over the $32,000 to him by the end of the day on Tuesday.

My God, Walter thought, what if other synthetics have been substituted for real gems in the store? That merchandise will have dropped in value by 99%. In addition, think of the lawsuits we can look forward to. Do I alert the staff? Should I ask the police to help solve the mystery? If I do that, the news of the jewel hunts will be made public. I have to get help from someone, someone intelligent, someone I trust, and someone who is independent of the store. He thought of Bernard.

An hour later, Bernard received a call from Walter. "Hi, Uncle Walter, this is a treat to get a call from you."

"Well not really. I have bad news...."

Walter's explanation of what had happened was interspersed with

Bernard saying "Oh no!"…"Oh crimy!"…"*Oy!*" Finally, Walter paused long enough to give Bernard a chance to confess what he had done. He said meekly: "I thought it would be interesting to see if the experts could tell the difference." Walter was furious with Bernard and let him know so, using words like "idiot", "prig," and "show-off." Walter slammed the phone down after saying that this younger generation was useless. A few minutes later, Walter had calmed down a bit and realized that this 'prank' meant that there would be no law suits or value reduction in Peacock's inventory. He even let out a chuckle. What a knucklehead William is, he thought. If he weren't married to Cornelia and father to her five children, he would be out on his ear.

Walter hoped that the news would not get to the public, but Sunday morning's *Tribune* revealed otherwise.

Prestigious Jewelry Store Sells Fake Sapphire

CD Peacock's, Chicago's finest jewelry store, in business since 1837, was caught trying to pass off a synthetic star sapphire as one found in nature…

Walter went out to buy the *Daily News* and three other papers. They all had articles about the "deception." Walter called all the newspapers to say he would hold a press conference at the store at 10:00 A.M., Monday morning. He insisted that Bernard take the day off from teaching so he could make a statement publicly explaining what he had done. Walter decided that William would not be there, placing him instead on a "leave of absence."

Someone in the press asked how the store's gemologist could make such a mistake. That was the question Walter dreaded, but knew it was coming. Walter answered, "Mr. Thatcher simply thought it was the same stone that had been evaluated years ago, so he didn't check it over."

The press then turned to Bernard with questions about how he synthesized a star sapphire. Of course, Walter didn't like attention brought to synthetics, so after Bernard had answered several questions,

Walter said: "I'm sorry to interrupt this but I would like to introduce you to Mr. Patterson of Smiths and Parker." Mr. Patterson said that he had the synthetic stone with him to return it to CD Peacock's. At the same time, Bernard produced the natural star sapphire. Everybody checked to see how they compared. The one Bernard had made was more blue-gray, the natural one was bluer.

The following day one newspaper commended CD Peacock's for trying to stay on top of the latest developments by having a family member learn how to synthesize a gem. Of course the reporter didn't realize that Bernard had acted on his own. Walter's statement about William helped the store to regain its reputation for expertise. All the articles commented that relations between CD Peacock's and Smiths and Parker were repaired. In short, the press interview successfully limited the damage the incident had caused. Walter was told that sales for the next two weeks were up. The publicity helped in this respect, but Walter feared that it focused the public's attention on the folly of paying big bucks for a natural gem that was no more beautiful and far more expensive than a manufactured stone.

Bernard took his star sapphire back and gave William and Cornelia the natural one. This act helped to sooth Cornelia and William's feelings of betrayal. Aunt Mamie made it very clear to the whole family to keep quiet about the jewel hunts at Sugar Loaf. She warned them that it could be devastating if the news got out. She got William and Cornelia to promise to wait a year before they tried to sell the natural sapphire and she ordered them to sell it abroad. Aunt Bertha said that she wished Mamie had never started the hunts. She confessed to Walter and Letty that she didn't know what Mamie was up to.

As for Bernard, the end of 1949 had been a disaster. He apologized again to Walter for letting the family down. Letty shared with Walter that Bernard was also miserable because he had lost Safi. Bernard's only compensation was that he had become a hero to his chemistry students at Chicago Latin School.

Chapter 15

In late November, Patrick Murphy walked down Peoria Street in Englewood with three younger boys, each with reddish-blond hair and a sprinkling of freckles. There was no mistaking they were brothers. From their home, Patrick and his family had heard shouting going on in the distance. Word had spread fast. By 10:00 A.M. they knew the issue. The entire parish knew the issue: Negroes were trying to push their way into their neighborhood and Jews were helping them. His younger brothers had begged him to walk with them to the focal point of the riot. It turned out to be just three blocks away from their three-room house. The boys wanted to see what the mob was up to.

His family was proud of their oldest son for being a policeman. Patrick had even taken some college courses, something that no other relative had achieved. Today was his day off, so he was in plain clothes. His shirt could barely contain his big shoulders and his trousers were too short, but even so, his confident stride and good posture gave him the aura of a policeman, a man of authority. Ironically Patrick was feeling uneasy, but years of training had taught him to conceal such emotions. He did not like what he was seeing and told his brothers so. "Where are the police?" he asked. "This place is heavin' with thugs."

"We have our police. We've got you," his youngest brother Timmy claimed, looking up adoringly at his older brother.

"You boys behave yourselves, now. This could get nasty fast." When they passed the Englewood Chipper their groans were audible. The smell of potatoes and hot fat made each of them aware of his hunger. Patrick's policeman's salary was not generous enough to adequately feed the six people in the Murphy family. His dad had been mostly out of work since the war ended.

"I've a mouth on me," Tommy said.

"Don't we all!"

"Yeah, but we need to teach these Blackies a lesson," said Shane.

"Come on Shane, the Murphys don't take the law into their own hands."

"Dad says that once them types move in, our property values go down the Swanee."

"Father Joe said that the number of Negroes in the city has doubled in ten years."

"The priest shouldn't encourage prejudice," Patrick said halfheartedly. Oh boy, this is supposed to be my day off and I have to deal with a riot in my own neighborhood without any assistance, and even my own brothers here are eager for a fight.

CHAPTER 16

On his way to picking up a book at the U of C's bookstore, Bernard had to walk across campus, passing a group of students handing out flyers. The students were calling out to people nearby, informing them that a race riot had just broken out in Englewood. The flash point was housing Blacks and Jews in a white neighborhood. Bernard stopped to read their flyer:

> *A new homeowner, a Jewish man, held a reception in his home on Peoria Street in Englewood to promote union membership. Among the many guests were eight Black workers. It is common practice among union organizers to encourage workers to identify themselves on the basis of their job. They believe that improving working conditions requires workers to band together and disregard barriers such as race, ethnicity, and religion. Within the first hour of the meeting, a belligerent mob gathered outside, shouting and throwing rocks at the house. The police and the mayor were called, but no help was sent to disperse the crowd.*

The flyer went on to explain the broader picture:

Chicago neighborhoods were more racially mixed before the southern states passed Jim Crow laws, requiring public facilities to be segregated. Since 1910, Blacks began moving north to find jobs in industry and to escape racial discrimination and segregation in the South. This relocation is referred to as the 'Great Migration.' Blacks who came to Chicago found that they could only live in a few small areas of the city—areas that are now tremendously overcrowded.

In 1923, the Chicago Real Estate Board urged white home owners

*to sign restrictive covenants.... White residents living adjacent to
the Black Belts were encouraged to resist racial integration.*

*The Depression caused Chicago's housing industry to come to
a standstill, further exacerbating the existing housing shortage.
Now that the war is over and the economy is bouncing back, some
new homes are being built on the outskirts of the city. Upper- and
middle-class whites are able to buy the new homes and are therefore
moving out of the city. Black families living in overcrowded conditions are buying the homes white families vacate, leading to the
integration of white neighborhoods.*

*Englewood is a typical lower-class white neighborhood. Its real
estate values have declined. Homes are old and need to be refur-
bished, but banks and insurance companies have redlined the district. Poor whites there can't borrow money to make home improve-
ments or get a mortgage so they can buy elsewhere. Residential
investment favors suburban areas at the expense of the city's poor
and minority sectors.*

This very topic was central to the housing action group that
Bernard was involved with. His group called themselves Advocates for
Equitable Housing Practices. It was a diverse group, who met once a
month on the U of C campus. Participants included some university
students and people from other sectors of the city. Their meetings kept
them informed and sometimes led them to take action on a particular
issue. Bernard joined the group after his father died.

The speed at which campus activists got the word out impressed
Bernard. The riot had just begun and they had already printed a flyer
explaining its cause and were busy circulating it among other students.
He wrote down some of their names and telephone numbers. Their
energy and enthusiasm was contagious.

"Maybe our two groups should merge," he suggested to one of the
students.

"Why don't you go to Englewood yourself to check out what is happening," a young girl responded. She's so young, Bernard thought, she must be a freshman, or has he aged that much, he asked himself?

The following day, Bernard was on the subway heading for Englewood. The ride would take at least fifteen minutes he figured. His thoughts wandered to his conversation from almost a year ago with Henry. Bernard had been standing in the entranceway to his apartment building waiting for a friend to pick him up. Henry, the doorman, stood by him. They started with small-talk about Alley and some comments about an obnoxious tenant. After a minute or two, Bernard realized he had an opportunity to find out something about Henry's personal life: "Henry, where do you live?"

"I's live where we's all live."

"What do you mean by that?" Bernard asked.

"Sorry, Mr. Peacock. I's complainin' because people won't let us live anywhere else and we ain't got no room where we is."

"Where is that?"

"Englewood."

"Englewood! I thought that was a white neighborhood."

"Yes, sir, whites of the worse kind, if you don't mind my sayin'. All's them there is Irish Catholic."

"Well there's nothing wrong with that, is there?"

"No, sir. One or two's just fine, but get a bunch together and they's mean."

"Why do you think they're mean?"

"They won't let any of us live in their neighborhood. Where we can live, we's all squished in—you can hardly breathe."

"Yes, I've heard that."

"They won't sell homes to us colored folk. They have these covenants—restrictions, whatever they calls 'em."

"I thought they were illegal. I think the Supreme Court just said covenants are unconstitutional."

"Do you think that will help us?"

"Well, it's a start."

"I suppose you's right. But I's ain't got much more time. For now, all's we can do is rent. You know what them realtors do? They buy a big house on the fringe of a white neighborhood and divide it up into ten tiny apartments and allows us to rent there. We's packed in like rabbits in a burrow. No space for us, and our white neighbors hate us. It ain't no good."

"Yes, that's not right," Bernard commiserated.

"And, by the way, the rent we's pay for that burrow is twice what a white man would pay. I ain't foolin' you. That's the truth."

Now, twelve months later, Bernard was on the subway going to Englewood. Walking up the stairs, out of the subway station, Bernard welcomed the fresh air as he made his way down Peoria Street. He was dressed casually like the others he saw—black trousers and gym shoes. A strand of brown hair persistently fell loose and hung in the middle of his forehead. He kept one hand in his jacket pocket clutching his camera as he walked. Soon the sidewalks could no longer contain everybody. People walked in the street. Eventually he had to push his way through the densely packed crowd. Angry shouts could be heard in the distance.

Once close enough to see the house that was the subject of this violent reaction, Bernard stopped and looked around. He saw groups of boys also scanning the crowd. The flyer had warned that there were gangs who were looking for Jews, Blacks, and outsiders to beat up. Englewood was now an Irish community. Its older residents probably had lived on the Near West Side when they first immigrated to the United States.

Bernard made sure to keep the flyer deep in his trousers' pocket as he stood watching the crowd. The door to the house at the epicenter remained closed. Some people carried placards. One read: *Coloreds Not Wanted*. Another said: *Our Parish, Our Community*. One two-word slogan was written in huge letters, it said: *Stay Out!* Then there were two signs close together that were probably intended to be one

message. A young man held the sign that said: *Remember Hull House.*
The sign right next to his said: *Neighbors Helping Neighbors.* Bernard
started feeling sad again thinking of Safi, remembering the times she
had taken him to Hull House.

He could see that a girl was holding the second sign. She had long,
bushy black hair like Safi. The girl turned toward him. Oh my God, it
was Safi! Bernard quickly pulled the camera from his pocket and took
her photo, making sure the sign's wording was legible. Immediately
he returned the camera to his pocket. He didn't want to look like an
outsider. He was touched by its sentiment: "neighbors helping neighbors." So like Safi, he thought, trying to get people here to recall how
they had benefitted from such decency. Then he noticed the man next
to her. They couldn't help but stand so they were touching each other.
Bernard himself was so packed in that he was always being jostled. But
that man was looking so fondly at Safi. In fact he looked somewhat
familiar. Bernard thought he might be that guy Mel, whom Safi had introduced him to when he went with her to Hull House. Oh, I can't take
this. He turned around, walked back to the subway, and went home.

Since Safi was in Englewood, Bernard knew it would be safe to call
Aunt Let. He needed a friend. Maybe she would know if Safi was seeing
someone else. When he called to ask if he could come over, he found
the telephone had been disconnected. Oh no, she hasn't paid the bill
again. Bernard put on his jacket and walked over to Letty's apartment.

He found his aunt disheveled and slightly tipsy. This depressed
him even further. He went to the couch and just sat quietly. He didn't
know what to say or where to begin. He couldn't even look at his aunt.
For once, she was also quiet. She sat in her wingback chair. He noticed
she had left her glass of sherry back in the kitchen. How long they both
sat there Bernard had no idea, but the buzzer brought them both to
attention. Bernard was ready to bolt, but his aunt assured him that it
couldn't be Safi. "She said she'd be gone all day." When Letty heard who
it was at the downstairs door, she buzzed him in and quickly went into
the bedroom. She came out again to open the door wearing her wig.

It was a policeman. Oh no, thought Bernard, had his aunt done something wrong? Letty introduced the man as Officer Murphy, who promptly removed his cap, exposing a large bandage on his head.

"Oh my heavens, what has happened to you?" Letty asked.

Patrick laughed, "That's why I'm here. I wanted to thank Safi for helping me yesterday."

"When was that?" Letty asked astonished.

"Well, there was some trouble in Englewood yesterday. That's where I live. It was my day off. Some punk conked me on the head with a rock. Safi helped to calm people down, and that little man she was with helped to bandage me up."

"That was at the riot—the Peoria Street riot?" Bernard asked.

"News travels fast."

Bernard felt the officer really giving him the once-over. He thought it best not to say anything more.

"So, Safi's not here, I assume."

"No," said Letty.

"Well I'm sorry to have missed her again. Please tell her that I am grateful for her help."

I bet you are, thought Bernard.

"I hope your telephone gets fixed. We need your reports." With that, the officer was out the door and gone.

"What did he mean 'your reports'?" Bernard asked. His aunt told him all about the crimes she had witnessed from the window. After a good fifteen minutes of hearing about Letty's spying, Bernard broke from the subject and asked bluntly: "Is Safi seeing another man?"

"No dear, I don't believe so. She has been downcast for a long time now. She doesn't speak to me much anymore."

Three days later there was a cold wind off the lake. Bernard stood inside the front door and watched Henry hail a cab for another resident. Henry was quite tall, thin, and somewhat stooped. Bernard estimated him to be in his late sixties. Once the cab pulled up to the entrance, Henry helped the old lady to the car, opening the door for her, trying to steady her against the force of the wind. When he came back inside, he hung his cap on a hook and said, "Hello, Mr. Peacock." Try as he had to get Henry to call him "Bernard," Henry always called him "Mr. Peacock." Bernard asked him if there had been any repercussions from the riot.

"I's don't know about repercussions," Henry said. "Don't even know what that means. But I's do know there was a few concussions."

"I hope no one you know got hurt."

"Everybody I knows is hurt … sick and tired of havin' no place to live but a postage stamp."

"I was there," Bernard said.

"You what?"

"I went to Englewood on the subway the second day of the riot."

"What's you go and do a thing like that fo'?"

"Well I thought it was wrong that the mob picked on that Jewish man."

"When the riot started, one big bruiser got a rock thrown at his head. Blood just gushed out. Someone grabbed me and shouted that I'd done it. A girl standing there with a sign said no, that it wasn't me. Thank God for that girl, otherwise I'd a been a piece of beef jerky. Yes sir, I was lucky. I'd only came out because the Missus wanted some milk. Should've kept waitin' for the streets to quiet down. If I'd known the danger, I sure woulda just stayed home."

CHAPTER 17

A week later, early in December, 1949, Letty got up, showered, and dressed. Safi asked her if she had some special plans.

"No, not really. Oh, I did want to ask you about the typewriter. I thought I would type a letter to a friend. Would you mind setting it up for me?" Safi looked bewildered but she got it down from the shelf. "Let's see if I know how to put the paper in."

"Do you want me to change the margins, because they're set for typing pages for the book."

"No, they're fine, but when you indent to start a paragraph, how many times should I press the space bar?"

"Well I've been using five for the book, but you can do it any way you want."

"To make a capital letter, what do you press?"

"You press the shift with your left hand and the letter you want capitalized with your right." Safi told her how to get special symbols and showed her where the paper was.

"Oh, one last thing, watch me while I put in a sheet of paper, to see if I do it right, and then I want to know where I should start typing, I mean how close to the top of the page?"

Safi looked worried. "Is my typing all right, Mrs. M?"

"Oh yes, Dear. I just have something I have to type." After Safi left for school, Letty started on her project. She knew she should do it before she began sipping sherry. She hoped there was only one page of her book that needed alterations, but the mistakes that she wanted to correct started at the middle of page eight and carried onto page nine. That meant she had to retype two pages. She had already written in longhand what she wanted to substitute in various places. She would put in Mary Kolze's name. For the parts that she now wanted to remove, she planned to add more descriptions or inconsequential little stories. When she finally finished the two new pages, she substituted them for those that Safi had already typed. She tried to put everything back just as Safi had left it.

Safi was almost through typing *One's Family*. Aunt Bertha had given Letty some money to have the book printed. She planned to have 30 copies printed in time to give them out at Sugar Loaf this summer.

Letty had read in a detective magazine how to decipher if someone has gone through your papers. She took two of her white hairs from her brush, cut them so they were no longer than an inch and laid one on top of the stack of papers and the other on page eight. She figured that Safi would realize quickly that she had made an alteration to the manuscript because the paper Safi gave her this morning was slightly whiter and thinner than the sheets Safi had used early on in typing the book. She didn't want to talk to Safi about what she had done. That was too embarrassing. But if Safi discovered the changes, she thought she would be able to tell by Safi's mood if she approved.

Two days later, Letty found the hairs gone. By the third day, which was a Saturday, Safi decided to go ice skating. As soon as Safi left the apartment, Letty called Bernard. "Bernard, do you know how to type a vertical line, I mean how do you make the typewriter do that for you?"

"I'm not sure. Let me think about it. Why don't you ask Safi?"

"I would but she just left to go ice skating."

"Really! Oh, well, I'll just take a quick look at my typewriter and see if I can figure it out … can I call you back later about it?"

The following Monday, after Safi went to her class, Letty took a cab to the public library. She went with sheets of paper, scotch tape, pencils, and an eraser. After researching genealogy records, she made a sketch that required an hour of false starts and erasures. When she thought she had the correct family tree of the Peacocks, showing all the descendants of Elijah, she still had to worry about how to make the vertical and horizontal lines using the typewriter, so she took her sketch to the librarian.

The following Saturday night, Bernard and Safi went out on a date. Letty knew better than to ask more than a few questions. She noticed that Safi took the greater part of an hour to get ready. Letty wished she could buy Safi some new clothes. She certainly needed them. On the other hand, when Bernard came to the door to pick her up, Letty was reminded that he didn't know how to dress. Nothing really matched.

Bernard had cut short his visit to Marjorie and Freddy's so he could get back to Chicago to take Safi out on New Year's Eve. They drove into the countryside west of the city to Black Hawk Lake. More a pond than a lake, it quickly froze over in the winter. Every year, the locals encircled it as best they could with Christmas lights, which they turned on in the late afternoon. For years, it had been a popular spot for ice skaters. Bernard and Safi skated for a few hours and then went to a nearby inn, Hubbard's Folly, which was famous for its home-style cooking. The inn was over a hundred years old and had had a few strange and exciting events in its history. It was a wonderful end to their winter vacation.

A few days later, they were both deeply involved again in school work. Whenever Bernard walked Alley by his aunt's apartment he would buzz up to see if Safi could join him. They both were usually free in the late afternoon. Most Saturday nights they also had a conventional date, but it was on these late afternoon walks with Alley that they really got to know each other and became attached. Letty, they noticed, was acting like Safi's surrogate mother. Safi told him that when she returned to the apartment, his aunt always asked about where they had walked. Bernard thought she was taking extra care of Safi because he lived alone and not very far away.

Bernard arranged that the next meeting of the Advocates for Equitable Housing would be at his apartment. They usually met in a classroom at the University of Chicago, but he convinced the group that it would be good to hear about Henry's housing experiences. They would start with a simple supper, which Bernard would provide, and then have their meeting. He talked Safi into coming and bringing with her some of her Hull House friends with similar interests. He wanted his friends to meet Safi.

Bernard worried that Safi would be put off by his apartment. He lived on the Gold Coast—an exclusive part of Chicago, overlooking Lake Michigan. The apartment had been bought by his parents many years ago. All he had to pay for was the monthly maintenance fee. To many girls, such an apartment might signal a life of wealth and security, but to Safi, the apartment could highlight his privileged lifestyle, one that she might want no part of. He knew he shouldn't think so far ahead, because Safi had given him no sign of committing herself to him for a lifetime. If she ever did, he hoped she would be willing to stay in the apartment, as it was a good deal for him. Selling it just to scale down wouldn't make sense. Though his parents had plenty of money, the furnishings had always been simple. They did not live a showy life.

That January evening in 1950, Bernard walked with Safi to his building an hour before the meeting. When they first entered the apartment, Safi went to the living room's big window which overlooked the lake.

"You get the morning sun, but then you have windows on the west side as well. Do you see the sunsets?"

"Yes." She notices weird things, Bernard thought, like his having a washer and dryer in the apartment.

"I've never lived in a building that you have to use the elevator to get to your apartment. I don't know if I'd like that … I mean do you feel trapped? What if there was a fire? Does that scare you?"

"I guess I'm so used to it that I never think about it."

"The highest up I've ever lived was five stories. It was a walk-up, of course." She smiled. "You're on the seventh story here." She spent ten minutes looking at the photos on the wall. "You look like your dad, don't you? Except you have your mom's hair."

Bernard had to stop himself from saying that she could look forward to his eventually being plump like his father. He had gotten carried away, assuming they would be living together in the future. Thank goodness he didn't blurt that out. He wanted to look at her and study her reactions, but he didn't have time. He had a lot to do.

The casserole was in the oven, and he was quite proud of himself on that score. It wasn't his first casserole. He was now getting rather good at making them. Of course it was always the same one. Several years ago he found a stash of index cards with recipes written by his mother. He cried just seeing her handwriting. It brought back so many memories of the wonderful years the three of them had together before she got sick. Since then, he had made her chicken fricassee whenever he entertained. He hadn't yet tried another of her recipes. Actually, he rarely had to cook for anyone. Safi helped with the tossed salad. She could be quiet. He liked that. He knew her well enough now to know that she was content when she was quiet.

They had set the table buffet-style. The last thing was the bread. He had bought a delicious loaf of Challah from the baker. He would pop that in the oven at the last minute, just to warm it up.

"Have I forgotten anything?"

"What are you serving to drink?

"Beer's in the frig."

When the buzzer rang, he put Alley in his kennel but didn't shut the door. He told Safi that he wanted to see if he would stay there upon his command. Safi rolled her eyes and smiled. One-by-one the activists arrived. Most had some connection to the University of Chicago. One was a student from the University of Illinois. Henry arrived after six, when he was through with his doorman's duties. Supper went fine. They soon settled down to business. Several of them reported on some action that they had undertaken since the last meeting.

A number of them stated facts that they all knew, but they couldn't resist expressing their frustration over various injustices. Racial segregation was entrenched in the North as well as the South. Violence and collective anti-Black actions like restrictive covenants and redlining helped to sustain it. "The government sanctions and supports ghetto expansion," another said.

"Yeah," said the student from the U of I, "the FHA neighborhood security maps are a prime example of that."

"Please explain how that works, since some of us here may not know," Bernard asked the young man.

"Well," the student expanded, "the FHA publishes color-coded maps of cities. The color of a region indicates the level of risk to invest there—red meaning the most risky. OK, I'm not saying anything new—it's just redlining, but how's 'bout the Home Owners Loan Corporation? It was created as a New Deal reform—to guarantee home mortgages—but it's been used to give only whites a $120-billion stimulus to become home owners, so they can build up equity and then have a way to pass on their wealth to their children."

Someone else made the point that urban renewal projects were also a problem. "They're designed to get rid of blighted neighborhoods, but something like 20% of Blacks have lost their homes that way and 90% of those can't find a replacement home. After being displaced, the only place they can find to live is in public housing."

Henry spoke for the first time: "Yes sir, we's call urban renewal, 'Negro removal.'"

One man stuck up for the director of the Chicago Housing Authority. He said the woman in charge had tried to relieve the pressure of overcrowding in ghettos by placing public housing projects in areas in which there was space, but white violence forced politicians to insist that such projects be built in ghetto areas.

Two of Safi's friends from Hull House came, Mel and an elderly woman, Cora, who had lived at Hull House most of her life. Bernard was impressed with her because she not only worked with poor people who needed housing, but she lived among them. Somewhere in the discussion, Cora explained that the Near West Side had a 130-year history as the Midwest's most important immigrant gateway.

Safi spoke, "The Near West Side includes Maxwell Street—my

neighborhood. It's constantly changing. It used to be largely Jewish, then Irish, Italian, and today, Blacks and Mexicans are moving in. Black musicians are starting to perform at the Maxwell Street Market. It's one of the few places they are allowed to perform. The market gives them a constant audience—a multi-racial audience. Shoppers there are entertained by artists singing and playing the blues. Our neighborhood is not only a gateway for new immigrants, it's also called the birthplace of Chicago Blues."

Bernard felt it was time for Henry to take center stage, so he asked him to explain what the housing situation was like in Englewood, and what he was doing about it.

"Well, first of all I's want to thank you for going to Englewood during that riot on Peoria Street."

Someone asked, "How many of us here tonight protested during the riot?" A lot of them raised their hands, including Bernard and Safi. Bernard smiled at her and said to her on the side, "Yes, I saw you there, you and Mel."

Henry kept his eyes on Safi. "It was real dangerous and we was glad for your support. I thought it was you who was there. Yes siree, you helped protect me. Thank you for your help that day. I was in mighty trouble."

Henry went on to explain how crowded Blacks were in his old neighborhood. "My wife and I, we's want to have no more violence, no more fear when we's go out, that we might be attacked. We's had heard about a black community called Robbins. It ain't got no paved streets, no sewers, but the lots cost only $90. We's bought us a lot there and we's startin' to build our own home there. It's a little like livin' in the country. There is nearby factory work for the Mrs. and my chil'en. I's want to keep my job here as doorman. The board has allowed me to sleep downstairs in the basement, four nights a week. I's go home on the weekend. On weekends, I work on buildin' our home. My wife, she has a vegetable garden and some chickens."

How big of a community is it?"

"About 5,000 people, I's been told."

"Where is it?"

"About 20 miles south o' here. It takes me a long time ridin' buses to git to and from, but it's worth every minute of it."

When their friends left for the evening, Bernard and Safi descended in the elevator with Alley. Safi said that it had been a perfect evening. "That's the kind of thing I want to do with my life.... Can I hold Alley's leash?"

"Sure."

"Alley was pretty good, wasn't he, once we put him in his kennel. He didn't seem to mind staying in there," Safi said.

When they opened the outer door to the building, they quickly realized that the wind off the lake had become quite fierce. From Lake Shore Drive, where Bernard lived, they had to walk directly west to get to Letty's apartment. The high-rises fronting the lake funneled the wind, increasing its force. During the day, rope railings would have been temporarily installed just to give pedestrians something to hold on to, but since it was already nighttime when the wind started its fury, no railings had been put up, and the walk to Schiller Street was treacherous. The actual temperature was around 6°F, but considering wind chill, it felt like it was -15°F. Icy sidewalks didn't help.

Before setting off, Bernard thought that maybe he should leave Alley at home, but decided against it. He asked Safi if she needed an extra scarf or gloves. Safi was grateful she had worn her stadium boots. She thought she could manage as dressed. After trying various arrangements, they decided the best was for Bernard to be on the street side with his arm around Safi's waist, with that hand holding Alley's leash. Bernard worried that the dog would become overly excited, but the opposite occurred. Alley seemed to realize that he was needed to keep Safi upright. He walked close to her without pulling on the leash. It was too cold to talk and as soon as Safi was safe inside, Bernard and Alley headed back home.

CHAPTER 19

In April of 1950, Letitia received a letter from Aunt Bertha:

Dear Charles, Walter, Letitia, Blair, Bernard, Cornelia, & William,

As many of you know, we recently received a tentative offer from the firm, Dayton Hudson, Co. Its senior vice president, GG Gordon, wrote us saying that the firm may wish to buy CD Peacock's. Dayton Hudson is a very large retail firm headquartered in Minneapolis, but it has stores all over the United States, some of which are jewelry stores.

Ella, Mamie, and I feel that all of the family members who would be affected by the sale should meet for a powwow, at which time we can explore the possibility and consider our various options. We would like each of you to be present at Sugar Loaf on July 15, for a full day of discussion, at which Charles will give us the situation of the Peacock treasury and costs of running the store, and Walter will report on the general trends in the jewelry business for the last 20 years. We should all be in agreement if we want to sell and, if so, if this is the time to sell.

When and if we do sell, the profits would be divided six ways for each of the children of CD. If one of you does not turn up for the discussion on July 15, then you must go along with what the others of us decide. I am asking that each of you send me back the second page I have enclosed with this letter, with your signature and date, stating whether or not you will be able to meet for the discussion.

Mamie is scheduling the hunt for the diamond two days after

our powwow, on July 17. The following year, 1951, she wants the
ruby hunt to occur on July 13. That will be the final jewel hunt.

The second page of the letter was the sheet they were supposed to
mail back to Boots. It said:

I _____ *(will/will not) attend the*

9:00 A.M. meeting on July 15, 1950, at Sugar Loaf

Signed _____ *Date* _____

Please mail to: *Mrs. Brode B. Davis*
The Pearson Hotel, Apt. 405
160 East Pearson Street
Chicago, Illinois

Letty was excited by this news. At last there might be some hope
of getting more money. Harold had worked so hard as an apple grower
in northern Wisconsin, but through the years he earned little money.
While her parents were alive, Letty and Harold never went without.
Once her parents died, Letty spent her inherited lump sum to take her
children to Europe for extended periods of time. When she returned to
the States, Harold was bankrupt and died within a year.

Letty was thankful to her father for setting up her trust, but she
never had quite enough money. Not only could she no longer afford to
travel or throw parties, but it was all she could do to keep up appear-
ances suitable to the Peacock name. There was a personal difficulty, but
she wasn't ready to tackle that one. Another problem was that her two
children lived far away in other cities. She visited them once a year, but
they seldom came to Chicago to see her and rarely called. The excuses
were myriad: the expense, the busy schedules of their children, there
was no place to stay if they did come. "Your apartment is certainly not
large enough," they would remind her. Letty felt like reminding *them*
that poor families squeeze into tighter spaces than hers, thankful just
to be together.

Safi was her bright spot right now. She was undemanding, eager to learn, and tidy. Letty felt that she had been given a second chance at motherhood. She couldn't help herself. She loved Safi as a daughter. Their relationship felt wonderful. She just hoped her sherry habit wouldn't turn Safi away. She was trying not to drink as much when Safi was around. Being involved in a project always helped, so now that she was finished with the book, she would have to find something else.

Why didn't her children take an interest in her book? They didn't respond to her letters, not even when a carbon copy of a chapter was included. Letty could understand it if they didn't like every part of the book. Maybe they could skip the chapters about the McLains and Rawsons, and perhaps even those about the Pennsylvania McLanes and the Helmers, but children should know their roots. She hoped Lucy, in particular, would take note that a woman is not a lady unless she knows the maiden names of her four great-grandmothers.

That night Bernard was picking up Safi for a date. They were going out every weekend now. Recently, in fact, Bernard had started to come over "to correct papers" on school nights. She loved having them both in her apartment, as long as Alley was left at Bernard's. Several weeks prior, Alley did accompany Bernard. What a disaster that was! Never again. Safi had made a light supper of cheese dreams and a tossed salad for the three of them. Bernard posted himself at the doorway to the kitchen to keep Alley out. They had moved the kitchen table into the living room to give them more room to eat around it. Safi asked Letty to guard the plates that she carried out to the table. You'd think that the dog had never been fed. It was alright when there was only one plate to guard, but somehow Alley thought that the second plate was brought out just for him. In the end, Safi and Bernie gave Letty the only cheese dream that escaped Alley's mouth. They apologized profusely, cleaned up the mess and went out to dinner. That night Letty had to admit she was glad to see them go. Bernard promised he would never come over with Alley again.

This evening when Bernard arrived, Letty asked him straight off what his thoughts were about Aunt Bertha's letter.

"Well, we had all better go, that's for sure. I've got to work to stay in her good graces after the sapphire disaster."

"Disaster?" asked Safi.

"Well yes, disaster." As he told Safi the story about switching his synthetic one for the natural sapphire, Letty could tell that Bernard was feeling embarrassed. He was ashamed to have to admit to her his colossal *faux pas*. Safi listened, at times grimacing, at others, laughing. When Bernard finished she asked: "In the end, you gave William the real one?"

"Yes, well, then Aunt Ella, I believe, had a word with William, who then offered to split the proceeds with me. We haven't sold it yet. It hasn't been a year." He turned to Safi and asked: "Are you ready to go?"

"Yes."

"Are you in favor of selling?" Letty asked her nephew point blank. She noticed that Bernard sighed.

"I could go either way," he answered, not looking at Letitia. He went to the coat closet to look for Safi's coat.

"I'd like to sell," said Letitia.

"Well, in any case, we should drive up together. I'll call you tomorrow afternoon, Aunt Let, so we can have a long talk about it."

After they left, it finally occurred to Letty that Bernard didn't want to talk about it in front of Safi. That's why he suggested calling her on Sunday afternoon, when Safi would be at Hull House. Of course, he wants Safi to go to Sugar Loaf with them, but he doesn't know if she will be welcomed by the aunts. I guess this is a bit awkward for him. Perhaps it is time for me to pay the aunties a visit at the Pearson Hotel, she thought.

With the apartment to herself, Letty sat in front of the window earlier than usual. Her interest in spying had fallen off recently. The last time she called the police station, the phone had been left off the hook while they looked for Officer Murphy. Letty overheard men laughing in the background saying: "Hey, Murphy, it's the peeper." Letty was crestfallen. After that, she didn't have quite the enthusiasm for snooping that she used to. It had been almost three months since she had called the police about anything.

It was a moonless night and difficult for Letty to make out what she was seeing on the street. Almost as soon as she was in position, with her binoculars on the sill and her notebook and pencil in her lap, she realized that she was seeing two young boys trying to steal a car. Later, when she called the police to make a report, Officer Murphy told her that usually kids try that type of crime late at night, after people were asleep. It was nice to hear his voice again. He was always polite to her.

In the morning, she phoned the three aunties to ask if she could come over to talk with them. Aunt Mamie was already doing something but both Ella and Boots were available. Ella asked Letty about Safi.

"I hope Safi is coming with you. I would love to see her." It was decided that Safi would have lunch with Aunt Ella and Letty with Boots.

When Bernard called in the afternoon, Letty was able to say right away that Safi was also invited to Sugar Loaf. What she didn't tell Bernard was that she and Boots had also agreed that this would be Alley's last chance to show he was well-behaved enough to visit the Loaf.

Chapter 20

Last spring, Safi had told her advisor, Jan Kalpinski, that her parents had been Communists and her dad worked to promote unions. Kalpinski said to her then: "Yes, the early '40s were the days."

He confided in Safi that his position at the university was somewhat precarious, "so you may want to choose someone else to be your advisor. Five years ago, when I first became an instructor at Loyola, I told them that I had been a member of the Communist party, and assured them that I never had any intention of working toward the overthrow of the government. That was sufficient to convince them that I was safe to hire.

"How things have changed in just five years, since the war ended. The Russians have tested their own atomic weapon. That, and Mao's conquest of China, and the Communists trying to take over the Korean peninsula, have all helped to bring about a 'red scare' in the U.S., and the red scare is being used to dismantle the Left."

Safi had trouble asking this articulate instructor a question. He never stopped talking. She finally got to ask: "Why has the Left been dismantled here and not in Europe?"

"We were näive at Yalta and were taken advantage of, yet we emerged from the war considerably stronger than other countries. We felt we had a duty to restore their security. Look, European countries were simply trying to survive. Their politicians installed systems of universal healthcare, but our leaders fomented an anti-communism hysteria so we would be willing to engage as the world's policemen. Three years ago, Loyola started requiring each faculty member to sign a loyalty oath. I signed one, but now I think Loyola is using my former

CPUSA membership as an excuse to not grant me tenure."

Kalpinski took a breath, so Safi leapt in with the question she really wanted to ask him: "Do you think that a major in labor history could lead to a good job with unions?" Safi asked.

"Well, this is a bad time for unions, too. Remember that the Taft-Hartley Act that was passed just three years ago requires all union officials to sign a non-Communist affidavit, which says that they do not belong to or sympathize with any communist or subversive organization. You probably know that just this year Congress established the Subversive Activities Control Board to monitor and track down left-wing radicals. Safi, you are getting into this at a difficult time. Trade unions are being purged as we speak. The repression is reaching an absurd level. People applying for licenses to fish in New York reservoirs now have to sign a loyalty oath."

"My boyfriend told me that the physics and chemistry students at the University of Chicago would like a Coke machine near their labs. You know how they often work there late at night, but they are afraid if they petition for one, they'll be considered disloyal." Safi knew this was a feeble attempt to contribute to the points that Kalpinski was making, but she didn't want to be just lectured to.

Kalpinski went on, not bothering to respond to her comment: "During the Depression employees gained the right to organize, join unions, and bargain collectively. Unions could elect their own representatives and employers were required to negotiate in good faith. Activists couldn't be fired for doing union work. But now, the red scare is being used as an excuse to weaken the Labor movement.

"Thousands are losing their jobs here. Families have been ruined. The Labor movement is being taken over by conservatives. Organizing is so difficult now, and what's really sad is that members of unions are losing the confidence to challenge their bosses.

"Safi, I hope you go into labor studies. We need talented students in this field more than ever."

In June, Safi and Bernard were able to attend the founding meeting
of the *National Labor Conference for Negro Rights* in Chicago. They
went in particular to hear Paul Robeson, who was the keynote speaker.
Robeson had long been a proponent of workers' rights. As soon as he
started speaking, both Safi and Bernard realized that they were hearing
in person one of the greatest speakers of their lifetime. Robeson said
it was tragic that conservative values had taken over the Labor movement. "Labor policies now actually block civil rights, and fair practice
clauses are a thing of the past." Robeson urged people to consider labor
rights as fundamental to civil rights. People of color deserve a level
playing field in employment. Safi kept a copy of his speech:

> . . . *Who built this land? Who have been the guarantors of our
> historic democratic tradition of freedom and equality? Whose
> labors have produced the great cities, the industrial machines, the
> basic culture and creature comforts of which our voice of America
> spokesmen talk so proudly? It is well to remember that the America
> we know has arisen out of the toil of many millions who have
> come here seeking freedom, from all parts of the world. The Irish
> and Scotch indentured servants, who cleared the forests and built
> the colonial homesteads, were a part of the productive backbone
> of our early days. The millions of German immigrants of the mid-
> nineteenth century, the millions more from eastern Europe, whose
> blood and sacrifices in the steel mills, the coal mines, and factories
> made possible the industrial revolution of the 1880s and 1890s.*
>
> . . . *The workers from Mexico and the East, Japan and the
> Philippines, helped to make the West and the Southwest a fruitful
> land. And through it all, from the earliest days, the Negro people,
> upon whose unpaid toil, as slaves, created the basic wealth of which
> this nation was built. These are the forces that have made America
> great and preserved our democratic heritage....'*

Periodically Safi reread Robeson's words, each time renewing her vow to have a career in workers' rights. Robeson had put aside his career as actor and concert artist to devote his life to the fight for Negro rights. Safi hoped to have that same dedication.

In July, Bernard, Mrs. M, Safi, and Alley drove up to Sugar Loaf. Bernard picked up Safi and Letitia in his green coupe with whitewall tires. Even Safi knew when she first saw the car months ago that it was a Pontiac. The Indian mascot and chrome stripes on the hood were dead giveaways. Bernard had told her that his father had bought the car in 1941. "A year or so later, Pontiac stopped producing cars altogether. Now that the war is over, they've started again,"

"I always thought that this car was too big for just Dad and me," Bernard said as they were loading the luggage. "Having a dog now makes a difference."

"Indeed," Mrs. M said with a sigh.

"It's a *sedan* coupe," Bernard stressed, "so it has a back seat. Safi and Alley will have to sit there."

"Sure," said Safi.

"I had to break Alley's kennel down so it would fit in the trunk. I think there'll be room for our bags too."

"I do appreciate being able to take the final copies of *One's Family*. It will be so easy to distribute them at Sugar Loaf. I haven't told anybody it's finished. I want to surprise them."

Safi was amazed to see Alley take so well to riding in the car. He stood on the seat for the first five minutes, then curled up and went to sleep. For once he wasn't jumping up. Although Mrs. M sat up front next to Bernard, Safi could have eye contact with him through the rear view mirror without Mrs. M knowing. She was sure Letty was glad to be as far away from Alley as possible.

About an hour into the 3-hour trip to Dartford Lake, Safi stopped worrying altogether about Alley. He continued to sleep peacefully. What a lamb pot! She thought about the two weeks she was to stay at Sugar Loaf. This time she was coming as Bernard's girlfriend but did the others know that? How would they feel about it once they did know? She dreaded being around that womanizer William Thatcher, but at least this time Bernard would be with her.

She raised her voice to ask, "Back in the 1880s, when CD bought the place, how did the Peacocks get to Dartford Lake from Chicago?"

"By train usually," Letty answered. "The few times they drove their surrey with a span of horses and a coachman, those trips would take three days, I've been told."

"I thought everybody loved going to Elijah's farm, back then. From what you described in your book, it sounded like there was plenty of room for all the relatives there."

"Yes, all the children loved Elijah's farm," Letty continued. "There was every conceivable type of animal on it, as well as orchards, a creamery...."

"And white peacocks!" Safi interrupted. "Bernie, would they have been albino peacocks?"

"Yes, I guess so."

"No," Letty contradicted, "they were not albinos. They were a color variety of the Indian blue peacock. They were totally white. Many people consider it to be the most beautiful bird there is."

"Do you know what they call a group of peacocks?" Bernard asked them.

"No."

"No."

"An ostentation! You know, like a murder of crows, a gaggle of geese, a pride of lions. Well, it's called an ostentation of peacocks."

Safi couldn't help but titter. Smirking, Bernard sought her eye in the rear view mirror. How appropriate, Safi thought. After a minute or two of silence, she continued to pursue her thoughts about the farm.

"I don't understand. Why would CD want to buy another place, and one so far away from Chicago? I would imagine once the family was ensconced at Sugar Loaf for the summer, they would not have gone back much to Elijah's farm." (Safi had just learned the word "ensconced" and was delighted to find an opportunity to use it.)

"That may have been the point," Letty said. Safi caught Bernard's eye in the mirror. "Except for Ella," Letty continued.

"Why—how was Aunt Ella different?" Safi asked.

"Boots told me once that Ella always begged to go to the farm." Each of them remained silent for a few moments, taking that in. Then Letty continued: "Bernard, in the early days at Sugar Loaf, it was your grandfather who provided a way to get provisions. He had a sailboat which he called *The Period*. About every other day, they would have to sail across the lake to get groceries, meat, ice, or the like. Dartford Lake is noted for its strong winds. More than once, *The Period* capsized. Neighbors came to the rescue in rowboats. Other days, Boots told us, the lake was so calm that by the time the family got back to Sugar Loaf, they had blistering sunburns and the ice had melted. Soon thereafter, my grandfather bought a 40-foot steam launch, so we had more dependable transportation. It was named after Aunt Bertha—*The Bertha Louise*."

"Everything gets named after Aunt Bertha—the garden, the bird bath, the grape vines," Bernard said with a smile.

"She does have a rather strong personality," Letty added.

Sitting in the back seat, Safi could afford to become deep in thought. She began to worry again that she and Bernard would never be suitable for each other. She could tell that her being Jewish was a source of discomfort for some of his relatives. Aunt Bertha's feelings on the subject were more extreme. Boots had more than just a strong personality, she was bigoted. She would never accept a Jewish woman into the family.

As they drove into Sugar Loaf, the house was on the right, at the bottom of a gently sloping hill at the end of a peninsula. It was a white frame building with green trim—a big rambling structure, and not as intimidating as Safi had remembered. It must have been added onto many times. There didn't seem to be any overall architectural plan. Safi loved the grapevines which trailed over the long, low portico flanking the front. They softened the entrance. The portico wrapped around two sides of the house and served as a porch. There was also a large screened porch at one end of the house. Safi didn't need to be told that the little woman inside who was waving to them was Aunt Mamie.

On her first visit to Sugar Loaf three years ago, Safi had been asked to address the relatives as aunts and uncles. She had no trouble doing so with Aunt Mamie, Aunt Ella, and Uncle Ed, but she knew she had better never address Aunt Bertha directly. That would be "presumptuous." Safi fantasized more cartoons of Bertha caught in the mayhem of Maxwell Street Market, flustered hearing a peddler call out: "Lady, I can see you have discerning taste. Get your kosher *sambousak* right here." Or another saying, "Indulge yourself, Madam, eat a flaky *boureka*—no buttering necessary." Safi would never call Bertha "Aunt" or "Boots," but she would also never leave her cartoons laying around again.

As she and Letitia walked up the steps to the porch, Safi couldn't help but notice Bertha's height and her excellent posture. She was in her mid-seventies, but had the commanding presence of a general. Both she and Ella had silky white hair, tucked in at the back of their necks in wavy loose buns. They were quite handsome women. Aunt Ella was soft-spoken and gentle. Boots greeted Safi with a firm handshake, whereas Ella put her hands on Safi's cheeks and looked lovingly into her eyes. "You are so welcome here, Safi." Ella's eyes were tearing up.

By this time, Mamie had come outside onto the portico. She was around five feet tall. Her hair was still dark brown, even though she was the oldest of CD's daughters. Her face was rather plain, but she had a twinkle that showed she might like a bit of mischief. Safi recognized the tall man behind the screen door to be Uncle Ed. She gave him a big smile.

"At last I have my walking partner," Uncle Ed said as he came out through the screen door.

A motorboat approached the front pier. Out poured the Thatchers, all seven of them. Little bodies with blond heads of hair came wiggling up to where they were standing. Towels were dragged on the ground. A couple mouths were decorated with chocolate ice cream. The youngest was crying. Cornelia was all smiles saying what a wonderful afternoon they all had. On seeing William, Safi instinctively moved closer to Bernie.

Blair Davis, Boots' son, came quickly out of the house with his Kodak camera. After kissing the three of them, he said, "Hold it everybody." He promptly positioned them according to height, using the front steps for staging, and took some pictures, after which he helped Bernie take the bags in. Safi heard Alley barking from the open car window, no doubt resentful he was not being welcomed along with the others.

CHAPTER 21

Rooms were assigned. Bernard was given a ground-floor room in a small side building, unattached to the main house but near the kitchen. Back in the days of CD, it had been the cook's room. It's inside wall was shared with the laundry room. Aunt Let must have warned the aunts to keep Alley as far away as possible. Bernard was pleased to note that he was quite close to Freddy and Marjorie's house, however.

The main house had an ell shape. The longer end of the ell faced the lake. The shorter end overlooked the garden and the lawn where the family played croquet. Bernard carried his aunt's bag through the living room to the front stairs. Aunt Mamie, the oldest of the three great aunts, and her husband, Uncle Ed, always occupied the one proper bedroom on the ground floor at the foot of the stairs.

At the top of these front stairs was a small landing giving access to two doors: one to Aunt Ella's room and the other to the room allotted to Aunt Letty. A window at the head of the stairs brought in light. It was at the crook of the ell, so that when Bernard looked through it he saw another window facing it no more than a yard away. Through it he could see Safi. He almost waved to her, but thought better of it when he saw Blair putting down Safi's bag in her doorway. He smiled, recalling Boots downstairs on the veranda pointedly directing Blair to carry Safi's suitcase to her room. Was she trying to make sure that the too-eager William didn't assume that mission? Or was Boots playing her usual house-mother role, keeping Bernard at a proper distance from his girlfriend?

Bernard remembered his days at Sugar Loaf when his parents were alive. His older cousin Stewart had been a hell-raiser. One time he was

so drunk he hit a rock, knocking him off his water skis just in time before he attempted to ski under the front pier. It was too bad Stewart had
such an affinity for alcohol because he was a natural athlete, winning a
cabinet full of awards in swimming. He had broad shoulders and a fine
physique, which girls could easily admire because he was always in a
swimming suit. Well not always—one night Boots caught him chasing
his girlfriend, both nude, through the garden. The girl was sent home
on the next train and Stewart had to clean the bird baths and weed
hollyhocks for the rest of that summer. Nonetheless, Bernard missed
Stewart—even the rows he had with Aunt Bertha. Bernard hadn't seen
him since he married and moved to Arizona. Sadly, Stewart rarely kept
in touch with Aunt Let, either.

Bernard unfolded the suitcase stand at the foot of Letty's bed and
put her heavy suitcase on it just as she walked into the room. He could
hear her panting slightly from using the stairs. She gets no exercise,
Bernard thought.

"I remember this room well," she said.

"It's good, isn't it? You have your own bathroom."

Letty walked over to the door to the adjoining bedroom on the
opposite side of the room and opened it. A release of giggles and small
shrieks took them both by surprise. "I beg your pardon," Letty said as
she quickly shut the door. "Oh God, the Ts!"

"Just the girls are sleeping in there. The three boys are sleeping in
'Tree Top.'"

"Oh, that makes it worse! They're right over me."

"Yes, the stairway up to Tree Top is in the girls' room."

"Every night will be a slumber party," Letty said despairingly.

"Would you like to switch rooms with me?"

Letty broke out in uncontrollable laughter. "Really, Alley and I
together!"

"What about switching with Safi, then? Of course, you would
lose the private bath. Good God, Safi will have to share a bath with
Cornelia's family. There better be a lock on that door."

"I'm sure Aunt Bertha has thought of each of these difficulties. Don't worry! She'll probably be sitting outside the door while Safi showers."

No one ever actually talked about William Thatcher's "problem," but everybody was on guard against it. The room that the Thatcher girls were in had three doors: one to Letty's room, one to Cornelia and William's room, and one to the stairs leading to Tree Top. Cornelia and William had access to the back stairs through yet another door. In effect, three of the upstairs bedrooms served as a hall. Boots always let it be known that she expected the doors to be kept open during the day, so people could pass through from one side of the house to the other. That meant of course that beds had to be made and the rooms kept tidy.

"May I help you unpack?" Bernard asked. He noticed Letty had spotted the water glass turned upside down on top of her dresser. He could read her mind. She had gone the entire trip without a drink and was probably dying to have him leave. So sad, he thought. She'll have to hide her bottles from Boots! Before he left her alone, he had to ask his aunt a favor. "How do you think people will feel if Safi sits in on tomorrow's powwow?"

"Oh, I already asked the aunts about that when we were back in Chicago. They thought it would be fine. She already knows so much about the family."

That night before dinner, the family met on the porch. Walter offered to make Old Fashioneds and Tom Collins for cocktails. Bernard and Safi helped Letty distribute copies of *One's Family* to everyone present. Letty had placed book plates on the inside front covers, so each relative already had their name in their copy. Blair gave a rousing toast to Letty. For the next several minutes the family quieted down and looked at their copies.

Aunt Ella said, "Thank you Safi for helping Letitia with the typing."

"This is splendid," Walter said. "We're very lucky to have this record." Bernard added that he was seeing to it that the Chicago

Historical Society got a copy. A cool breeze off the lake seemed to add to the accolades Letty was receiving. As she looked at each of her relatives assembled on the porch, Bernard felt his aunt's pride in her accomplishment.

Someone spoke out, "Oh here's the story of Uncle Brode reading on the train in his pajamas into the wee hours of the night."

"Oh yes," someone else added. "The railcar was disconnected and shunted on a side junction in Prairie Falls, Kansas." Everyone started laughing.

CHAPTER 22

Safi noticed Boots turn to the final page in the book, the page with the Peacock family tree. Safi froze. Oh my God, she thought, what if no one has told her? After studying the page for a while, Safi noticed Boots' face turning red. Safi dreaded what was coming, but was surprised to see Boots begin a ferocious stare at Ella. "Ella," she finally said loud enough that everybody stopped and turned towards Boots. "This is your doing."

Moods sobered and many family members quickly flipped to the last page in their book, mimicking Boots. A good minute passed before Blair started laughing. He came over and gave Safi a big hug.

Boots looked fiercely at Ella and said accusingly: "You purposely picked out Safi to help Letitia, didn't you?"

"Yes, Father asked me to make sure that the other side of the family was looked after."

"Nonsense, Father disliked Leo."

"Maybe at first," Ella turned to look at Safi apologetically, "I'm sorry to admit." She paused before going on and turned to look at Boots directly, "But not at the end," Ella declared. "On his deathbed," again Ella turned to Safi, "Father specifically asked me to look after the other branch of the family." Turning back to Boots, she added with considerable force, "Anyway, sister, your behavior is more than rude."

Safi heard Cornelia say under her breath, "Good God, she's related to us."

Bernard became furious. He went over to Boots and Cornelia and took their books away from them. "If this family isn't good enough for you, get another one."

At that very moment, Marjorie entered the porch with a big smile on her face, ringing the dinner bell and announcing that dinner was ready. People left the room quickly to go to the dining room without looking at Boots.

There were seventeen at the dining room table that night. Uncle Charles, Cornelia's father, came in from fishing on the lake just in time. He was exuberant about having caught a lake trout. Usually people were bored silly with explanations of his angling ventures, but tonight they questioned minute distinctions between lures throughout the soup course. Boots didn't say anything.

Safi felt the sting from the scene on the porch throughout the meal. Bernard and she had talked things over back in Chicago and decided that they would not sit next to each other while at the dining room table, as a way of easing the family into their relationship, but Bernard had abandoned that plan tonight. In fact, on the porch, after putting Boot's and Cornelia's books down on a table, he took Safi's hand, held it firmly, and walked her from the porch to the dining room and insisted on sitting next to her. This comforted her.

For the first half of the meal, Safi couldn't look at Boots. In spite of what happened on the porch, Safi knew she had friends here. She started enjoying watching Bernard eat. She could tell he loved what they were served: roast beef, Yorkshire pudding, roasted potatoes, green beans, biscuits, and apple pie à la mode for dessert. These days, the aunts hired local people to do the cooking. Back in CD's time, she knew from Letty's book, there was live-in help, if she remembered correctly. Even a butler named Leroy, was brought up to Dartford Lake from Chicago. Safi recalled reading that there used to be four courses at the dinner meal. Each table setting had, in addition to the dinner plate, both a salad plate and a butter plate. Bernard told her he remembered as a child sitting next to Leroy in the kitchen, helping him make the curlicues of butter.

The dining room table was made of walnut and had comfortable chairs to match. Safi noticed that there was always a little scurry among the Ts while people were sitting down to the table. It seems that each of the Ts wanted to sit in the one chair with a high seat. Later, when she was alone with Bernard, she asked him why one chair was made higher than the others.

"Great-grandmother Mary Ann, CD's wife, was about five feet tall. CD had a chair especially built for her so she wouldn't feel like a child."

"That's probably why Aunt Mamie is so short," Safi suggested.

"Yes, no doubt. Each of the younger children wants to sit in that chair. They are supposed to take turns, Cornelia told me, but somehow they always 'forget' whose turn it is.

"I hope all this family business is not too awkward for you," Bernard said to Safi. "Boots was despicable today, but remember, she is just one."

"Cornelia is another," Safi replied.

"They're sheltered and ignorant, both of them," Bernard said.

"Actually in some respects I find it fascinating, having worked on Mrs. M's book for three years."

"Do you mind sitting in on the powwow tomorrow?"

"No. Aunt Ella already asked me to participate. I love her." They kissed each other good night. Then, found a good excuse to move into a dark corner and kiss some more.

Safi had trouble falling asleep that night. She knew she was in love with Bernard, but she would not allow herself to expect that things might work out between them. Oddly enough, just before falling asleep, she sensed that Boots must feel isolated from the rest of the family....

At 7:00 A.M. sharp, Safi woke up to a little bell ringing on the second floor. She recognized Boots' voice calling out loudly: "Rise and shine and hear the little birdies sing their songs of praise so early in the morning."

"Oh my God," Safi said yawning, "this deserves another cartoon." She had forgotten that Boots always awakens the children at Sugar Loaf with this message. She had definitely missed her calling as a drill sergeant, she mused.

Safi actually was glad to get up. She went to the bathroom with her towel and shower cap but found William waiting outside the door. She quickly turned around to return to her room when he said: "Too bad we can't double up in the shower. It would be ever so much quicker."

Safi didn't know how to respond. Before she could think of what to say, the bathroom door opened and Cornelia stepped out. Her hair was wrapped in a towel and she had another towel wrapped around her. Even in this state Safi thought she was pretty. Too bad she had such a *schmuck* for a husband. Cornelia looked at the two of them and gave Safi a disgusted look. Safi turned around and went to her room. She would bathe later in the day.

Bernard came to breakfast after Safi was seated. He put his hand on her shoulder, smiled as he said "Good morning," and sat down next to her. Safi realized that was as much as he dared to do with Boots watching. After breakfast, the family went out to the screened porch to start the powwow. The room was big enough to accommodate the eleven adults assembled. A few comfortable chairs had been brought out from the living room. A table for Charles was placed at one end.

Before he started the meeting with a financial report, Cornelia spoke up and asked if it was appropriate that Safi was present. Safi felt her cheeks turn scarlet. Before anyone else replied, Aunt Ella looked pointedly at Cornelia and said: "Safi is very welcomed." Ella's eyes passed on to Boots. "She is a member of our family and her great-grandfather was also in the jewelry business. Besides, she is a close friend of a number of people here, and having helped Letitia with her book, she already knows a great deal about our family." Ella looked at Cornelia and said loudly: "Rudeness has never been appropriate behavior for a Peacock."

There was stunned silence. Finally, Cornelia said in quite a meek voice: "It isn't that I don't want you here, Safi, it's just that I was hoping that you could watch over the children so I could be here." Safi was saddened by the thought that Cornelia saw her as a servant.

After some hesitation, Uncle Ed said loudly: "What? What did Cornelia say?" Mamie shouted to him an abbreviated explanation. "Well, holy mackerel, I'll take care of those little guys. I'm taking a back seat here anyway, what with my inability to hear much. Marjorie might be able to help me." He got up to leave. "Never can hear a dang thing any of you say anyway," he said, and walked out.

Everyone started to feel better again, although Safi was still upset. Despite Cornelia's disrespect for her, Safi felt sorry for her. Safi had been lucky to have had a mother who cared greatly for the well-being of her family. Once again, Cornie could have used her mother's help with her five children, but Aunt Gertrude had not come to Dartford Lake this summer. Some excuse was given, but everybody knew it was the height of horse racing season.

Her own thoughts distracted her from listening closely to Uncle Charles. She thought he was supposed to give a financial report, but by the time she could concentrate on what he was actually saying, she heard him talking about "white flight" to the suburbs. Evidently he at- tributed the downturn in CD Peacock's business to that! He went over the finances of the various divisions of the business, holding up big charts for each department: gold, silver, gems, jewelry repair, watches, stationery, stemware, china.... Sales were down in each one.

"Well, we've just been through a war, and before that, a depression. Won't sales soon bounce back?" Blair asked.

"I see no sign of that. Some of the other jewelry stores are building branch stores in the suburbs. Do we want to do this?" Charles asked.

William said: "Wouldn't that be convenient not to have to go downtown each day?"

"How much would it cost to build a store? Would we want to build in a new shopping center or buy an existing building in a well- established wealthy neighborhood and remodel it to fit our needs, so that it becomes our type of jewelry store?" Blair asked.

"Actually our store has moved several times since the business was founded in 1837. Let's see, Father used to make us memorize this,"

Aunt Mamie said:

> In 1837, it started as a frame store on the south side of the river
> at 155½ Lake Street. In 1843, it moved west with the business dis-
> trict to 195 Lake Street. Then to 199 Randolph in 1849, which had
> become the leading retail thoroughfare. In '57, Elijah moved The
> House of Peacock to 205 Randolph Street. At the time of the fire,
> in 1871, the store was located at 221 Randolph Street. The fire de-
> stroyed everything, except the jewelry vault. After the fire, Peacock's
> temporary quarters were at 96 West Madison. In 1873, the store
> was at State and Washington Streets. In 1894, the store moved to
> State and Adams. The year Father died, 1903, we were incorpo-
> rated under Illinois State law. Now it is at State and Monroe.

William clapped: "What a memory, Aunt Mamie!"

She went on: "Anyway, I think we've moved nine times in 113
years. We always moved so the store would remain in the fashionable
business area. My point is we have a long history of moving and estab-
lishing a new store."

"Does that mean you are in favor of starting some stores in the
suburbs?" Bernard asked.

"No it doesn't. I think the young people here should be influential
in making such a decision, because you are the ones that are going to
have to live with it."

"Well, as I see it," Bernard said, "there are four options: keep our
store as is and don't sell, but get more talent in so we can increase the
sales. Secondly, we could start some suburban stores and keep the
downtown one, but then we would certainly need more talent. Or we
could sell the store but insist that those of us who want to continue
working in it are hired by the new owners. Lastly, we could just sell the
store, take the money and run, so-to-speak."

Safi was surprised that Bernard entered into this discussion, since
he maintained that he didn't care much for the business. Bernard did
tend to show off his intellectual skills. She actually sympathized with

William when he said looking directly at Bernard: "It's easy for you to be flip about this. Your livelihood doesn't depend at all on our decision. You've never worked at the store, even though you're the last Peacock."

"You're right, William. I'm sorry if I seemed flip. Can I just make another comment? Isn't it a shame that inheritance of businesses always went to the men in the family. If women had been allowed to work, we would have twice as much Peacock talent available to us today."

"That 'University of Chicago twaddle' doesn't really advance our discussion," William sneered.

Bernard is right there, Safi thought, but so is William. It's water over the dam, now.

Ella didn't stand for this turn in the dialogue: "We can have differences of opinions and attitudes, but please, we must maintain the Peacock tradition of politeness and respect."

"If I may say one other thing along this same line?" Bernard continued. There were sighs and shifting of positions. "Family members can change their last names. Blair, William, Cornie, you could each change your surname to Peacock, if you wanted to."

"Thank you, Bernard. We know we can always count on you to have a different approach," said Boots.

Was Boots being sarcastic? Safi couldn't tell for sure.

"Perhaps we should go into the synthetic gem business," William added. "That could enhance our reputation."

Mamie suggested that they have silence for a few minutes while members of the family recovered their manners.

Finally Walter resumed the discussion by saying: "Do we have the energy to become engaged in suburban stores and still run our downtown store?"

"Perhaps *we* don't have that energy, but we could hire people who would have that kind of drive," Cornelia suggested.

"I think we have to be realistic," Letty said, "we don't have many young family members that want to go into the business, so why should we continue to try to run it if it isn't doing well in the first place? And, if it doesn't stay as a family-managed business, why should we continue to own it?"

"If it comes to that," Charles continued, "we can still be proud. Most family-owned businesses last only for two generations. We have lasted more than four."

"I have heard," said Blair, "that family-run businesses tend to have better survival rates because they are not in business for quick profits. They can ride out storms because they are managed by people with long-term vested interests."

"That is very true, Blair. What tends to undo them are family quarrels and lack of interest and expertise among the family members who run the business," Walter added.

The discussion went on all morning. When they broke for lunch, Safi noticed Mrs. M slip upstairs, no doubt for her glass of sherry. Uncle Ed led the five little ones into the house. They quietly took their places at the table: hungry but exhausted. Evidently, Uncle Ed not only got Marjorie's help, but they took Alley and walked the children through the woods to a Winnebago Indian burial ground. He said that Marjorie told them about the effigy mounds. The Thatcher kids started repeating eagerly what they had learned.

"Effigy mounds are where they buried things they had made."

"They were made by Winnebagos. I like that word."

"Some mounds were in the shape of turtles."

The oldest said: "The effigy mounds were usually built in the shape of an animal, but if they buried people in the mound, it would be in the shape of a cone." Cornelia was delighted and thanked her great-uncle profusely.

Aunt Ella perked up to say: "The last Winnebago chief to rule the Dartford Lake area was Chief Highknocker." Some of the Thatcher kids giggled.

"Chief Highknocker," one repeated. Then they all had to say it.

"That was the name people in this area gave him, because late in his life—I think he lived for over a hundred years—anyway, late in his life he started wearing a stovepipe hat.'"

"Oh boy, I'd like to see that—a stovepipe hat with braids and war paint on his face." The giggling continued.

"The Winnebagos believed Dartford Lake was a sacred area because it was the home of the 'Water Spirit,'" Ella added.

"Oh, that's why Bernard wanted to dig the well—to tap the 'Water Spirit,'" William said.

The more Safi heard William, the more she felt he had innumerable ways of being obnoxious. Bernie must want to retaliate, she thought. She was glad he didn't. Boots did it for him: "William, bury the hatchet!" Two of the children laughed until they saw Bertha's expression.

The lunch was simple, as Boots had promised. She said it had to be light so no one would fall asleep in the afternoon. Safi knew Bernard could have eaten much more. At least the two of them had time for a quick stroll in privacy before the meeting resumed.

"I didn't know your family was in the jewelry business."

"I only realized it myself when I discovered that Leo Glitz was my great-grandfather. But how does Aunt Ella know anything about my family?"

"I'm guessing that she followed the request of my great-grandfather and tried to know what was happening to your side of the family. She and Uncle Ed are both keen on history."

"Do you think Aunt Ella was referring to something in particular, when she talked about rudeness?" Safi asked.

"I have no idea."

After lunch it was Walter's turn to discuss the history of the jewelry business and what the present-day trends suggested for the future. Safi expected to be thoroughly bored by Walter because the topic didn't interest her, and she thought Walter's monotone would put them all to sleep, even if they'd only had a light lunch.

He began: "Jewelry is not static. The jewelry business is continually evolving, reflecting our society, which is continually changing. Politics, wars, scarcity of materials, new methods of production, new materials, and new attitudes all affect the jewelry business. To reach a wise decision today about selling the store, we can't assume that in the future we can have the same store as we had in the past, or have today. We have to predict, as best we can, how society is changing.

"There are two reasons why, in the past, jewelry has been especially important to women. Not very long ago, a woman could not own other types of property. There were only two ways for her to secure her future: marry well or acquire jewels. With jewels, she could get out of a difficult situation. Being light weight, jewels could be easily hidden and transported. Being durable, they kept their value. Besides security, jewels had an additional value to a woman. She could use them to draw attention to herself. By displaying her jewels she could maintain or improve her social status."

Safi immediately thought of Mrs. M.

Walter continued: "Recent changes have given women other avenues to acquire security and status. They've gained the right to vote. Politicians now have to consider their needs. The war gave them job opportunities that were never available to them in the past. Why are these changes important to CD Peacock's? Well, because most jewelry is purchased *by* women and most jewelry purchased by men is purchased *for* women."

He paused, probably to make sure that his point had sunk in, before going on. Safi had always assumed that Walter was not very intelligent. To her, he had seemed a bit stodgy, dull, and slow-witted. Walter continued: "You see, CD Peacock's is doing just fine in terms of the quality of what it sells, in terms of the honesty of its salespersons, and in terms of our service in general. For over 100 years our store has had an outstanding reputation."

William directed a daggering look at Bernard. Safi did her best to minimize its effect by not looking at Bernard to see his reaction.

"Perhaps we can improve in the knowledge of some of our salespersons a bit." Safi heard Boots say with a sigh as she fixed her eyes briefly on William.

"We always have to remember that we are in a retail business. Marketing is important. Jewelers created a market for birthstones, gems for specific anniversaries, wedding rings for women, and recently, those for men. I believe something like 85% of weddings today are double-ring ceremonies. These trends won't last. All fads have to blend in with the mood of society at the time. I remember Grandfather telling us that the Arts and Craft movement of the 1870s was a reaction to mass-produced goods of inferior quality. In jewelry the reaction took primitive forms with floral or Celtic patterns.

"Then in the 1880s to the 1910s, Art Nouveau came in to jewelry production. We sold brooches with highly stylized designs of plants, especially flowers, using curvilinear forms. Art Nouveau stressed the beauty and harmony of everyday life. It tried to get away from classical ideas of what art should be. We responded to that trend—hence our lovely peacock doors.

"During the '20s, cocktail jewelry came into fashion. Today we call it costume jewelry. The Art Deco movement produced a desire for jewelry with bold color and geometric shapes. The style celebrated the machine age. Thank God it passed quickly! I always thought it was gaudy. But for a few years before the austerity of WWII set in, Peacock's had to sell jewelry with clean lines, stepped edges, and arced corners. Geometrically shaped stones were set in white industrial metals, such as platinum and palladium.

"Now that the war is over, there's interest again in the arts and leisure pastimes. New materials such as plastic and innovative coloring techniques have led to a variety of novel styles. You've all seen that.

"I have two more points to make. Although we didn't appreciate Bernard's sapphire stunt, it did serve as a wake-up call. I personally think that people in another forty years are not going to care whether a stone is real or artificial. We now can synthesize rubber and penicillin, make aluminum foil, and buy frozen dinners. Consider how fast new materials and devices are being created: the atomic bomb, the electron microscope. We're soon to have television with a colored picture.

Commercial air flight is regular now. Mark my words, I think we're at the beginning of a new age. People are going to want to travel and have new devices. As these inventions multiply, I believe jewelry is going to have less appeal. Increasingly, the public will choose to buy synthetic gem stones, which you must admit can be beautiful. People will always want stunning designs and jewelry that is well made, but I believe they won't care if the stones were found in nature.

"My second point is that people are not as formal as they used to be. Women rarely wear white gloves or hats. Many put on trousers when they are at home. I've come back to women. Remember, jewelry is largely bought by or for women. In a few decades, women won't need jewelry. They may want to buy it as art work, but they won't need to have it. I say we get out of the business while we can. Sell. We've had a good run. In two or three decades, stemware, crystal, silver services, and flatware won't be wanted. Changes are occurring too rapidly. Our lifestyle will soon be old and obsolete. Sorry. I've talked too much."

There was a long pause. Letty was the first to speak: "Although I want to sell too, I don't believe our lifestyle is obsolete."

"For me, everything depends on whether or not the new owners will hire us, in more or less our current capacity," said Blair.

"We three aunties don't work in the store, but we would like to sell and sell soon, before we lose our fine reputation. I want us to go out on a high note," said Mamie.

"I forgot to say, that the downturn in our sales pretty much matches that of our competitors in the city. But in fact there is one department in which we have increased sales in recent years and that is in men's jewelry."

Safi noticed Blair's cheeks turn pink.

"Like Blair, Cornelia and I would like to know if the buyers will hire us, and if so, in what capacity," William said.

"I suppose we can always enter into discussion without committing ourselves," Charles offered. "I think for my part I'd like to just retire. Gertrude, of course, thinks I should keep on working."

Safi had been dying to ask a question. "I know I have nothing to do with your decision, but I wonder if I could ask a question, because of something that I just learned in a course." Mamie and Charles welcomed her to continue. "I believe money to run the government during the nineteenth century was raised through tariffs and excise taxes. For much of that century there was no tax on property, as I understand it. Business monopolies had developed which controlled industry. Americans were free to acquire unlimited amounts of wealth. My labor professor says that during the nineteenth century, America was involved in a class struggle between the super rich and workers."

William interrupted: "Communism is being taught at Loyola too, not just the U of C."

Safi smiled but didn't respond to the remark. "Labor thought that the income tax would level the playing field. Since fine jewelry is something only the wealthy can afford, can you attribute the downturn in sales to the fact that the wealthy are now being taxed?"

"That's a good question Safi," Charles responded. "But the wealthy can still dodge taxes by channeling their fortunes into tax-free foundations. Those are commonly thought of as charitable institutions. However, the grants that they give often advance the interests of their founders. The Carnegie and Rockefeller Foundations were in place even before there was an income tax. So I would have to answer that the income tax has not reduced the percentage of super rich people in this country. I believe Walter is right. Sales are down because people don't aspire to owning fine jewelry as much as they used to."

Walter added, "I believe the top marginal tax rate is 94% on income over $200,000, or something like that." The three aunties gasped. Walter chuckled. "It's not as bad as it sounds because income tax is graduated. Let's not get into that. But I want to tell you, Safi, that in addition to forming charitable foundations, wealthy people can dodge income tax by transferring wealth to their children and by setting up family trusts. I think there are still plenty of wealthy people."

Safi didn't know much about these things. She was starting to feel uncomfortable, not only for being an outsider, but because these techniques of hoarding wealth were against her socialist values. Bernard's parents must have used these techniques because he obviously had no financial worries. Although he was generous with his money, if he lived on only his salary from Chicago Latin School, he'd be living on Wells Street rather than Lake Shore Drive. She didn't want to be lured into a lifestyle which ignored poverty and workers' rights. In fact she wouldn't let herself.

The day after the powwow, Safi walked into the kitchen and found Aunt Ella standing alone by the gas stove, making herself a cup of tea. Safi realized that this aunt actually spent much of her time in the kitchen. It was Ella who supervised the preparation of dinner each night. She ordered the food to be purchased and made sure the kitchen was kept tidy. The two of them exchanged greetings and a few comments before Ella asked Safi, "How long did you live at Hull House after your mother died?"

Safi was taken by surprise, but welcomed the question, "About three years."

"I suppose you went to school in the neighborhood."

"Yes, it was the same school that I had been going to before, because we'd always lived in that neighborhood."

"What was it like?"

"The school or the neighborhood?"

"Both really, I want to picture what your life was like then."

"The school was very crowded." She chuckled. "Actually the neighborhood was very crowded too. The streets and sidewalks were packed with people walking and shopping. It was a place where you could get everything from a screwdriver to a fur coat."

"Yes, It has the reputation of being the busiest shopping area in Chicago," Aunt Ella said.

"We lived just off Maxwell Street, in between Hull House and Maxwell Street. It was always noisy. Mom and I lived in a two-room apartment above a shop. It was very small. My bedroom at Mrs. M's is bigger than the one Mom and I slept in."

"Did you and your mother have to move there after your father died?"

"Yes, but we just moved next door, into a smaller apartment. We knew the owners well."

"Nonetheless, it must have been hard for you and your mother to fit into such a small place with all your belongings."

"No. We never owned much. You know my father was a Communist. Well, my mother was one too. They were both activists, but they weren't subversives. Everyone today thinks that Communists want to overthrow the government, but we were never like that. My dad even thought anyone advocating the use of force, violence, or terrorism should be expelled from the party. He was a union organizer. My mother worked for years at Hull House. She typed for them. Then after Dad died she also typed theses, mostly for the University of Illinois students. Both my parents read a lot, but they got their books from the library. Dad always said that he saw no point in owning things."

"Your neighborhood was largely Jewish when you grew up, but now it's changed hasn't it?"

"Yes. Many of the Jews and Germans moved out, even by the time I was born, I think. I remember my mother making a distinction between her German Reform Jewish background and that of the Eastern European Jews who came later."

"Maybe like the difference between the Protestants and the Irish Catholics who immigrated later?" Ella threw in.

"Yes, exactly, well no, not exactly because of anti-Semitism. According to my dad, German Jews felt obligated to support the Jews from Eastern Europe because anti-Semitism in Europe and in the United States was on the rise, even though their religious views were quite different."

"Hmm, that's very interesting. So because there was no anti-Christian movement, Protestants and Catholics could afford to be at each others' throats." They both laughed.

"I think the Eastern European Jews started coming over in the 1870s. They tended to be Orthodox." Safi went on to tell Aunt Ella that her family was not religious and why. "So let's see, I think originally the Near West Side was German with many of them Reformed Jews. Then it became Irish, Orthodox Jewish, and now it's increasingly Black. I learned in my course that the Near West Side has always been an 'entry neighborhood.' That's what it's called because new immigrants move into it, pushing the older ethnic group out. Maybe I should turn that around; earlier immigrants move out to a so-called 'better neighborhood,' allowing new ones to take their place. That's more like it, I think."

Safi found out that Aunt Ella had been to Hull House a few times. "I never suffered the type of losses that you have. The hardest thing for me as a child was not being able to go back to my grandfather's farm."

Increasingly confident of Aunt Ella's sincerity, Safi mustered the courage to ask her some questions about the farm. "I heard from Mrs. M that it had everything—such a variety of plants and animals. Why couldn't you go back?"

"Well, for some reason, it didn't appeal to my father."

"Is that why he bought Sugar Loaf?"

"Yes, I think so."

"Did you like the white peacocks?" Safi asked with a smile.

"Oh yes, we all did; and the orchard. We grew our own vegetables. You know, they were delicious! Emily was wonderful to us."

"Emily?"

"Grandmother Mary and Grandfather's oldest child."

"That was Mary Kolze and Elijah's first child? Mary Kolze was my great-grandmother."

"Yes, that's right, my father's half-sister."

Safi realized that she had come a long way in understanding Peacock relationships. Three years ago she would have been helplessly confused, but not now. Ella went on: "Emily was wonderful to all of us children but especially to us girls. She taught us how to take care of the vegetable garden and all the flower beds. That's how Boots became such a good gardener, although she will never talk about Emily."

"Why not?"

"Father wanted little to do with Mary Kolze. I think he was embarrassed that she was a German immigrant. But anyway, Boots always went along with whatever Father said. You may have noticed that she's a bit keen on discipline. Even though Mamie is older, Boots could always keep Mamie in line. She didn't have that control over me, but I suppose she didn't have to because I learned to keep my thoughts to myself. Well anyway, getting back to Emily. She taught me how to make apple strudel. Do you know how to make it?"

"No, I'm afraid not. That was a little fancy for our tastes when I grew up. What was special for us were *sufganiots*."

"What is that?"

"Deep fried jelly doughnuts covered with powder sugar."

"They sound good!"

"It was always such a production. Like us, none of the families around us had the money to make their own *sufganiots*. All that oil would have been too expensive for any one family, so we did it together. That was fun. They were good times."

"Would you like to make apple strudel together? I would love to try to make one again. I think I still know how."

Two days later Safi and Ella were again alone in the kitchen making apple strudel. Ella continued telling Safi of her special feeling for Emily. "It was funny, but she was more like a mother to me. It wasn't that my own mother wasn't lovely, but to her I was the youngest of six children, whereas Emily had lost all of her brothers and sisters. She had two children herself to care for. Her youngest, Miriam, your grandmother, was just a year younger than me. We became close. I just loved to play with her. I never understood why, but Father didn't like that."

"You remember the opal necklace story in Letitia's book?"

"Oh, yes. It was a strange story, I thought."

"What nobody knows is that the woman who gave me the necklace was Emily. I think Father knew and that was why he made me throw it away. It wasn't a fear of opals. Somehow he sensed that it was Emily who had given it to me."

"I wonder if you would mind my asking something that I don't understand about Mrs. M's book?"

"Not at all!"

"Well, in the first draft, Mrs. M didn't even bother telling what Elijah's second wife's name was."

"Yes, well that's connected to the other peculiarity. I mean that Father wanted nothing to do with his half-sister. I ... I do have a theory about it, but I really don't know the answer."

Aunt Ella was about to explain her theory when some of the Thatcher kids walked into the kitchen, no doubt attracted to the aroma of the apple strudel baking in the oven. Safi never recovered any time alone with Aunt Ella before she had to return to Chicago. The strudel was a hit with the family. Bernard took a big piece of it over to Freddy and Marjorie's.

That evening, some of the Peacocks started a game of croquet to relax before they were called to dinner. Blair and Bernard enjoyed a beer while they played. Walter joined the game as did some of Cornelia's children. Safi was amazed to find Walter to be such a pro. Then, to even off the teams, Charles joined in, although he was at a disadvantage starting late. He hit the ball with a sideways swing. All the others swung the club between their legs. Safi soon realized why Charles didn't care if he started late. He could hit an opponent's ball that was forty feet away. To her surprise some family members who were generally so gentle became quite aggressive. Walter didn't hesitate to knock Blair's ball so far that it almost landed in the lake. There would be great moans from a player who missed a loop. The level of skill that they demonstrated could only be explained, Safi thought, by having spent years playing the game.

Someone who wasn't playing must have removed Alley's tether to a hickory on the other side of the house. By the time they saw him coming, Alley was going at top speed. With consummate skill, he intercepted Charles' ball neatly, just before it would have hit Walter's. The reaction was mixed.

"Three cheers for Alley!" shouted a T on Walter's team.

Bernard was laughing uproariously until he saw that Charles was furious. He quickly responded by picking Alley up and carrying him back. At the dinner table that night Blair explained to the aunts and others what had happened.

One of the Ts spoke up. "I saw you untie Alley, Uncle William."

"Yes, I thought the dog needed a walk after being confined all afternoon."

"Well thank you, William. I didn't know you would like to walk Alley. Next time, let me know when you want to do it and I'll give you a proper leash."

Safi thought his demeanor and drooping eyelids made Bernard appear innocent and sincere, yet she knew he was intentionally pointing out what a louse William was. Mrs. M's eyes narrowed as she looked at William.

Chapter 23

Two days after the powwow, Aunt Mamie announced that she was ready to have another jewel hunt, this time for a six-carat diamond. Letty wanted so much to be the first to find it. She really needed money. Even if the family agreed to sell Peacock's, it would probably be a couple of years before any money from such a sale would be distributed.

Only immediate family members were allowed to help a contestant find the jewel, so Letty was on her own. Cornelia, on the other hand, could call on the help of her father, Charles, William, and her 5 little ones. In fact, Letty had noticed that there was always one T or another in the presence of Mamie. Perhaps they thought they could catch her in the act of hiding it. Letty was quite sure, however, that Mamie would have taken the precaution to hide the jewel before the younger generations arrived.

The night before, Letty went to bed early and had one less glass of sherry than usual. She set her alarm clock for 7:00 A.M. In the morning, after eating a piece of toast and a quarter of a melon for breakfast, she had an hour to kill before the clues would be placed on the dining room table, so she wandered around trying to anticipate where Aunt Mamie would have hidden the diamond.

She thought of it being frozen in ice, say in an ice cube tray. However, some unsuspecting person might throw the ice cubes into the sink. Mamie could have hung it so that it blended with the crystal pieces in a candelabra. She walked casually around the kitchen and into the side room where the refrigerator was. Having satisfied her curiosity, she left this small room and planned to turn right down the hall to the dining room. In doing this, she glanced straight ahead into the trunk room where the telephone hung on the wall. There she saw Elijah's trunk. She had been asking for years if she could look inside it, but Boots said that they had lost the key and Mamie said it was private. As if I would hurt anything, she thought. Honestly, the aunts sometimes treat me as if I'm still a child. Then she noticed that the key was in the trunk's lock. So, it wasn't lost after all!

Precisely at 9:00 A.M., the tray was placed on the dining room table. Each slip of paper on the tray had the same three-word clue:

line, boot, elephant

No other directions were given, just those three words. Charles, Blair, Walter, Bernard, Letty, Cornelia, and William each took a clue. Walter couldn't win again. Since Bernard and William were to share the money from selling the sapphire, did that mean that neither of them could win again? She didn't ask because she didn't want to open up sore wounds.

Letty thought about the three words. What did they have in common? Of course, she thought: trunk lines, a boot is the trunk of a car, an elephant has a trunk. *TRUNK!*

Letty tried not to look directly at any of the other people in the room. She put on a pensive demeanor while making her way through the dining room into the living room. She paused, looked around, then casually walked out onto the veranda. She paused again. From there she walked slowly around the house, the long way, so as to not give anything away. Then she entered the trunk room which also had a door to the outside. She shut that door, crossed the small room to the other door which led to the hall and closed it quietly. She unlocked the trunk and lifted the lid, which was quite heavy. There sat the diamond on top of a blue damask tablecloth. She put the gem in her dress pocket and relished her good fortune. She had to admit, had she not been thinking of Elijah's trunk, just an hour earlier, it could have taken her all day to think of the solution. After a minute, it occurred to her that she had an unusual opportunity. She could look into Elijah's trunk and see what was underneath the damask tablecloth. The fact that the aunts had refused her request to do so in the past made this idea all the more enticing.

She carefully removed the tablecloth. Underneath she found albums and a few pocket folders containing letters. Some documents were carefully preserved between pieces of cardboard. She thumbed through the pocket folder and took out a letter that had her puzzled. It was from Leo Glitz. The letter was addressed to Samuel Peacock and referred to the theft of some "Hanover gems." Were they jewels from the House of Hanover, perhaps? The connection with nobility did not surprise her one bit, but it was something she wished she had known about earlier so she could have put it in her book. Now her book was already distributed. How fascinating, Letty thought, but she had better not get carried away before first getting the general feel as to what was in the trunk, so she put the letter back and went on to other items. Towards the bottom was a large CD Peacock's box. It was the type of box that customers received if they made an expensive purchase. The outside was a solid dark blue color. The lid had a gold rim and in its middle was the Peacock coat of arms. Inside, Letty found two water colors and some pen-and-ink drawings. Each had been carefully wrapped in tissue paper. This trunk was a gold mine. Just as she was about to open an album, she became aware of voices coming through the heating duct. It sounded like Mamie and Boots talking. They're probably in the dining room, she thought. Without a second's hesitation she put everything back into the trunk, placing the damask cloth on top. She quickly opened the door to the hall and barely got the one to the outside opened before Boots appeared at the threshold to the hall. Letty put on a broad smile, reached into her pocket and showed Boots the diamond.

"That was fast," Boots said rather suspiciously.

"Yes, well I noticed the key was in the lock. I thought you said it had been lost."

"I thought it had been. Mamie said it was. She thinks of Grand-father Elijah's trunk as her property."

"Well, once I looked at the trunk...." Letty explained how she solved the puzzle. "Very lucky, wasn't I?"

Mamie came in and gave Letty a hug. The top of her head brushed against Letty's chin, allowing Letty to look beyond at Boots who, unlike Mamie, did not seem pleased.

"Letty, Dear, don't lose it now. Do you want me to keep it for you until you go home?"

I'm still the child to them. "Yes, thank you, but first I want to show everybody." As Letty passed through the outside door she saw Mamie take the key out of the lock and put it in her pocket.

Heck, thought Letty. Now I'm not going to be able to really examine what's in the trunk.

Once all the excitement over finding the diamond settled down, it was time for Bernard to take Safi to the station in Princeton. It had been planned that Safi would leave Sugar Loaf that morning to return to Chicago. Her summer school course at Loyola started the very next day. Fortunately, Letty did have a minute alone with her, long enough to tell her that the trunk was full of interesting things about the family. "I don't have time to explain now, but do you think when you are back in Chicago that you could do some investigating for me?"

"Sure. What do you want me to find out?"

"I want you to find out about your relative Leo Glitz. He was..."

"I know. He was my great-grandfather." Safi finished Letty's sentence for her. Letty noticed Safi's mouth took on an enigmatic smile. Letty told Safi that she had found a letter written by Mr. Glitz in the trunk.

"Oh, what did the letter say?"

"It said something about some 'Hanover gems.' I didn't have time to read it carefully." That was all she had time to say before Ella came up to them to say goodbye to Safi.

CHAPTER 24

The entire Sugar Loaf household was pleased that Letty had found the diamond. It was generally agreed that of all the contestants, Letitia was the one who could benefit the most from having a diamond to sell. Safi, however, thought differently. She was convinced that Mrs. M did have enough money. She just didn't know how to manage what she had.

When she was on the train, Safi had time to think without interruption. She considered the jewel hunt and realized that it made her feel uncomfortable. She liked the intrigue and the puzzle solving aspects of it, but why have such an expensive prize? That just encouraged greed. She wasn't used to being around people who were so wealthy that they could have a jewel be the prize of a treasure hunt. So far, she had kept these thoughts to herself, but one day, she would express them to Bernard. Criticizing the Peacocks, while a guest in their home, would not be right. She could tell that Bernard didn't care about jewels or wealth really, although he must actually have plenty of money. She heard him say once—she had forgotten to whom he was speaking—that "The purpose of wealth is to help others, not to show it off." Bernard caught her eye after he made that statement. She had the feeling that he wanted her to have heard what he said.

Safi laughed, thinking of the attitude some of them had towards Bernard. To them he was a maverick—out in left field. That was good, she thought. That was exactly where she wanted to be, too. Was she truly in love with Bernard? And was that wise? Maybe love can't, by its very nature, respect wisdom. Did he love her? That uncomfortable thought persisted: Was he just a rich man taking advantage of her?

Their backgrounds were so different. Whatever the outcome of their relationship, she would not sacrifice her principles just to fit in with the Peacocks.

Three days later, Safi was back home and in the routine of going to class and studying. Summer school courses were always more intense than those given during the regular school year, so she actually didn't have much free time. Yet she was so glad that Letty had asked her to find out more about Leo Glitz. She was relieved that she wouldn't have to keep what she knew about him secret anymore. One thing Safi definitely wanted to investigate was his disappearance in 1893—was he murdered in Bughouse Square for his wallet, or trampled by a horse being a good Samaritan, or was he lost fighting the Cold Storage fire? She had seen so many conflicting reports.

She decided to go to the police department and ask to see the reports concerning Leo's disappearance. She had recently found out that police reports were open to the public to a certain extent. Once at the station, she was directed to the missing persons desk. It was such an old case that the man behind the counter had to rummage through the archives to find the file. It took much longer than she expected, and without the exact date of the report (which Safi was able to provide from her prior research), it might not have been possible to even locate it, according to the clerk. "I can't believe I found it," the man said when he finally returned, "but here it is. I don't know if this will be much help, though, there is very little here. The case was transferred to the homicide division, it appears."

"Homicide?" asked Safi. "Then he was murdered?"

"Yes, it's possible. Apparently, the original investigator linked his disappearance to a body found in Washington Square, and thought there were enough suspicious circumstances surrounding it that he sent it to homicide."

Safi looked through the report quickly. There were only two pages. The first contained the original report by Leo's wife, along with an interview of the firefighter who had seen Leo fighting the Cold Storage blaze. The second page was dated over a month later, and detailed how the detective had followed a subsequent lead passed along from a precinct station about a possible identification of Leo Glitz as the body found in Bughouse Square that evening. It concluded that the missing wallet and the nature of the wounds could indicate a robbery/murder, rather than an accidental trampling, and referred the case to homicide for further investigation. "How do I get to homicide from here?" she asked.

The officer at the homicide desk who brought her the record stood closely by, watching her while she thumbed through the material in the report. "It says here that a letter was found in the victim's pocket, can I see that letter?" she asked.

"No. That would be evidence in an unsolved murder case. We are not allowed to show that to you." The officer didn't realize it, but the letter had been written in German, and on the next page, there was a translation of it. Safi figured if he didn't know, he wasn't doing anything wrong, nor was she, since the report was public, so she just continued reading it as if she wasn't that much interested:

[the royal seal of the Dukedom of Hanover]

Dear Mrs. Peacock,

I was most intrigued by your letter. This is the first I have heard of this 'Hanover Collection.' I want to assure you that the jewels you have described have never been owned by me or by any of my relatives in the nobility. I took the liberty to ask my good friend the Grand Duke of Oldenburg in the neighboring dukedom if the jewels had belonged to him and he assured me that they had not.

I hope you will be able to recover them and determine their true owner. You may consider making inquiries among the English nobility.

Sincerely,

Friedrich August, Duke of Hanover   *May 5, 1893*

Seeing the Duke of Hanover's name, and the "Hanover Collection" mentioned, Safi knew immediately this was important, and connected somehow to the letter Letty had found in the trunk at Sugar Loaf. This one was addressed to a Mrs. Peacock. No time to think this through now, she told herself. Safi asked if there was a list of witnesses and/or people interviewed as part of the investigation. But again, the officer said he was not free to give that information.

Safi took out her pencil and paper and began noting details from the report. Leo was bludgeoned to death with severe blows to the side of the head and face. No wallet was found, so the police had assumed that he was mugged, in order to rob him. Safi asked the officer if the police had any indication what kind of a weapon was used.

He smiled and said: "Young lady, if it's not written in the report, they either didn't know or they kept it from the public record for investigative reasons. Sometimes we need to keep things secret."

"It says here that the wounds were extensive, yet not very deep. The weapon wasn't round, so much as u-shaped. Does that suggest anything to you?" Safi asked.

"I'm afraid not."

"If his wallet was taken, how did the police identify him?"

"Probably somebody there identified him."

"But shouldn't the police report say who identified him?"

"This happened almost 60 years ago. Maybe the person didn't want to be known. It sounds like it was just another hobo who got mugged, or perhaps not. Being Bughouse Square, that was the place all the extremists went to preach—someone with opposite views could have been waiting to get him. So many possibilities."

As Safi was leaving the police station, out of the corner of her eye, she became aware that someone was waving to her. She saw that it was Officer Murphy. Oh no, she did not want to get involved with him. She waved to him briefly, but hurried on down the street. She pretended not to notice that he was trying to catch up to her. Fortunately her bus was at the bus stop, giving her the legitimate excuse to start running. She caught it just in time.

On the bus, she became so deep in thought that she almost missed her stop at Loyola. Who was the Mrs. Peacock in the letter? She could be Mary Kolze Peacock, Elijah's wife, or Mary Ann Peacock, CD's wife. There was no explanation of what the Hanover Collection was. Did the police think the letter found in Leo's pocket was irrelevant to the case? If that were true, an explanation should have been given in the report. Safi wondered if these omissions were indicative of sloppy police work. Maybe in the 1890s the homicide department didn't think Leo's case was important enough to investigate such leads. The police may have dismissed Leo as a troublemaker. He had been arrested during the Haymarket Riot. Perhaps they associated him with the killing of eight policemen. Or maybe the police had made a more thorough investigation but were induced to leaving the case unsolved. The obvious person to have given such a bribe would be CD himself. *Oy!* That scenario would undo Mrs. M and the Peacocks.

That night, Bernard called her from Dartford Lake. Safi thought she would tell him what she had found out that day, but at the last moment decided not to. *What if Bernard's great-grandfather was somehow responsible for my great-grandfather's death? There are secrets that no one is discussing—the mysterious Hanover jewels, for example.* Safi thought it was likely that they were the same jewels that Aunt Mamie was hiding. Safi really hadn't learned much more about Leo Glitz. For all these reasons, she thought it best to not discuss all this with Bernard over the phone. It would have to wait until he got back to Chicago.

"Did Mrs. M ever get to look at what was in Elijah's trunk?"

"Funny that you should ask, she's been begging me to pick the lock."

"Does she say why?"

"No. You know she can't rest until she knows every facet of this family. She thinks there's something of utmost importance in the trunk. And she thinks the aunts don't want her to know about it."

Safi wanted to say: "She's right," but resisted the temptation. Safi began feeling uneasy. "Bernard do you know why Aunt Mamie is having the jewel hunts?"

"Well no ... I don't think any of us do.... She said she would explain after the last one, which will be next summer. Why do you ask?"

"It seems a bit strange to me. What do you think?"

"Yeah, it sure does. Aunt Mamie has always had a bit of mischief about her."

"Do you think the jewels are those that were stolen, the Hanover Collection?"

"The Hanover Collection, what is that? ... Oh hi, Aunt Mamie. I'm just talking to Safi. I'll be off soon."

"Oh no, did Aunt Mamie hear you say 'Hanover Collection?' Please don't say anything about it, because I could be very wrong and I don't want anyone to think I'm suspicious."

"Suspicious, what are you suspicious of? Now you are being mysterious."

"Bernard, just be quiet. Don't say anything more. Please. Forget the Hanover Collection. I'll explain everything when you get home. Ah ... how is Alley?"

"Oh, he's having a great time, but yesterday he got into a bit of trouble."

"Oh dear, what happened?"

"Evidently Uncle Ed had hung his hat on the rocker he was sitting in on the veranda. Alley probably jumped up, knocked it down, and then chewed on it for whatever time it took to make three prominent holes. Uncle Ed was unaware that anything was happening until Boots came out and caught Alley in the act! Boots immediately laid down the law. Alley must now be on a leash, tied up, or kenneled ... so I run with him every day and only let him loose when we're in the woods."

"I miss you, Bernard."

"I know. I miss you too, and think about you all the time."

CHAPTER 25

Patrick wished he had time to go out with girls. He could tell that some of them in his neighborhood wanted his attention, but too often, when he had made an arrangement to meet a cutie somewhere, he would have to send his younger brother around to tell her he was called out at the last minute. Once it was three days before he had enough time to go to the girl's house and apologize. That sort of thing happened twice to Sarah Callahan, and now she wouldn't even look at him. The boys on the force even had a name for this occupational hazard—the DBDs (Duty Before Dames).

When he saw Safi leaving the station, he had tried to catch up with her, but gave up when he realized she was determined to catch her bus. What a wasted opportunity. For a long time he had sought an excuse to talk with her. The peeper was always watching them. He wished she would just go back to her window and snoop at others.

What was Safi doing at the police station? His curiosity was roused. Patrick went inside the station and asked the desk sergeant what she had wanted, "the one with the long dark hair who just left the building."

"The pretty one?" the officer teased.

Patrick pretended that he was in no mood to fool around: "This is an important matter."

"Oh, right! She asked to be directed to missing persons."

"That figures," Patrick responded, to make it appear that he was fully aware of what she was up to. A minute later he was asking the same question of the desk clerk there, and being directed to homicide.

"Oh, yes, it was a murder from way back in 1893. Can you imagine someone caring about a man who was clubbed to death 60 years ago, and in Bughouse Square, no less?"

"Do you remember the victim's name?"

"Let's see, I have to write each inquiry down. Yes, the man's name was Leo Glitz."

"God, what a name!"

"Right, *Murphy*," the desk clerk scoffed.

Caught off guard, Patrick realized his mistake. The facial features of the homicide desk clerk indicated he might be Jewish himself. Patrick asked to look at the file on the Leo Glitz murder—this time more politely. When he signed the log, he saw he was signing in under Safi's name. Oh, Winter, she might be Jewish, too.

Reading the letter in the report from the Duke of Hanover, Patrick wondered if there was any connection to CD Peacock's. When he had spare time (ha! as if that ever happened), he'd have to go to the store and ask some questions. Going to the Palmer House beats going into pawn shops, he thought. What does this have to do with Safi Winter? Oh boy, life is never simple.

He took down the details of the case. Not that he cared much about what happened 60 years ago, but if it helped him get to know Safi, he'd be fascinated.... Was she trying to avoid him or did she really have to catch that bus? The first thing he had to do was find out about this Hanover Collection and its connection to CD Peacock's, if any. He was about to go to robberies when he was called over by the clerk.

"Hey, Murphy, they've just called for you. You're supposed to get your rosy bottom up to Sergeant Donahue's office, on the double," the clerk said with a smug smile. Patrick thought he was enjoying interrupting him and telling him what to do. Oh well, he resigned himself, got to go.

"Thanks," he said to the clerk, walking quickly to the stairs. He took the steps up two at a time. That clerk has to stay behind a desk all day. He must be so bored. He's probably too spineless to be involved with the public and chase up the nasty types, Patrick told himself.

CHAPTER 26

After Murphy left homicide, the desk clerk still felt annoyed with him. So what the hell, before he returned the Leo Glitz file to the shelf, he would read it himself. He didn't just read it, but truly studied the case. He knew he was supposed to sign the log, but who would care if an old geezer like him knew something he wasn't suppose to know? He wasn't going to investigate anything, was he?

After a minute or two he still had nothing to do, so he stepped over to the robbery department and asked his friend, Stefan, the desk clerk there, to pull the case on the Hanover jewels robbery, if he could find it. "It was probably in the 1890s sometime and it may have been associated with the CD Peacock's jewelry store."

In the last few years, Stefan and Bob had fun browsing old cases and challenging themselves to solve them. They weren't seriously interested, but it helped them pass the time. They understood each other perfectly. The two men often went out for a beer together on Friday nights. "For what?" they would ask each other. And then they would answer in unison: "To celebrate getting through another boring week." They would both laugh. Then they settled down to a game of Scrabble. Recently the two of them started bringing their *New York Times* crossword puzzles to work. On lunch breaks, one often checked with the other for the answer to a particular clue, making sure that no one else in the staff room caught on as to how they passed their time on duty.

Bob used to be a detective. Stefan never made it that far. He went straight from being on patrol, walking a beat, to a desk job. "We could have made fine detectives," Bob told Stefan once, "but these Micks only advance their own."

"Sure and have ya noticed now?" Stefan loved to mimic the Irish accent.

Stefan took several minutes looking for the file. Bob went back to his desk. He didn't want to be away from the homicide desk too long. Ten minutes later Stefan walked over to him.

"Found it, I think. Oh yeah, but not much to this one. It looks like the police went to the store because the owner's brother, Samuel Peacock, reported a theft of five jewels, which he called the Hanover Collection. When the police arrived, Samuel was carrying his coat over his arm already wearing one of his gloves, in a hurry to go home."

"That doesn't sound like *nothing* to me," Bob responded. "What kind of jewels?"

"Oh that's all here." He passed Bob the report. "The jewels are described in detail: the types of stones (all different), the number of carats of each, their cuts, and values. But then they couldn't figure out how the jewels could have been stolen, or even if they were really ever stolen at all."

"Hmm, Charles Daniel Peacock, the owner, oh yeah, CD Peacock, was adamant—ha, I love it—'adamant,' that comes from diamond doesn't it?" Bob was proud of his wordsmith skills.

"OK, he was 'adamant'—about what was he adamant? Stop showing off and finish the damn sentence," Stefan said.

"He was adamant about not letting any news of the theft get out, Bob continued. "He thought it would be bad for the store's reputation."

"It also says," Stefan added, "if you read on, that the police were suspicious that the jewels were stolen so the store could collect the insurance money for them."

"Really, a high-class place like Peacock's?" Bob said. "Did you read that final comment by Officer O'Malley?"

"*A broch!*—O'Malleys back then, too."

"Something to the effect that O'Malley got the impression that the Charles fellow wanted the police to leave the store and just drop the case, right? Most peculiar," Bob said.

"But it says somewhere in the middle of the report that O'Malley checked with the insurance company and CD Peacock's never did put in any claim to collect the insurance money for the missing jewels," Stefan explained.

"Well it appears that they did drop the case. There is no follow up in future years. You'd think there would be something," Bob said.

"But wait a minute, what about this fellow Leo Glitz? How come he's in the picture?" Stefan asked.

CHAPTER 27

While Safi was at Sugar Loaf, Bernard didn't take his daily swim in the lake first thing in the morning. He just wasn't sure how Alley would react. If he stood on the shore and barked, everyone still in bed would be livid. If Bernard jumped in the water, and Alley started acting up, then he'd have to come out to calm Alley down before he could even get used to the cold temperature. He would get no exercise. So he never took the chance. Now that Safi was gone, he could run the risk of annoying people at least once, to see how Alley reacted. So at 7:00 A.M., on the first morning after Safi returned to Chicago, Bernard walked out on the front pier with his towel over his right arm, pulled by Alley, leashed to his left hand.

Bernard had planned the order of his actions. First he put his towel on the bench at the end of the pier and took off his tennis shoes. He put his shoes in the mailbox because Alley loved tossing them around by the laces. Next he released the leash and put it in the mailbox also. Then Bernard jumped off the dock. To his great surprise Alley jumped in after him and started dog paddling. He followed Bernard everywhere. When Bernard swam back to the steps, Alley came and started to climb up, until he saw Bernard change his mind and swim away from the dock. After a good half-hour of this, both Bernard and Alley had had enough. Perfect! Alley shook himself off after Bernard helped him climb back onto the dock, then he laid down panting. What a great way to start the day, Bernard thought.

A few days later, Bernard decided he was not up to par on his family's history. Letty and even Safi knew much more than he did. Maybe he should start by taking a real interest in *One's Family*. So far he had given Letty's book only a cursory read, just so he could say he had read it. It wasn't particularly interesting. He had heard some of the stories a thousand times, those about the relatives he knew, and it was hard to care about stories of people he didn't know, especially those who had been dead for 50 years. But maybe he was missing something.

So far he was having a wonderful summer vacation. He had already read a few books that were "good for him." He could afford to take some time out to read something frivolous. So he found an Adirondack chair under a tree far from the house, brushed off the hickory nuts and leaves that had collected in the seat, and settled there for a good read. He took pencil and paper with him, as his student days were too recent to turn away from the habit of taking occasional notes. Oops, he had better get Alley. He needed companionship, so he tied him up on a long lead, long enough to allow him to lie down beside him. Ha, as if he would do that, he thought, but surprisingly that is just what he did. Alley allowed him a good three hours of peace and quiet.

In the book, Aunt Letty mentioned the fact that CD was the campaign manager for "Long John" Wentworth's candidacy for mayor in 1860. In college, Bernard and his friends always joked that Wentworth was Chicago's own Ozimandias. His ego matched his 6'6" height. There were several examples, but the story that Wentworth had built the tallest monument that Rosehill Cemetery would allow said it best. It was a 70' stone obelisk and reportedly cost something like $40,000. Wentworth made sure it was erected before his death. Upon his orders, after his death a small headstone was placed in front of the obelisk whose only inscription was "J.W." Evidently there was no plan for his wife and children, for they were not buried anywhere in Rosehill.

Later in the book Letty spoke about a family dispute over Elijah's will. Apparently, when Elijah died in 1889, he left $25,000 to erect a granite shaft for the cemetery site that he had purchased for the Peacock family. The lot had 60 burial sites: half were for his first family and half for his second family. Apparently the second family didn't want to spend the money on a shaft and tried to break the will. CD insisted on carrying out Elijah's wishes and took the matter to court. He won the suit and had the monument erected. Bernard couldn't help but question if CD was truly concerned about Elijah's wishes or had he caught a fever from Wentworth? Had this conflict started or just exacerbated the rift between the two sides of the family?

One thing that was odd about Aunt Letty's book, he thought, was that there was very little mentioned about jewelry. The only stones she mentioned were the diamond ring that the gambler never paid for and Ella's opal necklace. Bernard was disappointed to find no reference to the so-called Hanover Collection that Safi had talked about. There was no theft discussed in the book. Perhaps women Letty's age and before were not included in "shop talk." Letty certainly cares about jewels. She wears her entire assortment whenever she can. Where would the jewelry business be without people like Letty? It absolutely depended on ostentation.

This reminded Bernard of the annual Peacock Christmas parties that his family and all the other relatives had attended. Being an only child, Bernard loved the opportunity that the party afforded to play with his cousins. His parents enjoyed socializing as well, but were put off by the elaborate display of silverware (nine pieces per place setting), Baccarat crystal (water goblets, wine glasses, and after-dinner liqueur glasses), and numerous other pieces made of either Sterling or silver plate (butter plates, individual salt and pepper shakers, candelabras with crystal bobeches). Bernard remembered his mom saying on the way home that the table gear alone could have paid for an iron lung for some poor child stricken with polio.

For years his mother had worked tirelessly as a volunteer at the Home for Destitute Crippled Children. She worried constantly that Bernard would catch polio. After she died, in her memory, his father refused to continue going to the Christmas parties. Together, the two of them, he and his dad, found other ways of celebrating "more in tune with the Christmas spirit."

Early on, his father must have realized that strutting was part of the jewelry business. His dad preferred books, but being a librarian had its drawbacks too, Bernard thought. His father was too quiet and withdrawn from people. He had become dependent on his mother for social contacts, so when she died, he didn't know how to make friends. By the time Bernard had lost both parents, he already knew the importance of fighting against loneliness, not just accepting it. He became an activist on the U of C campus.

Bernard heard a commotion in the garden. He went over to see what the matter was and found Boots with smoke coming out of her ears.

"Just look at what the deer have done to my tomato plants!"

"Oh, no, all the shoots have been nibbled on. I'm so sorry," Bernard said, while walking around inspecting plants and commiserating with his aunt. Then it occurred to him that this situation could be turned to his advantage. "Weren't the plants fine until last night?"

"Yes, I thought the plants had gotten big enough that I no longer had to worry."

"I've heard that tomatoes are a favorite plant of deer."

"Yes, but this year I thought I was going to be successful."

"Aunt Bertha, you know how deer feed the heaviest in the early morning or just before dark?"

"Yes, I am aware of that."

"Well, up until yesterday, I let Alley out at the first light of the morning and then while we ate dinner. I let him off his tether, because I knew he wouldn't bother any of us then, since we'd all be inside. In other words, Alley was free to run around just when the deer like to eat." Bernard stopped then and there, noticing that Boots' mouth had tightened and her eyes had narrowed. She rose to her full height which was considerable, put her hands in her apron pockets without taking her eyes off Bernard. He fought off an urge to laugh and tried to keep his eyes fixed on hers.

"OK, we'll try it and re-evaluate the situation in three days."

To diffuse the tension, Bernard began asking about other plants. He pulled out a few weeds. He knew she was on to him and was glad when she finally went back in the house.

He returned to the Adirondack chair and *One's Family* to read the description of the purchase of Sugar Loaf and the additions to the house. Bernard had never known before that Tree Top, the single room that was the third story of the house, was constructed so CD could get away from his six children. All the summers that Bernard had come to Dartford Lake, he had never slept in Tree Top. His curiosity was piqued because he read that CD spent hours each day in that room. Too bad the Thatcher boys were sleeping in it. On the other hand, the entire Thatcher family had gone across the lake to spend the day in the town of Dartford. Why not go take a look now?

He went in the house through the trunk room, up the back stairs, through William and Cornelia's room, and into that of their two girls. He opened the door to the staircase which he ascended to Tree Top, where the three brothers slept. The room was an utter disaster: cots unmade, toys and feathers permeated all levels. Hmm, pillow fights, Bernard thought. I would have loved this when I was their age.

Once his eyes had adjusted to the clutter he was able to concentrate on the structure of the room. It was really quite lovely—or it could be. The room was square with a steeply slanted ceiling. On the side where the ceiling was about twelve feet high, there was a large picture window that overlooked the lake and took up most of that wall. The ceiling descended to a height of about seven feet at the opposite wall, which was windowless, but contained the door to the staircase. There were matching windows at the center of each of the other walls. Bernard, enjoyed analyzing architecture. He thought the design, with its lean-to or shed roof, was quite modern.

From this third-story vantage, viewing the swaying of branches and leaves was mesmerizing. He immediately thought of Safi. How she would love this room. From up here they could spot birds and perhaps a nest or two. In her three short visits to Sugar Loaf, Safi had become enthralled with its trees, birds, and all the creatures she never got to see in the city. He remembered her reaction when she saw her first redheaded woodpecker: "I didn't know that there could be a red that bright in nature."

Hearing a motor awakened Bernard from his daydreaming. He looked out the picture window toward the pier. Good God, a boat was pulling up. To his relief, it was only the mailboat. The mailman was opening the mailbox when his normally complacent black labs started barking. With paws on the gunwales, they looked ready to leap out. Oh no, Alley had pulled free of his tether and was running at lightning speed across the lawn toward the pier. Bernard ran downstairs to get things under control. He heard Aunt Bertha calling him from somewhere outside. By the time Alley was on the pier, the mailman had adroitly made his delivery and pulled the boat away. Alley might have jumped in the lake in pursuit had Bernard not gotten hold of his collar. He swept him up in his arms and carried him to the house, passing Aunt Bertha on the way. She had one word for him: "Kennel."

After taking care of Alley, Bernard intended to return to Tree Top. But first, he thought, he would enjoy looking at the unusual structure on the outside, from ground level. Of course he had looked at it before, but he had never paid much attention to detail. That's funny, he said to himself. Those side windows are not centered. They are decidedly closer to the picture window by at least a foot. He quietly ascended the back stairs again and made his way to Tree Top. He thought he was safe to explore the room further in private because the Thatchers had not returned yet, and he had seen Aunt Mamie and Boots seated on the front porch.

Once in the room again, he looked at the side walls. The windows were definitely positioned in the center of their walls, which were paneled with beadboard that went from floor to ceiling. The door to the stairs, when shut, was flush with the short wall. There must be space behind the rest of this wall. He knocked on the wall and then started inspecting the beadboard to see if it opened. He realized that any one of those straight grooves with half-round detail could actually be an opening without appearing different from the others.

There were three cots in the room, two across the back wall. Bernard lifted both cots out of the way, leaving a passageway for him to move along the wall. He pressed systematically along each of the vertical grooves hoping one would give way and swing open, but no luck. He looked over the room again to see if any other ideas would come to him. One thing did. The walls were topped with four-inch crown molding but there was no base molding anywhere. Perhaps the panel that opened was hinged from the top. Maybe the crown molding could move with the paneling, in which case he should press near the top of the wall. Ten minutes later, applying pressure along the top, Bernard almost stumbled as a section of the wall suddenly gave way. The panel swung out from the wall. Bernard lifted it up. He noticed that there were two sticks to prop the panel open. He quickly looked out the picture window to be sure the Thatchers had not arrived.

Inside the cupboard, Bernard brushed away cobwebs to reveal shelves. They were mostly empty but held some ledgers, magazines, and boxes of letters. There was a fancy eight-inch square box made out of mahogany. It had a combination lock which Bernard assumed wouldn't open, but he gave it a try anyway. Surprisingly, he could lift up the lid. The lock was not engaged. When he looked inside, the explanation was clear. The box was empty, although beautifully lined in black velvet. There were five compartments with black velvet cushions in each. This must have been for displaying jewels Bernard thought. He closed the box and turned it over. It was inscribed on the bottom as being made by the firm "Rudy Ruggles and Co."

He opened a ledger and saw that the dates went far back to the late 1880s. He read the same man's name, George Aide, at the top of each page. Perhaps he was the treasurer? Turning to the facing page, Bernard read: "George Aide: Treasurer of CD Peacock's." Why would these ledgers be here? Shouldn't they be kept in the store? Let's see, the ledgers are for the years: 1885-1893, nine books in all.

One small box held just a few letters, all from the same man: Leo Glitz. Wasn't he Safi's great-grandfather? He took the letters and put them in his shirt. He was getting awfully nervous, feeling like a criminal who needed to get away. He closed the secret cupboard, put the beds back, returned the room to its disorderly state, and quietly descended the two sets of stairs. Before he had reached the trunk room he passed Aunt Ella in the hall.

"That Alley is certainly a free spirit," she laughed, "but you have to come up with a solution or Boots won't allow him back next summer. I thought it was best to warn you, Bernard."

"Thanks, Aunt Ella. I am trying to keep him under control."

"I know you are, Dear, but that dog is a little rambunctious for us older types."

CHAPTER 28

Letty was still determined to get into Elijah's trunk. Why would Aunt Mamie be so perverse, unless there really was something that she didn't want people to see? Letty considered her options. In her opinion, Bernard could do anything mechanical, but unfortunately, he refused to try to pick the lock.

"I got into enough trouble with that sapphire," he said. "I am not risking anything else, even to help you."

Letty couldn't ask Marjorie and Freddy to help. If they got caught it could jeopardize their jobs, and that would be most unfair. There was no one else she could ask. Her only choice was to find the key. Where would Mamie hide it? She is short and feeble, so that narrows the field some. It couldn't be in a place where the family spent a lot of time, or else, sooner or later, one of us would discover it. She next tried to concentrate on Mamie's way of thinking. Letty loved the woman. There was something she knew about her that she didn't think the others fully appreciated: Aunt Mamie was smart. Her smartness had nothing to do with book learning, but she was smart about people. Everybody in the family thought that it was Boots who managed things at Sugar Loaf and she did, but the subtle mastermind behind Sugar Loaf was Mamie, all four feet eleven inches of her.

Letty thought that Mamie had wanted her to find the diamond because she hid it in the very place that she had been obsessed about. Over the last four years or so, since she started writing *One's Family*, she had asked Aunt Mamie several times if she could look at the things in Elijah's trunk. The answer was always, "No," and no explanation was ever given. All Mamie had to do was place the key in the lock and she knew I would notice. Yet she still didn't want me to explore its contents. That might be why she and Boots stayed in the dining room, ready to stop my investigation.

Then there was Mamie's cleverness in the family story about the gates. Letty herself could remember the numerous gates—as many as seven that separated Sugar Loaf from the main road. Each time they drove up to a gate, someone would have to get out, open the gate, wait until the vehicle passed through, and then close it behind. The road out of Sugar Loaf went through two other farms. At least the Peacocks could access their land from the water, if need be. The owners of the middle farm, the Bixlers, were at the mercy of the Henshaws who controlled the last five gates before the road to town was reached.

Mr. Bixler had heard what a fine lawyer Brode, Aunt Bertha's husband, was. Once, years ago, Bixler rode through the woods to Sugar Loaf so he could discuss with Brode what could be done about Henshaw's belligerent attitude of late. Mr. Henshaw had actually threatened to refuse the Bixlers passage to the road to town. On hearing the story, Brode became furious. With Boots at his side, Brode phoned Henshaw's lawyer, a local man from Princeton, and shouted into the phone: "*Mandamus*, I'll sue Henshaw for *mandamus*." Letty laughed because even now, no one in the family understood what "mandamus" meant.

Without explanation, Aunt Mamie placed a jar of grape jelly made from Boots' arbor, a bottle of shelled hickory nuts, and a loaf of Aunt Ella's zucchini bread into a basket and put a clean dish towel on top. She left the house, basket in hand, and walked through the woods. It took her more than a half-hour before she reached the Henshaw's farm. A fierce-looking German shepherd met her at the path leading to the house. Mamie walked slowly toward the house while the dog growled and barked at her. The door to the porch opened and a woman came out to call off the dog. Aunt Mamie walked on at her slow pace. The woman looked suspicious. When Mamie got within twenty feet she said, "I heard you were not feeling well."

"Who are you?" the woman said with a sharp tone to her voice.

"I'm Mamie Smith, a neighbor down the road."

"Are you one of the Bixlers?"

"No, I live at Sugar Loaf."

"Oh, a Peacock then."

"Yes, that's right. How are you feeling?"

"I am feeling fine. It must be Mother that you heard was sick. She lives with us."

Mamie finally reached the porch steps and stopped. "I see. I'm sorry she isn't well. Has she been ill a long time?"

"About seven years," the woman answered with a smirk on her face.

Mamie laughed, "News takes a while getting through the woods. I wonder if we could give you a few things we made at Sugar Loaf." All the while Mamie kept her eye on the woman at the door, who had not introduced herself. "Are you Mrs. Henshaw?"

There was a pause, but finally the woman answered: "Gladys Henshaw. Won't you come in?"

Mamie went in and spent a long hour talking to Gladys. She met Laura, her mother. Gladys said that she didn't know what had gotten into her husband, threatening to keep the Bixlers from getting to their property. "I think when he was younger, Harvey had the idea that he would eventually own all the property from here to the lake. Things ain't ever that easy. I've been so busy tending to Mother here and the garden that I haven't paid much attention to him lately. I heard him say he wasn't going to let the Bixlers through, but I really didn't take him seriously."

By the time Mamie left, the three women were chatting away like old friends. Gladys gave Mamie a jar of her watermelon pickles to take back to the rest of the Peacocks. The quick and simple end to the story was that Harvey Henshaw dropped his threats to the Bixlers. Brode and Boots, of course, were convinced that Henshaw and his country lawyer had caved in to Brode's legal expertise. And that would have been all that Letty would have known if she hadn't noticed Mamie leaving the house one day carrying a basket. Letty was about 14 at the time. She went to Aunt Ella who was in the kitchen to ask where Aunt Mamie was going. Ella told her the story. The incident of the threat had occurred four years earlier. Aunt Mamie had continued to visit Sugar Loaf's neighbors with a basket once a year.

So where would she have put the key? Marjorie had told her once that Aunt Mamie locked the door to hers and Uncle Ed's room when they went back to Chicago. Maybe the key was in their bedroom? She knew she shouldn't go in there without their permission, but a few days later, when Boots, Mamie, and Ed were taking a stroll through the garden at the very time that Aunt Ella was preparing a loaf of bread in the kitchen, she thought it wouldn't be so bad if she took a quick look in the bedroom. She knew detectives always wore gloves in such situations, but if she were caught in the room with gloves on, everyone would know she was not innocent. Instead, she prepared a story. If caught, she would say that she had mislaid her detective magazine and, knowing Uncle Ed liked to read it too, she thought she would look for it in his bedroom.

Once there, she quietly went through the drawers, looked on top of the wardrobe and in the medicine cabinet and finally under lamps. Then it occurred to her that because the key was large and old, anyone who happened to discover it would find it puzzling. Mamie wouldn't risk that if she truly wanted to keep the key hidden.

Letty quickly left their bedroom. Further analysis should be done in a safe location, she told herself. Once in the dining room, Letty was able to reason calmly. She decided that Mamie would have to hide the key in a place where it would never become visible, but be easily retrievable, quickly used and hidden again. She decided Aunt Mamie was most likely to hide it in the trunk room itself, but where? She went into the trunk room and thought about Mamie being so short. Think low, she told herself. She could tape the key to a flat low surface that is out of sight, like the ledge of the wooden box of the wall telephone, but someone might run their fingers under that surface when cleaning or just fiddling around while talking on the phone. Where is a flat surface that would never be cleaned? How about the bottom of a door? That would never be cleaned or even painted. But a key taped there could interfere with shutting the door. There were two doors to the trunk room. The one to the hall was not a tight fit. Letty had to be quiet because Aunt Ella was close by in the kitchen. Only the pantry was between the kitchen and the trunk room. Letty bent over, not an easy task for someone of her height and weight, and ran her fingers along the door's base. Halfway to the end, she felt tape and then something under the tape. From the feel it was definitely a key—THE KEY!

In her excitement Letty lost her balance and tried to recover it by pushing on the door, which she inadvertently slammed shut. Before Aunt Ella came from the kitchen, Letty had managed to get up off the floor and open the door.

"Is everything all right?" Aunt Ella asked.

"Oh yes, I'm sorry, I let the door slam shut," Letty said looking over her shoulder at the outside door.

As it was ten in the morning, Letty was afraid if she dislodged the key from the tape and opened the trunk, she could easily be discovered by anyone passing between the dining room and the kitchen. She didn't dare. There was no telling when someone would show up and ruin all her plans. Her sleuth work would have to be at night, but that was difficult for other reasons. Letty didn't want to admit it, but once she laid her head on the pillow at night, she was sound asleep instantly. Her husband, Harold, had always said that she simply passed out, having consumed so much sherry. She tried not to think of those conversations with him. He was wrong, of course.

If only she could get Bernard to help her, but she knew he would refuse. He didn't care what was in the trunk. Three days from now he was going to drive her back to Chicago. She had two nights to accomplish her mission. The Thatchers were leaving tomorrow morning. Would it be easier with them here or not? She thought that any unusual sound at night could be easily attributed to one of the little imps. That would mean tonight would be best. However to avoid passing through two bedrooms of Thatchers, Letty would have to use the front stairs by Aunt Ella's room. At the base of those stairs was the bedroom of Aunt Mamie and Uncle Ed. The boards of some of the steps on the stairs squeaked. No, she couldn't risk it. Uncle Ed couldn't hear a thing, but as often happens, his partner Mamie had unusually good hearing, almost to compensate.

This meant that she must try to get in Elijah's trunk tomorrow night. Tonight she could have her sherry as usual.

CHAPTER 29

It was a hot muggy day, so typical of Chicago's summer weather. Safi was torn between having a breeze move some air around and keeping the apartment free of soot. There were three windows that actually opened (the three that hadn't been painted shut). The soot could easily be wiped off wooden furniture with a damp cloth, but it made upholstered furniture and pillows grimy. The way around that was to cover the couch and the wing-back chair with sheets. She had tried to explain this to Mrs. M, but Letty would have no part of it. Her rejection came with no explanation, so Safi thought that Letty must consider sheets on furniture beneath her class. However, while Mrs. M was still up at Dartford Lake, Safi used sheets and opened up the windows. There were no screens, but few insects came in this high off the ground, and as for the increase in noise from the streets, that didn't bother Safi. She had lived with far more noise than that in the past.

She couldn't help but smile, thinking about Mrs. M. Long ago, Safi sensed that Letty herself was somewhat embarrassed by her snooping activities. Unless Safi walked into the room while she was at it, Letty would never admit to doing it. This was probably why she preferred peeping at night, while Safi was studying in the kitchen or was asleep. The irony was that for all Letty's trying to hide her sleuthing, she never realized that during the summer months, Safi always knew the next morning what she had been up to. The soot on the windowsill gave her away.

Mrs. M was due home in a few days. Safi thought she had better write up what she had already found out about Leo Glitz. She jotted things down in chronological order:

1870 Silver Skates Contest & newspaper article about it

Leo journalist

Leo arrested Haymarket Riot

Letter about stolen jewels (to Mrs. Peacock?)

Leo's murder, cause of death?

Safi couldn't wait for Bernard to get back. She wanted to share her findings with him. It was going to be awkward to tell all of this to Mrs. M. There might be a scandal here, perhaps worse. On the other hand, nothing had really been established yet, so maybe it would be better if Letty knew now.

Safi thought there was one other piece of information that she should try to collect before the two of them returned to Chicago. The Hanover Collection sounded like the set of jewels that Aunt Mamie was giving to family members via the jewel hunts at Sugar Loaf. According to the date on the letter from the Duke of Hanover, they must have been stolen from Peacock's some time early in 1893, or before. If she had the date of the robbery, she could look up details in newspaper articles. Even better, she thought, why not return to the police station and check their files again? If records are open to the public, someone there must be keeping files on robberies that I could see.

The following day Safi walked past the homicide department on her way to robberies. She was enjoying this venture, but she hoped she would not see Patrick. The clerk at the homicide desk recognized her and called out: "Hello there, Miss Winter."

This took Safi completely by surprise. She was embarrassed, but at least there was no one else around.

"I'm Officer Feldman. I remember you were here about a week ago. Sorry, I didn't mean to stop you. On your way to robberies, are you?"

"Yes, as a matter of fact I am."

"Well good. We need the public to get interested in these old cases. Then we'll get more of them solved." Officer Feldman looked down at his desk. Safi thought she could see that he was working on a crossword puzzle.

According to the report, the Hanover Collection robbery occurred in March of 1893. It was reported by Samuel Peacock, who appeared ready to leave the store for the day, putting his gloves on, carrying his coat, when the police arrived. Safi took detailed notes. Four of the jewels described in the report exactly matched the ones Mamie had given away in her hunts: alexandrite, emerald, star sapphire, and diamond. Safi had heard the fifth gem was to be a ruby—also the final jewel in the Hanover collection. There was no doubt in her mind now that Mamie was distributing these same stones in the hunts at Sugar Loaf!

There was one thing she would have overlooked, had Officer Waschewsky not pointed it out, and that was that the police felt that CD Peacock wanted to down-play the robbery. Grateful as she was for his help, she found it annoying that Waschewsky kept looking over her shoulder to watch what she wrote down. "Are you already familiar with this case?" Safi inquired.

"Certain cases puzzle me. This is one."

But when Safi asked him for an explanation, he said he could not say anything more, so she thanked him for his help and left the station. She went straight to Loyola, hoping she wouldn't be late for her class.

That afternoon, thinking back on her experience at the station, she recognized that both the officer in homicide and the one in robberies had been extraordinarily friendly and helpful. She wondered why. Usually when that sort of thing happened, she attributed it to young men on the make, but these two officers were old enough to be her father. That was kind of nice. She was becoming aware that she had been brought up to be suspicious of policemen. On the other hand, Patrick, she was afraid, *was* on the make.

When Safi got back to the apartment that evening after her class, she filled out the timeline on Leo with more of the details. Now she was ready to present it to Mrs. M, but she wished Bernard would be there with her, as the topic may be awkward to discuss with Letty.

CHAPTER 30

With Alley still in his kennel, Bernard went to his room, where he could be alone to read the letters he had taken from Tree Top's secret cupboard. He pulled them out from inside his shirt and started to examine them. They were all written by Leo Glitz. He wondered what had made his aunt so curious about this man, who was Safi's great-grandfather. All five letters were written to CD. He put them in the order that they had been written and read them one by one:

Letter 1

Dear Charles,

A few months before the fire, I remember hearing that you talked Elijah into buying a fireproof vault. Then the night of the fire, story has it that you told Elijah to place the House of Peacock's most valuable items in the vault for the night. Although that dreadful conflagration destroyed a third of the city and all of the business area, your beloved vault protected the store's gems. In gratitude to you and, perhaps equally due to his yen to get into the real estate business, Elijah turned the store over to you. Having saved all the items of large value, you were able to open up for business within months of the fire at your new location at State and Washington Streets, and changed the store's name to CD Peacock's. All of this foresight has given you such a head start over other businesses in recovering from the fire that one wonders if you hadn't put Mrs. O'Leary's cow on commission.

Congratulations on your good fortune,

Leo   *August 3, 1873*

Hmm, thought Bernard, this is a veiled criticism of CD. Perhaps, as Aunt Letty says, CD was an astute business man, but Leo also paints him as an opportunist without much soul.

Letter 2

Dear Charles,

It has been so long since you have joined Mary Ann and your children when they visit the farm. Elijah and Emily long to see you. We have many funny stories to share with you. Elijah has just purchased two fine horses that we all enjoy riding. Dick, the pony, never gets to rest when we're all here, but he loves the attention. Emily teaches the young ones how to garden.

Come join us sometime,

Leo   *June 20, 1881*

Letter 3

Dear Charles,

After disappearing for 15 years, your brother, Samuel, has come home. Apparently, he has been living in California all these years. We think he got into some trouble there with the law. Sam is of great concern to your father as his behavior is both unpredictable and, at times, disreputable. He has taken over a small shed for his science experiments with his large vacuum pump. Your father seems to think you could have a good influence on him, especially since Sam has always adored you. Elijah could use and would appreciate your help.

Leo   *April 2, 1886*

Letter 4

Dear Charles,

Now really, a theft of five stones—the Hanover Collection, bought from the Duke of Hanover! There was no sign of a break-in. They went missing in broad daylight when on display in a viewing room that could only be entered through one door. Only three people had the key to that door. I'll wager one of those three people was Samuel.

Charles, how could you have succumbed to this publicity stunt? No doubt Samuel was behind it. Do you plan to find the jewels five years from now hanging from a chandelier or in a message container that comes from the gift wrapping department? Only Sam could get an 'elite jewelry store' like Peacock's to pull such a trick.

Sorry, my commiseration is boundless,
Leo *March 10, 1893*

Letter 5

Dear Charles,

Emily's mother thought all along that it was unlikely that the jewels came from the Duke of Hanover. She decided to write the Duke herself, in German, of course. She just received a letter with the royal seal of the Dukedom of Hanover in which the Duke said he has never had those specific jewels in his collection. I will gladly show you this letter if you would care to meet me in Washington Square on Wednesday evening at 7:00 P.M., July 12. I realize that you may be uncomfortable at the thought of going to this place where 'anarchists rant and rave,' but the square is only two blocks from your home, so it is a convenient location and it is still light and quite safe in the early evening.

Please let me know if you are not planning to meet me.
Sincerely,

Leo *July 5, 1893*

Bernard was stunned. Now he realized that the five jewels—the Hanover Collection—must be the prizes of Aunt Mamie's treasure hunts. So Leo thought the robbery was a hoax. I've never heard of anyone in the family mention a robbery. Keeping this quiet was so important to CD that he built a secret cupboard to conceal the mystery. Bernard felt that there were probably other things in the cupboard that he should look at, but he realized that he would have to wait for the Thatchers to leave Dartford Lake before he could safely go back to Tree Top. He wished he could share all this with Safi. And Aunt Let, oh my God, she would love coming up with a theory that explains all of this. Yes, this is right up Letty's alley.

Alley! Yeow! I've left Alley in his kennel much too long, he suddenly realized. He put the letters under his pillow and left the room, shutting the door.

Two days later, the day before he was scheduled to drive back to Chicago with Letty and Alley, Bernard made his move to explore the cupboard once again. He went straight to Tree Top after the Thatchers left. The room was a mess, but less of a mess than the last time because the toys and clothes were gone. If anyone caught him, he was prepared to say that he wanted to help Marjorie clean up the room. He tried to be as quiet as possible.

When he had the door to the secret cupboard propped open, he took out the ledgers again. He couldn't tell if anything was wrong without careful scrutiny, but he figured they wouldn't have been kept here if there wasn't something that needed to be covered up. It would take him some time to make an analysis, so he decided to take the books back to Chicago with him. Where could he put them for now? What about under Aunt Letty's bed? She would never look under it and from there, he could take them one by one down to his car, carrying each under his jacket. That wouldn't be too conspicuous, he hoped.

The only other thing that Bernard thought might be of interest was a manila envelope. Inside were letters from a Sheppard Pratt Asylum near Baltimore, Maryland. The letters were addressed from the asylum's director to Elijah and some to CD. They seemed to be reports concerning the patient: Samuel Peacock, Elijah's son! Omigod, Bernard thought, this is really getting murky. Why am I doing this? If people don't want me to know these things, maybe I should just mind my own business. He noted that Samuel died in the asylum in 1901. He decided not to take these letters and quickly closed the cupboard and carried the ledgers down to Letty's room. He then brought them down to his car. An hour later they were all inside his trunk and he could relax at last. He passed Aunt Let on the veranda. She said: "I don't feel too well, Bernard."

"Oh, I am sorry. Is there something I can do for you?"

"I'm just going to lie down for a while. I may not come down for dinner. I'll see how I feel, but if I don't show up, please make excuses for me. I think the best thing I can do is rest."

"What's wrong?"

"I'm just feeling a little queasy. Please tell the aunts I don't want any of them to fuss over me. Just let me sleep."

After she left to go to her room, Bernard couldn't help but think that she was not very good at lying. I'm sure she's up to something. That little smirk was a dead give away. I'll bet she's planning to get into the trunk. Why go to bed now? Aha! I'll bet she's planning to get up in the middle of the night.

That night would be their last night at Dartford Lake. He wouldn't return until Christmas time when he visited Marjorie and Freddy. As much as he loved visiting them, maybe this year he'd give it a pass. He wanted to spend the time with Safi. How would she feel about spending so much time with him—say the rest of her life? This was a big step. Does she love me? Is she serious about me? After dinner, he walked over to the Fabers' house. He wanted to say goodbye to Freddy and Marjorie. Once he sat down with them, he felt awkward. He couldn't get his nerve up to ask what he wanted of them. Marjorie broke the ice: "They say this is going to be a cold winter."

"How do they know?" Bernard asked.

"I just read that prediction in the *Farmer's Almanac*." After an interlude, Marjorie continued: "Did Safi enjoy herself at Sugar Loaf?"

"Yes, I think she loves it here. Everybody was so welcoming."

"What does she do for Christmas? I understand she has no family."

"Yes, that's right. I don't know what she does. I've only known her for eighteen months."

"Is she your first girlfriend?"

"Oh, I've had others but none I care as much about...." He just blurted it out: "I think I'm in love."

Marjorie and Freddy both laughed. "Yes I think you are."

"Can you tell?"

"Oh yes," said Freddy. "Can a beaver swim?" They all laughed.

"Do you think she loves me?"

"I bet you want to be with her over Christmas."

"Oh, I do.... You know she's Jewish. So Christmas doesn't mean much to her. In fact she's not religious at all."

"Does that matter to you?"

"No, not at all!"

"What's Aunt Letitia going to do for Christmas? Are her children coming to Chicago to see her?"

"No, I doubt it, but maybe she's going to visit them. I'll ask Aunt Let on the way home."

"Well, whatever happens," Freddy said, "You and Safi are both welcome here."

"But you don't have room for both of us."

"Yes, we do. There's plenty of room in this old house. We've had as many as ten people here staying for three weeks, right Marjorie?"

"Yes, twice."

"How could you do that?"

"We have three trundle beds, you know, and two hammocks that we hook across the sewing room. Don't you worry now! We can do it. When it gets close to Christmas time, just give us a call and tell us if and when you're coming. Having you come is one of the highlights of our year."

Bernard was greatly relieved. He explained that he couldn't be sure how it was going to work out between him and Safi. They said they understood. An hour later he was still on their couch talking away. They gave him some hot cocoa. That was deadly for Bernard. Cocoa always put him to sleep. Maybe the early swim and the tension of taking the ledgers from CD's secret cupboard had wiped him out. His head was bobbing. Marjorie propped a pillow behind it and placed a light blanket over him. She and Freddy saw no reason to wake him, so they turned off the light and tiptoed off to bed.

Around 2:00 A.M. Bernard awoke and realized where he was, and more importantly, that Alley had not relieved himself in a long time. Quietly, he walked with Alley around the house. Someone must have left the light on in the trunk room. Then he remembered Letty's early retirement and smiled. He thought it was best to pretend he didn't know what she was up to. For one thing, he would frighten her if he popped into the trunk room. Then there was Alley. It was next to a miracle that he hadn't already barked. He led Alley to his bedroom next to the laundry room. He got him into his kennel, put on PJs, and had just rested his head on the pillow when he heard a horrible scream. Bernard leaped from the bed. Three seconds later, he opened the trunk room door. No one was there! He turned out the light and made his way into the hall where he found Letty crouched in a corner. He turned on the hall light, just as Boots arrived at the head of the back stairs. She started to descend: "What's wrong? I thought I heard a scream."

"Yes," Bernard said to Aunt Bertha, "I think Aunt Let has been sleepwalking again." Looking at Letty he said, "Are you alright, Aunt Let? Come let me help you up."

"Oh dear, I don't know what happened. Why am I down here?"

"Come on, let's help you back to bed. Do you feel strong enough to walk up the stairs?"

"I think so, with your help." They started going up, forcing Boots to back up herself. When they were in her room, Letty called out to Aunt

Bertha: "Thanks Boots, I'm sorry I woke you. I'll be fine now. I haven't sleepwalked for two years, at least."

"Perhaps you've done it more often, but you just didn't know it."

"Maybe so, but I think Safi would have realized, though." Once Letty was sure Boots had gone back to bed, she begged Bernard to go back to the trunk room and tape the key which she handed him to the bottom of the door to the hall.

"Is the trunk locked?"

"Oh yes, I got that done before I saw the mouse."

"The mouse! That's why you screamed?"

"Yes, a horrible furry little thing. Thanks for covering for me. That was fast thinking on your part—sleepwalking—perfect."

"Well I hope it was worth it. Did you find anything interesting in the trunk?"

"I'll tell you when we drive back tomorrow."

Once in the car and on the road back to Chicago, Bernard asked his aunt what she had found in the trunk. She told him that there wasn't really anything of particular interest. "In fact, I can't see why Mamie didn't want us to look in it all these years."

Bernard took his eyes off the road to scrutinize his aunt's face, to look for signs of prevaricating. She seemed her normal self. "Well, what was in there? Tell me anyway."

"Oh, albums, some marvelous pictures, going back to the 1880s."

"Any of Elijah's farm?"

"One or two. Many of us at Sugar Loaf."

"Any of Mom and Dad?"

Bernard kept on quizzing his aunt. If she were telling him all she knew, he would have to agree that there wasn't much of special interest in Elijah's trunk. He thought he wouldn't mention anything about CD's secret cupboard. The further he drove, the more pleased he was with making that decision. He would eventually tell her about Leo's letters to CD and the ledgers, but once she knew about the cupboard, she would pester him to return to Sugar Loaf. She'd probably want to turn around right now and go back. He was curious about Samuel Peacock. As far as he could remember, nobody had ever mentioned him. He would have remembered hearing about a relative with psychosis. It must never have been talked about. If I say or ask anything about Samuel Peacock now, she'll want to know how I've heard of him ... best to wait, he thought.

CHAPTER 31

Safi had one of her appetizing dinners ready for them when they arrived in the afternoon: pot roast, mashed potatoes, green beans, and lemon meringue pie for dessert. Over dessert, Letty asked Safi what she had found out about Leo Glitz. She started to answer, but glanced at Bernard. Those two can't keep their eyes off each other, Letty thought.

"Not much," Safi answered, "but I'll tell you later. I want to tell you first that Patrick, you know, Officer Murphy, came by and asked me to have you be on the lookout for a nicely dressed woman who walks up to someone on the street. She distracts the person while her male companion attacks the victim from behind, usually stealing a wallet at gunpoint. They tell the victim to just keep walking down the street as if nothing has happened or else they'll kill him. They have performed this stunt now twice in neighborhoods near here. The same *modus operandi* was used by a similar couple in Cleveland three years ago, and they were never caught."

Letty was already looking forward to checking up on all the neighbors on whom she had been unable to keep tabs while she was at Dartford Lake. But now she had the added incentive of being given an assignment by the police. So when Safi and Bernard announced that they were going out, she was glad to have the chance to do some investigating. Early evening was when everybody came home from work, and some had to do last-minute shopping. There were many people on the sidewalks. It was the time of day when the most was going on. While sitting poised with her binoculars and notebook in front of the living room window, her mind drifted back to Dartford Lake. She already missed the tranquility of Sugar Loaf. She wished she could still hear the waves lapping the shore. Tomorrow she would start the process of selling the diamond.

Three weeks later, Letty found the highest valuation for her stone from Jacobs Appraisals. Mr. Jacobs told her that he knew of a potential buyer: a Japanese industrial magnate who was only in town for a few days. Mr. Jacobs made the arrangements and Letty sold her diamond to Mr. Yasushi Mutou for $43,000. Then she had the delightful task of deciding what to do with the money. Safi and Bernard wanted her to invest it in stocks and bonds. How dull!

Letty had been thinking for some time that she would buy a piano. She had always thought of herself as a talented pianist. For most of her teenage years, she had spent five hours a day practicing. Chopin's *Minute Waltz* was her party piece when she gave intimate concerts for her friends and relatives. Seven years ago, she had to sell her baby grand, when her husband went bankrupt. Now the apartment she lived in was so small that only an upright might fit. She had saved a few pieces of her favorite sheet music.

At times, she even dreamed of giving music lessons. The problem was that most children and adults would only be able to take lessons in the late afternoon, and Letty knew she couldn't stay sober that long into the day. If the parents ever smelled alcohol on her breath, she would lose their business. Perhaps she could give lessons through the elementary school that was only three blocks away. The lessons would have to be scheduled before her first sherry at 11:00 A.M.

She shouldn't get excited by all of this, she warned herself. She didn't even have the piano yet.

CHAPTER 32

Safi was pleased that ever since Bernard discovered the secret cupboard in Tree Top, he had become very interested in both the mystery surrounding Leo Glitz's death and its connection to the Hanover Collection. For the last few weeks, Bernard had been going over the ledgers to see if there was some discrepancy that CD might have wanted to hide. When he called Safi that night, she asked him if he had discovered anything unusual yet.

"Yes, I think I have. Is this a good time for you to come over so we can put our heads together about this? I could walk Alley over and pick you up."

Safi did not respond immediately. There was nothing that she wanted more than to be alone with Bernard in his apartment, but the last time they had a good length of time together on their own, they had become quite intimate. They ended up lying on the couch. Safi finally pulled herself away. Now she knew how easily she could be overcome by passion for Bernard. She was afraid she would succumb to his charms, and one-half of her didn't want to become tempted. The other half was excited at the thought of being alone together again. By now, she had no doubt whatsoever that she was in love with him, but how was she to know if he was in love or just playing her along? She knew what men could be like.

"We do need to compare notes and see if we can come up with an explanation," Safi answered, "but could we go to Bernini's? You know, that coffee house on Rush Street that we went to a few months ago, instead of your apartment."

He sighed. "Yes. I know what you mean. If only we could ask Aunt

Let to chaperone us. But we have to figure this out without her being present, and I can't carry all the ledgers to the coffee house. Let's see, well, we have many other things to talk about, but I don't want to discuss them over the phone. Can I come over now?"

"Yes, sure, but Mrs. M is here."

"I know, but I want to see you. I'll be right over."

Safi was excited. She hoped he might be coming over to ask her.... Oh, she shouldn't think about it. She freshened up in the bathroom and then told Mrs. M that Bernard was coming over. "Is that alright?"

"Yes, of course, Dear." She is smirking again, Safi thought.

The doorbell rang. That was fast, Safi thought.

CHAPTER 33

Two weeks had gone by since Patrick had seen Safi running to catch her bus, and he still hadn't had a chance to follow up on her investigation. His partner, Sean, knew all about it. Over a year ago, Patrick had told Sean about his aspirations concerning Safi. Sean knew what was behind Patrick's visits to Mrs. Mercer. Patrick was confident of Sean's loyalty. He didn't worry that Sean would make fun of him to the other guys in their division. And he didn't worry that Sean would go for Safi himself. Sean Callery was a happily married man with four kids. They had many hours to kill when they were on patrol. Cruising along, they could scrutinize the people they passed for criminal deviations while talking to each other. They had mastered the art of truncated conversations. Both understood the other's delays. The sentence would be completed eventually, or the question would be answered, but for that instant, something had to be checked out.

They discussed various ploys Patrick could use to get to know Safi. Even if their schemes were half-baked, discussing such possibilities helped to pass the time.

"Too bad I'm not in homicide," Patrick said.

"We could always pretend. You go in as the detective in charge of the case and I'm your side-kick who takes notes." They both laughed. Patrick was too young to be in charge. Visualizing the salty Sean with his potbelly taking notes in a little notebook was equally funny.

"That could get us into heaps of trouble."

"I'd almost be willing to try it just for the laughs."

"Mrs. Mercer would catch on. I have to give it to the old lady, she's pretty alert. She loves to pick up on clues. I told you about the notebook she keeps next to the window."

"Yeah, yeah. It wouldn't … be good … to pull her leg, especially when she takes our work so seriously.… How's about you go in with the possibility of helping her with her inquiry."

"That's maybe a possibility," Patrick said pensively. "Why in hell does the girl want to know about a murder that occurred 60 years ago?"

"If you knew the answer to that, maybe there'd be all sorts of things you could help her with."

"You may be right."

Sean stopped at a gas station so Patrick could use the men's room to freshen up, then he let him off at the corner of Dearborn and Schiller. They didn't want Mrs. Mercer to know he was coming. Patrick was prepared to announce himself through the speaker system, but after pressing the button to Mrs. Mercer's apartment, he was immediately buzzed in, no questions asked. *That's better. I will take them completely by surprise. One of the perks of being a policeman is that people can't refuse to talk to me.* Walking up the stairs to the second floor, he decided to carry his cap. His family always said that his wavy red-blond hair was one of his best assets, so why not show it off.

He no sooner had pressed Mrs. Mercer's doorbell when Safi opened the door. Her reaction to seeing him was unquestionably one of disappointment.

"I'm sorry to take you by surprise, but you did buzz me in without asking me to introduce myself."

"Oh, no … I'm sorry, I was expecting somebody else … so it was quite a surprise to find it was you at the door.… Please come in."

"Is Mrs. Mercer here?" he asked.

"Yes, just a minute. Please come in and sit down." By the time Safi called Mrs. M into the living room from her bedroom, Patrick had composed himself. He noticed that Mrs. Mercer looked freshly made up with powder and lipstick. Her hair was almost beautiful. Then he realized that she was wearing a wig. She was still in her bathrobe, however, and her obvious embarrassment was probably due to that, Patrick thought.

"Hello, Officer Murphy. It's nice to see you again," said Mrs. Mercer.

"Please, call me Patrick. Thank you. It's nice to see you both again too." The buzzer sounded. Safi leapt up to let the person downstairs in. It's probably the guy she's expecting, Patrick thought. Things are not going well. Safi stayed by the front door. She didn't come back to sit down with him and Mrs. Mercer while the visitor climbed the stairs. Then he thought he heard her go out the door, not waiting for the person to ring the doorbell. When Bernard showed his face around the hall, Patrick knew what he was up against. Sure enough, it's that good looking guy, though he's a little out of shape. As they were re-introduced, Patrick continued to size up Bernard. He is somewhat overweight. I'm taller, stronger. I could take him down anytime, if only that sort of thing mattered with these people. He noticed that this fellow Bernard had not taken his eyes off of him since he entered. He doesn't look too pleased, although he's trying to act casual. Safi doesn't take her eyes off of him. Oh my God, this is a disaster. I had better cut and run.

"I'll leave you in peace, but I came over to offer my assistance. I know you were inquiring into the murder of a Leo Glitz." He paused because all three of them seemed to be caught off-guard....There is something funny going on here, he thought. I should be in homicide. Oh, what the hell, I can't get what I came for, but maybe I can get something else. "I just have a few questions I'd like to ask, but if you don't mind, could I call my partner, Officer Callery, to come up and take some notes while we talk?" Without really waiting for their response, he walked over to the open window and signaled for Sean to come up.

Once Sean entered the apartment, Patrick established that Bernard's last name was Peacock—"Hmm, the same as Mrs. Mercer's maiden name."

"Yes, Bernard's great-grandfather was my grandfather: CD Peacock," said Letty.

"Safi, Miss Winter, why were you interested in Leo Glitz's murder?"

As he asked the question, Patrick noticed Bernard and Safi exchange glances.

Letty turned to Patrick to say: "I asked her to look up Leo Glitz."

"How did you learn that he was murdered? I mean you must have first found out he was murdered and then decided to go to the police station."

"Yes, that's right … sort of …" Safi answered, looking at Mrs. M. "I first looked him up at Newberry Library, and there were conflicting reports on his death in the newspapers. Some said he might have died fighting a fire and some said he was killed in Bughouse Square. It was only when I went to the police station that I found out his death was classified as a homicide."

Patrick turned to Letty and asked: "Why did you ask Miss Winter to look up this man who died in 1893?"

"You have to realize," Bernard contributed, "that my aunt here is quite a writer. She's just published her first book. Safi does the typing and some research for her …"

Before Bernard could go on, Patrick again asked, "Why Leo Glitz?"

"Leo was married to my grandfather's half-sister," Letty said. "Although it's another branch of the family, I still would like to know something of that side as well."

"Have you told Mrs. Mercer and Bernard what you learned from the police report?" Patrick asked Safi.

"I believe I told you both that he was clubbed to death in Bughouse Square in July of 1893. His wallet was missing so the police thought he was mugged for his money. It is possible that somebody present knew him and identified him for the police."

"What about the letter?" Patrick asked Safi.

"Oh yes, there was a letter found in Mr. Glitz's pocket," Safi explained. Patrick noticed a flicker of alarm cross Mrs. Mercer's face. "But the officer said that I wasn't allowed to see it because it was evidence in an unsolved murder," Safi added.

"Well, as I said, if there is any way we can be of assistance to you, please let us know."

"Are you still trying to solve that murder, then?" asked Bernard.

"Oh yes. Of course we don't have much time to work on such old cases, but there is no statute of limitations on murder. If anything comes up from your own investigations, we would expect you to let us know," Patrick answered. "Well, thank you for your time. We have to go now."

"And thank you," Bernard said. "We know how busy policemen are, and this must be of low priority to you both."

CHAPTER 34

After the policemen left, Bernard couldn't help but say: "That was strange! Were they investigating the murder or did Officer Murphy come for one reason then change his mind?" He himself had come over to his aunt's to ask Safi to marry him. "This sudden drama over Leo Glitz seems drummed up. I never thought the police would continue working on a murder case that happened 57 years ago." Safi looked dejected. He smiled at her and took her hand. She lifted her head, smiled, and squeezed his hand. Even Aunt Let looked disappointed. "How's about I take you both out to dinner tonight."

"That would be lovely," Letitia said.

Safi smiled but still looked a bit deflated. "I wonder, Safi, if you could come to my apartment first and then we'll come back and pick you up, Aunt Let?" He didn't explain why he wanted to talk with Safi alone.

Bernard noticed excitement in Safi's voice when she said to his aunt: "I was going to prepare a ham slice with au gratin potatoes for dinner tonight, but that will keep for tomorrow night."

"You two go on then and call me just before you're coming back to pick me up." It seemed to Bernard that perhaps having Safi over alone in his apartment was not a problem for his aunt, as long as it was during the daytime.

They didn't talk much while they walked. The wind off the lake was quite gusty and made it difficult to hear one another, but a somber mood had spread over Bernard. It was around 4:00 P.M. when they walked through Bernard's door. Alley announced his need to go out. They both said almost simultaneously: "Oh no!"

"I can take him," Safi offered.

"Well, thanks, but you wouldn't be able to hold him, although he is getting better. Have you noticed?"

"Yes."

When they were in the elevator together with Alley, Bernard realized he could no longer hold back his concern. The elevator door opened out into the large entrance way. Trying to keep his voice casual, he asked: "So, have you known Patrick Murphy long?" Safi stopped dead in her tracks. He turned to look at her and found her smiling from ear to ear. She explained what had happened the day she went to the police station. Walking out of the building Safi slipped her arm through Bernard's and squeezed it affectionately. "You haven't seen him since then?"

"No," she answered. He started smiling.

They walked towards Lincoln Park along Lake Shore Drive. Bernard spotted Priscilla Campbell walking her dog and coming towards them. It always puzzled him why she dressed so stylishly and wore makeup when she was just out to walk her dog. Priscilla lived in the building next to his. After a year of many coincidental encounters he became suspicious that she was trying to engage him in conversation whenever possible. The dogs always offered her an excuse. As she came closer, her smile withered and finally seemed somewhat forced. Lacking subtlety, she looked over Safi while Bernard introduced them.

Priscilla had actually wangled a few dates out of Bernard: "Why don't you join us tomorrow night, we are going to hear Odetta on Rush Street;" or "I'm having a few people for dessert and coffee. Please join us." The offer of food was hard for Bernard to resist. He shouldn't be hard on Priscilla, but Safi seemed to have so much more to her, without even trying all those tricks. On the other hand, he was kind of pleased to have someone who was attracted to him show up just when he was ready to propose to Safi. He didn't want Safi to think he was a pushover.

When they got back to his apartment, Bernard got up his nerve to ask the big question. He led Safi over to the couch where they sat next to each other. Bernard held both of her hands. He appeared to be blushing. When he started to talk he was looking at the coffee table. "I don't know what it is about sapphires, but I seem to be drawn to them. At first all I wanted to do was to synthesize one and that was stimulating, but once I met a real sapphire in person," he turned to look directly into Safi's eyes and through a big grin he said, "I am no longer in control of my thoughts or passions. I can't live without you. Will you marry me?"

Safi squeezed his hands and said: "Oh, yes, Bernie, of course." For the next two hours they couldn't keep from smiling at each other. They decided not to hurry with making plans for the future.

"Let's tell Aunt Letty tonight."

"Oh yes. She'll be very happy.... How will the rest of the family feel?" Safi asked with some concern.

"Are you kidding? They'll be ecstatic." They kissed again and decided that they wanted a summer wedding at Sugar Loaf. "Where has the time gone? We have to go to pick up Aunt Let." Bernard gave her a call and the two of them went down into the building's garage so Bernard could drive his car.

"Did you tell Mrs. M that we are going to Antoine's?"

"No. Do you think that matters?"

"Maybe. I don't know. I've never seen her casually dressed."

"Oh, I see. Well, it's too late now. I've already called her. She said she'd be waiting outdoors by her entrance."

They turned from Lake Shore Drive to go west down Schiller. As soon as they crossed Dearborn, Safi called out: "There she is. Oh dear, she's dressed to the nines and now she's spotted us and is walking toward the car. Can you pull into that empty space there so she can get ... Oh! ... Oh! ... What's happening? Oh my God! Quick park here. I'm getting out."

"What are you doing? I haven't stopped the car yet!"

Safi started screaming as she scrambled out of the car: "Help! Help, Police, Help!"

Bernard could see she was running toward Letty. A well-dressed woman was near his aunt. He got out of the car and started running toward them, not knowing what was going on. Now there was a man behind Letty. It looked like he was attacking Letty from behind. Bernard was still fifteen feet away. There was a police siren. He heard screeching of brakes. Two policemen were running toward them, guns out: "Drop your gun!"

"You're surrounded. Drop your gun!" Another police car rounded the corner from Clark Street. The man dropped his weapon. Policemen had him in handcuffs in no time.

Bernard looked for Safi. "Where's Safi?" he called out. Then he spotted her running up Schiller after the nicely-dressed woman. He started running in pursuit at top speed. The woman Safi was chasing suddenly stopped in her tracks and opened her pocketbook. Bernard saw something shiny flash through the air at Safi. A policeman ran up from nowhere and tackled the woman. Safi stumbled and would have fallen down had Bernard not caught her. The knife had grazed her upper arm and blood was slowly oozing out. Bernard and the policeman, who turned out to be Patrick, quickly assessed her injury. Both men relayed to the other through glances that it was merely a surface wound. Certainly no artery had been cut. Nonetheless, Safi had turned white and was trembling. Bernard held her head in his lap while his aunt took off her fancy brocade coat and put it over Safi. The gesture was kind, especially since the coat would surely be stained by the blood.

Even at that dramatic moment, Bernard felt annoyed with his aunt when he saw she was wearing every piece of jewelry she owned. In this part of town, one should not advertise one's possessions. His aunt should certainly have known better. Patrick had gone to his police car and now brought back a blanket to cover Safi.

Separate police cars took the two culprits away. Patrick and Bernard helped Safi and Letty back to the apartment. Once Safi was lying on the couch, Bernard washed her arm and then called his doctor. When he knew the doctor was on his way, Bernard turned to his aunt and said crossly: "What did you think you were doing, wearing all your jewelry? You're inviting people to mug you, the way you're dressed."

Almost ignoring what Bernard said, Letitia turned to Patrick and declared: "We got them, didn't we?" Bernard could tell she was terribly pleased with herself.

"You're almost implying that you knew they would attack you," Bernard said. "Oh, I get it. This was the couple the police asked you to look out for."

"Did you spot them from the living room window?" Safi asked.

"Yes. I was pretty sure it was them. They were walking and standing around together talking ever since about 4:30. Then, when people were starting to walk home from work, they walked up Schiller toward the Lake, but soon split up. The woman stayed at the corner of Dearborn and Schiller, looking down Schiller. She leaned on a stone wall while she waited. He sat on a garbage can in the alley. I could see both of them, but they couldn't see each other. I don't know how she could let him know that someone was coming. When you called, Bernard, to say you and Safi were coming, I called the police because, even though the couple hadn't done anything yet, it was my only chance to call. Then I went down to wait for you. It never occurred to me that I would be their target."

Patrick was looking somewhat sheepish. "I didn't intend you to be their victim, but just to report it if you saw them," he said.

"Well, that was my first assignment. How did I do, Officer Murphy?"

"You did good, Mrs. Mercer, but you shouldn't have waited outside the building for Mr. Peacock, especially when dangerous people like that couple were around. You didn't tell the police you were going to wait outside, did you?"

"No."

"Well we didn't expect you to do that. Thank God, you have never done that before. You inform. That's the peeper's, I mean informer's job. We catch the bad guys. That's our job. Are you all right, Miss Winter?"

"Yes, Officer Murphy, I'm fine."

Looking at Bernard, Patrick said, "Is the doctor on his way?"

"Yes," Bernard answered.

Patrick said good bye and left, thanking Letty once again for being so alert.

After the doctor came and went, Bernard suggested that they just have a Chinese dinner delivered, since it was late. Bernard could tell his aunt was trying not to show her disappointment. She doesn't get out much, he thought.

Sitting at the kitchen table, they shared the contents of the little cardboard containers: bean curd with mixed vegetables, chicken fried rice, shrimp egg foo yung, and moo shu pork. There was a spring roll for each of them. After they had eaten, Bernard and Safi told Letty that they were engaged. Of course she was delighted. "I'm so happy for you," she said, but Bernard could see that she was having trouble smiling. Then tears began to well up in her eyes. She half-laughed and said: "I'm so happy for you and I'm crying. Isn't that ridiculous?"

Safi took her hand. Letty would miss her. She probably did not look forward to living alone again. "We won't be far away," Safi said.

But Aunt Let probably realized that it wouldn't be the same. Safi had made his aunt feel loved again. Bernard realized how much the two of them cared for each other. He would do what he could to have them remain close, but he also knew he could not tolerate his aunt's drinking, and that would mean she couldn't live with them. Then there was Alley. Letty would hate dealing with Alley everyday.

Recently he had been reading a book on Quaker thought and he remembered the phrase: *To Proceed as Way Opens*. He felt that meant that one should just wait patiently and a solution will become apparent. He liked that idea. Good God, I'm not becoming religious? No, absolutely not, he thought. He agreed with Safi and her parents on that score, but he also saw the value of reflection, of recognizing problems honestly, and then having the faith that they can be resolved. Is that a contradiction? No: *chemists have solutions*, he chuckled.

The next day Safi and Bernard were again in Bernard's apartment. They planned to buy an engagement ring at Peacock's on the following Saturday. A simple one would be all Safi would tolerate. Could they find something suitable at Peacock's? Bernard had no idea.

Even though they avoided sitting on the couch, knowing what had almost happened recently, conversations didn't progress far before they were interrupted by kisses and hugs. Finally, they realized that a whole hour had gone by and they still hadn't dealt with the ledgers. Safi dragged Bernard over to the dining room table where they were stacked in chronological order.

"OK, here's the thing," Bernard said, opening each one for inspection. "The head buyer for Peacock's would be an expert in jewels. He might make one trip a year to New York to buy gems from wholesalers. There were also wholesalers in Chicago. In addition, the store would purchase gems from estate sales and auctions. Anyway, the buyer knows the type, quality, weight, and cut of gems that the store needs for the coming year. He would buy what are called in the business "parcels" or "lots." One parcel might have twelve diamonds each about .25 ct in weight. Another parcel might have eight rubies, all around .35 ct, etc. Larger stones are bought individually. Their type, weight, and cut are always recorded in a ledger, along with the source of the purchase and the date. Usually there is a note as to the quality: fine, good, fair, etc.

"Now here is the interesting thing. We know the specifics about the five jewels that were supposedly purchased from the Duke of Hanover, thanks to your research at the police department. We know the details of their types, carats, cuts, and sizes. Let's see, you gave me a copy of their descriptions. Where is it? Ah, here it is:

Gemstone	Carats	Cut
alexandrite	5.20	step cut cushion
emerald	5.61	oval
star-sapphire	6.60	round cabochon
diamond	6.03	brilliant
ruby	6.14	cushion

"But not one of the purchasing sheets indicates that the stones were bought at the same time. I have been able to locate each of the five stones somewhere over the years. The ruby was purchased in 1890. See—here it is on the 1890 purchasing sheet for rubies. The emerald is on a sheet from 1888. Both the star-sapphire and the alexandrite came from an estate sale in 1891. And lastly, the diamond was purchased in 1887. According to Leo's letter, the robbery took place in 1892. I believe Leo was right, that there was no purchase from the Duke of Hanover. There must have been a deliberate deception, one that required the books to be hidden, in case someone wanted to check on the purchase of the stones. This was so important to CD that he had a secret cupboard built at Sugar Loaf."

"I think the family didn't want people to know about Samuel as well," Safi added. "I have never heard Mrs. M mention anything about him. Anyway, it looks like we have two mysteries. Who killed Leo Glitz and why; and why did they make up the story about the Hanover Collection and then pretend that it had been stolen?"

Bernard added: "And why are the same jewels being distributed among CD's offspring in the guise of prizes for treasure hunts? I guess it is still important to continue pretending that those jewel were stolen?"

"You know it all seems carefully orchestrated. I don't want to make it sound as if I think your family is devious, but when you think of it, the five jewels will be distributed before the sale of the store. That way, they'll be sold by separate parties, each a year apart, and so won't draw the attention of the new owners.

"You know, when Officer Murphy came to see Mrs. M about Leo's murder ..." Safi started to say.

"I think his purpose was to visit you, not Aunt Let, but please, go on, sorry to interrupt," Bernard said.

"Well," Safi continued, smiling, "he didn't say that the letter was written to Mrs. Peacock or that it referred to the Hanover Collection."

"You're right but why is that important?" asked Bernard.

"So as far as Mrs. M knows, we have no inkling that Leo Glitz's murder might be related to the 'stolen' jewels."

"Do you know why Aunt Letty asked you to look up Leo Glitz? Because she asked you right after she had looked in the trunk that first time, when she had only a few minutes to examine its contents."

"Yes, she said that there was a letter from Leo which mentioned the 'Hanover gems.' I believe that was all she said at the time."

"OK then, now that she has had a good look at the contents, and considering Officer Murphy's visit, she does suspect that there is some kind of a connection between Leo's death and the Hanover jewels now."

"That could explain why ever since she's been back in Chicago, she has hardly shown any interest in Leo Glitz," Safi said.

"She doesn't want you to find out about the connection," Bernard surmised. "Tonight, maybe Aunt Letty can tell us something about Samuel."

Safi asked, "Didn't you say that Samuel died in 1901, at that mental institution? Let's see, Mrs. M was born in 1892, so she knew both Samuel and her grandfather."

It amazed Bernard that Safi knew so well these dates and relationships within the Peacock family. Of course she'd been working on the book for the last three years with his aunt. "I don't think that the great-aunts would help us much with these mysteries," Bernard said. "In fact, they seem to be covering them up, the way Mamie guards the trunk." Instinctively, Bernard lowered his voice when he added: "I bet Aunt Letty did find something in that trunk that she's not telling."

"I do know Mrs. M well enough to believe that if there was any disgrace to the family involved, she would not want it exposed."

"You're right, and that's what makes this so difficult. Ordinarily Aunt Letty would want to help us, but when it comes to the Peacocks, she recounts only what is positive."

"Perhaps while we are visiting Marjorie and Freddy after Christmas, we'll have a chance to look in the trunk ourselves."

"Good thinking, Sapphira. That will also give me a chance to return the ledgers, inventory books, whatever they're called, to the secret cupboard."

"Oh, I keep meaning to ask you, did you ever find out about the box that you found in the cupboard? Do you think it might be the one the Hanover jewels were stored in?"

"I'm working on it. The trouble is that Rudy Ruggles & Co. went out of business ten years ago. Now that you mention it, we should probably bring that box back to Chicago with us when we leave Sugar Loaf this winter. I have located two men in Chicago who used to work for Ruggles. If they saw the actual box, they may be able to say something more definitive."

"What do you hope to find out about the box?" asked Safi.

"I don't know, maybe I can find out who placed the order for it and when it was made. It would have been custom-built. Probably nothing will come of it."

"You know this business is starting to be creepy. I don't know if I'll want to get married at Sugar Loaf."

That comment made Bernard realize that he had to do whatever it took to solve these mysteries. He wished he could engage Aunt Let's help, but she may not want to help bring some things out in the open. What if CD did kill Leo? Oh my God, then the marriage might be off.

CHAPTER 35

Before Saturday, Safi had suggested: "If we can't find a ring that is simple enough at Peacock's, would you mind if we went to another type of store?" She wanted to say that even a pawnshop might have interesting rings. "I don't want to hurt the feelings of family members. Is there someway we could look around without the others wondering what we are doing?"

"I'll call Blair. He'll understand. He could meet us as soon as the store opens. The others are usually a little late arriving at work."

"Isn't there a private showing room?"

"Yes, that's right, there is. Remember? That was how they supposedly displayed the Hanover Collection."

"Maybe if we're in the showing room before the others arrive at the store, they won't know what we're doing."

The first several samples that Blair brought in did not suit Safi at all. "I don't think I want a stone," Safi said.

"Usually the engagement ring is a little fancier than the wedding ring. The wedding ring can be just a simple gold band," Blair said.

"What about a sapphire, a small sapphire that doesn't stand out much?" Bernard asked Safi.

"I can't imagine that not being showy," Safi said.

"What about an antique setting? I think we might have some that you would be comfortable with." Blair left the room, before Safi could answer. He came back with a tray of unusual rings. They were not large. One was a filigree setting and the small stone, a very small sapphire, was set flush with the filigree. Only if you looked directly down on the ring could you see the stone. Safi tried it on. "The ring's a little loose."

"That can be adjusted," Blair said.

"I do like it, but, oh dear, how much is it?"

Bernard put his hand on top of hers. "It's $170 and that is inexpensive," he answered.

"I think I heard you say 14K 'white gold'. What does that mean?" Safi asked.

Blair explained that pure gold is designated as 24K. "Although it is a beautiful yellow color, the metal is too soft to make a durable piece of jewelry. Gold jewelry is almost always a mixture—an alloy—of gold and some harder metal such as palladium, zinc, or nickel. Those metals are the same color as silver, so when they are mixed with gold, the color lightens. The alloy is called 'white gold.'"

"So karat refers to the amount of gold, but then you said the sapphire was 0.15 carat. What does that mean?" Safi asked Blair.

"Aha, good question," Blair answered. "That type of carat, spelled with a C, means something very different and it's only used to tell you the weight of a gemstone. One carat is exactly one-fifth of a gram. The value of a gemstone, however, is not based only on its weight. Its clarity, color, and cut also help to determine its worth. For instance, in this ring that you're considering, the stone is small, but very clear. It has a lovely deep blue color and it has been cut with many facets. Its so-called 'brilliant cut' reflects light from many angles."

"It's so pretty," Safi said.

"I like the Art Deco look about it," Bernard added.

"It's lovely." She finally looked up a Bernard with a broad smile, "Thank you, Bernie."

While riding the bus back home, they discussed how they could help Letty. "She really needs to get out of the apartment everyday, to walk and explore the neighborhood," Safi concluded, "but at the same time, she has to be dressed right. She has to learn how to dress so she's not so conspicuous."

"Could Patrick give her another 'assignment'?" Bernard suggested.

"That's a great idea! An assignment that gets her outside."

"Just so she doesn't go out lit up like a Christmas tree."

"I think I actually have Patrick's number in my purse."

"Oh you have, have you?"

"He gave it to me when he knew I was coming home sometimes at night from Loyola."

"Yeah, I bet that was his reason!" Bernard laughed. "Why don't we stop at my place so you can call him?"

Later that afternoon when Patrick was off duty, he came over to Bernard's apartment. He and Bernard had a beer while the three of them put their heads together. It was decided to put it to Letty that the police would like her to extend her peeping to a radius of several blocks. The area would include the corner of Clark and Division Streets—a busy subway stop and a heavy crime area. Safi said that the police would have to give her some undercover clothes to wear and insist that she wear them. "If the police ask her to wear them, I think she'll do it," Safi said. "You have to be adamant that she not wear any jewelry."

"She'll have to look scruffy," Patrick said.

"That really goes against her nature," Bernard said, "but perhaps we can draw on her training as a drama student. I believe she studied drama and the fine arts after going to college in the '20s—Mount Vernon Junior College, I think it was. She did her drama training here in Chicago."

"Well, here's the thing," Patrick continued. "This will take two visits, I believe. First, I'll come over and present the idea, requesting that she help us. I'll bring a map of the area that we hope she will cover. Then if she likes the idea, I'll come back a week later perhaps, with a woman detective named Rose. Rose will bring an assortment of clothes. It would really be best if Rose would come back again and walk Mrs. Mercer around the area, suggesting a few places she could stop and have a cup of coffee. Rose will have lots of tips for Mrs. Mercer."

"Would she be willing to put so much time into training Mrs. M?" Safi asked.

"Yeah, she would. Rose lives nearby on Sedgwick, and those boys that Mrs. Mercer nailed over a year ago had stolen cars in her neighborhood. So Rose is grateful to Mrs. Mercer. I know some of the guys down at headquarters call her 'the peeper,' but in all seriousness, we need people like Mrs. Mercer."

The summer was closing. Bernard would soon be back teaching and Safi would be starting two more courses at Loyola. This fall she would officially be a junior and a full-fledged history major. Her emphasis would be labor history.

Chapter 36

Letty was getting used to the shoes now. In fact she had to admit that walking in these lace-ups was much easier than heels. The slacks made her feel unfeminine, but where she was going she would never bump into any friends. Even if she did, they surely wouldn't recognize her. Rose told her not to wear powder or lipstick, and her hair should just be collected at the back of her neck in a tie. She wore an old, ratty cardigan with pockets over a dreadful man's shirt. She looked terrible but that made it fun. She was invisible. It was like having two lives. Right now, she was walking down Clark Street and had just crossed Goethe. Rose had suggested that she carry her money and keys in her pocket, but have in her hand a mesh shopping bag with a magazine in it. She got to Tony's Coffee Shop but decided to walk a block further down Clark, turn west on Elm, north on La Salle, and east on Division. Each day she went out, she made it her business to try a few new blocks. She also didn't want the people in Tony's to always think of her as coming from the same direction.

She ordered a cup of coffee. She was getting to know the regulars and had written down descriptions of each. Rose suggested that she have a piece of paper in her magazine so it didn't appear that she was taking notes. Then when she got home, she could transfer her notes to a notebook. She knew where certain people sat in Tony's, and was getting so she could recognize who they were just from their voices. Her favorite place to sit was at a table where she could keep an eye on the news kiosk at the head of the stairs down to the subway on the opposite side of the street. Rose said that good surveillance took a long time, like weeks and weeks, but she said it could really pay off.

Two weeks into her surveying the neighborhood, Letty noticed for the second time a man jump out of a car, talk to the news vender, then jump back in the car and take off. Both times that happened between 10:00 and 10:30 A.M. on a Tuesday morning. It was probably nothing significant but she would watch out for it.

She wondered if she would ever be able to walk to Newberry Library. It was about 10 blocks away from her apartment. That was a mile. She thought she could do it some day. There was something there she wanted to look up without Safi knowing about it. She thought she knew why Aunt Mamie kept such a close watch on Elijah's trunk. She didn't want the others to know about the Hanover Collection. She was worried that CD had something to do with Leo Glitz's death. She wanted to do a genealogy search on the Glitzes.

A week later, Letty was having a cup of bitter coffee at Tony's late in the afternoon. Bernard and Safi were having a little engagement celebration at Hull House around 5:30. Letty figured she would have to be back home at 4:30, in order to have time to get ready before Bernard picked them up.

She had already paid for the coffee and was just getting up to leave, when she spotted a pickpocket helping himself to a man's wallet from his back pocket. Letty went charging outside Tony's. The man ran right by her. All she could think of doing was to trip him. In so doing, she was knocked off her feet as well. She yelled, "That man just picked somebody's pocket." She repeated herself. Nobody seemed to hear what she had said except the pickpocket himself, who got up and started running off.

"Stop that man. Thief!" Letty yelled. By the time people realized what Letty was saying, there was only one man quick enough to chase the thief down the stairs to the subway. The man who had lost his wallet realized it was gone. He and others helped Letty up. Letty thought for sure the thief had gotten away. Within a few minutes however, two huge guys almost lifted the villain up the stairs and held on to him, tight. The police had already been called. The man did not have the wallet on him, however.

"He must have thrown it away," Letty said. Several people went down the steps into the subway station to look around for the wallet. Finally one man spotted it tucked behind a trash can. By the time the wallet was returned to its rightful owner, a police car had driven up. Neither of the policemen inside was Patrick, however. Perhaps that is just as well, Letty thought, because she didn't want to blow her cover.

Letty had bruised herself in a couple of places. The police took notes from all the witnesses. A waiter came out and congratulated Letty. "Did you see her?" he asked the crowd that had gathered. "She stuck her foot out, and down that scumbag came," clapping his hands for emphasis.

Letty couldn't help but smile. The thief chimed out, "Yeah, she attacked me officer. This old bag needs to be prosecuted for assault."

"Shut up, Greasy," the policeman said. "Who do you think the judge will believe: you who's been in the slammer before for pickpocketing or this nice old lady who couldn't get out of your way fast enough?" He turned to Letty and asked: "Lady, are you all right?"

"Yes, Officer," Letty replied.

He said to her quietly, "Did I hear you say your name is Letty Mercer?"

"Yes, that's right. Rose Donahue and Patrick Murphy are my friends," Letty said quietly.

"Well done. I'll let them know." The policeman took a statement from Letty. By the time the thief was handcuffed and in the car, Letty was free to walk home. Once in her apartment, she only had ten minutes before Bernard would pick them up—no time to change clothes.

"I think you look fine," Safi said.

Before she did anything else, however, Letty went to the kitchen to pour herself a well-deserved glass of sherry. She was looking forward to going to the engagement party that Hull House was giving for her two lovebirds.

Safi and Bernard drove the Pontiac up to Dartford Lake after Christmas. This time Alley had the back seat to himself. They already knew that Alley loved riding in the car. He just slept the entire way, giving the two of them three hours to talk in peace.

They had spent Christmas day with Letty in her apartment. "I was glad we were there with her when Stewart and Lucy telephoned," Bernard confided. "Stewart said at one point that he was surprised we weren't celebrating in my apartment, remarking how small Letty's apartment is. I told him that Aunt Let's apartment is fine, that we spend a lot of time there. I made sure both of them knew about Aunt Let's work with the police."

"When you and Mrs. M were out of the room, I told Lucy that it would be very important to call Aunt Let once she is living alone again. I don't think they were happy with me calling Letty 'Aunt Let,'" Safi revealed.

"They'll get used to it," Bernard replied.

"I've been thinking," Safi said, "there are other ways of being an orphan than not having parents."

"How do you mean?"

"Well, I think Mrs. M sometimes feels she doesn't have a family. She feels the loneliness that both of us do, but in addition she's hurt. In our cases the abandonment was accidental, but not in hers."

They went on to rehash the Christmas Eve party. This year it was held in Charles and Gertrude's big home on Hibbard Road in Winnetka. "I heard some of the relatives saying how nice Letty looked wearing her pearls and a wool dress," Bernard commented.

"Didn't she love telling them about her crime-stopping adventures?! At first several of them just smiled to be kind. I don't think they believed that the stories were all that true."

"Yes, I noticed that too. But then about halfway into the evening, I think they started realizing that they were true. I overheard Boots say to Mamie: 'Remember when she was a child, how she always led the other children on imaginary adventures?'"

"Weren't all the relatives lovely to us?" Safi said. "I mean the way they toasted us. Cornelia didn't seem too happy, but I'm not going to let that bother me."

"Yes, yes, and they seemed really pleased that we want to be married at Sugar Loaf," Bernard said.

"Don't you think that Aunt Mamie rather quickly requested that the wedding happen well after the jewel hunt?" Safi said. "She probably doesn't want any wedding guests to witness it."

"Yes, that will be the last jewel hunt—the ruby."

"The last of the Hanover Collection," Safi said.

"Yes, with all the goodwill on the part of the family, I'm feeling a little guilty trying to uncover the mystery about Leo and CD when they obviously don't want us to," Bernard said.

"True, but we have to go after the truth, no matter how painful." Safi reminded him.

"Right, but I just hope it won't be an embarrassment for the family."

"Maybe nothing will be found that will embarrass them," Safi replied.

"I doubt it," Bernard said.

The road leading to Sugar Loaf was slippery in patches. The temperature was lower than in Chicago, well below freezing, but there was no wind. The snow cushioned sound, and although the branches had lost their leaves, they gleamed with ice. Safi saw it as black and white photography. Without color, Safi thought, differences in textures and shapes predominate. It's more dramatic. They passed by the two farms: first the Henshaw's, then the Bixler's. At last, the Peacock's white house was visible. Snow was piled high up around it so you couldn't see the two steps leading up to the veranda. Marjorie and Freddy had cleared paths to their glassed-in porch. Smoke drifted from the chimney. Part of the parking lot in front of the garage had also been shoveled.

Freddy emerged wearing a thick, woolen, red and black plaid shirt and a stocking cap. Why are his gloves so big? His hands couldn't be that large. He must be wearing two pairs of gloves. Safi was glad she brought her ear muffs. Too bad they weren't available right now. Her scarf would have to do. She hoped they would go into the house right away. Marjorie came out buttoning her jacket. Then she put on her hat and mittens, with her breath making clouds of steam. It was two days after Christmas. A small spruce was decked with lights, ready to be turned on once it got dark. After five minutes of greetings, Bernard asked: "How thick is the ice?"

"Plenty thick enough," Freddy said. "They even started driving over to Dartford on Christmas Eve. This has already been a colder winter than last."

"Is it all right if I let Alley run around a bit?"

"It's fine with me." Alley was ecstatic with such freedom.

They took the essentials out of the car and carried them into the house. The rest they left outdoors or in the car.

"I have to put Alley's kennel together, and I had better do that right now so if trouble comes, we'll have a place for him to go," Bernard said. Actually Alley was quite good during the entire visit. The combination of having all the freedom to run around and people who didn't care much what he got into was his recipe for bliss.

That night after a supper of soup and bread, they played Scrabble and Parcheesi.

"I see you brought several books with you, Safi. How are your studies going?"

"Fine . . . I have a term paper due the first day back at school, so I'm not entirely on vacation. I'll have to do some reading, unfortunately." Safi's "unfortunately" was not sincere. She loved to read, but wasn't sure if Marjorie and Freddy would be comfortable with her doing so. She worried that they might consider it rude. In the car, Bernard had told her not to worry about it because the two of them were very relaxed and would not be offended: "Besides Marjorie probably has several sewing projects that she'd like to work on while we're there."

Several days went by, with Bernard ice fishing a bit and skating more. When they were in the city, Bernard and she had gone skating at least once a week, so by this time, Safi could skate reasonably well, but she didn't like ice fishing. The Fabers had a steady flow of visitors.

One morning Bernard asked Marjorie for the key to get into the main house. He said he wanted to show Safi a few things. "Last summer, Safi didn't get to see all of the house. We want to have a plan in case it rains on the day of the wedding, that sort of thing." Safi noticed that Freddy gave Marjorie a smirk. He had caught them kissing the night before, so she could imagine what he thought.

"It's going to be horribly cold in there. There's been no heat on since the first of October."

"We won't be long and we'll wear our coats," Bernard said. Again Safi saw Freddy purposefully look at Marjorie and laugh. Marjorie gave Bernard the key for the trunk room door. Safi wished it had been the key to any other door to the house. While going through Elijah's trunk, Marjorie and Freddy could walk through that unlocked door anytime and take them by surprise. Fortunately Freddy and Marjorie seemed fully occupied by guests and people who wanted to go ice fishing.

Bernard opened up the door, then he and Safi returned to his car to retrieve the ledgers while Marjorie and Freddy were down at the lake. They stacked them in the kitchen in a corner until they could take them up to Tree Top. Elijah's trunk was their first objective.

Safi had a pad of paper and pencil. When they came to an album of CD's era, they looked at the pictures and tried to discern who were the people in them. During the last decade of CD's life, his brother Samuel had come to live with him. Both Safi and Bernard commented that Samuel looked out of place in the pictures. If the others were smiling and relaxed, Samuel looked gloomy and dejected. Once they were all looking off to one side, almost as if to shun Samuel who was laughing uproariously.

"Look at that house! It must be CD's house," Bernard said. "Let's see, the address is given as 285 N. Dearborn. I wonder if that was before or after the street numbers changed? The building has probably been torn down by now, but it would be fun to try to find it. Here it says "near Newberry Library." Oh, and the architect was Henry Ives Cobb. He was the architect of Newberry Library as well."

"How do you know that? You amaze me," Safi said.

"Remember my father used to work at Newberry. I spent a fair amount of time there myself. It was a quiet place to study after school."

Safi then remembered that Bernard went to Chicago Latin School from elementary through high school. That embarrassed him no end because he knew it was a school for privileged kids. At times, she was aware that Bernie's education was definitely more cultured than her own. Just the way he described the details of CD's house: "rough hammered greenstone with a slate roof, three stories on a battered basement." She'd have to find out what a battered basement is. "It has a balcony on the second floor," Safi contributed.

"Look at those tall stone chimneys, three of them. They give the house added height," Bernard observed. He said how much he would like to have pictures of Elijah, Mary Kolze, Samuel, and CD, but he didn't feel right about removing them from the album.

"Wait a minute, there is no picture of Mary Kolze, is there?" asked Safi. "I wish there were. I'd love to see what she looked like. Oh my goodness, look at this. Here is the letter written by Leo Glitz to Samuel:"

Dear Samuel,

Why have you gotten Charles in such a bind that he has faked a robbery of the Hanover gems? I have never even heard that Peacock's owned such a collection before the talk of robbery in the newspapers. You should be grateful that your brother gave you

a job in the store. Instead you jeopardize his business with your
shenanigans. You're lucky that your brother is overly cautious about
bad publicity. I am not. I will take you to the police myself if there is
any talk in the public about the Hanover jewels or the robbery.

Leo Glitz   *March 8, 1893*

"So, if Aunt Mamie is keeping this out of sight from the rest of us, do you think it means she is afraid that either CD or Samuel killed Leo?" said Bernard.

"Aunt Mamie herself may not believe that either Samuel or CD is Leo's murderer, but she may worry that if outsiders had this information, they may think one of the two of them killed Leo." Safi clarified.

"OK, we now know that Aunt Letty is on-board herself with the cover up. She doesn't want anything negative to come out against the Peacocks."

They pushed on until they had examined everything within the trunk. They came across two walking sticks. Both had the name of the owner engraved in the metal handle. CD's handle was silver and Samuel's was brass. "Look at this," Bernard said to Safi. He pushed a button on the silver handle and out popped a flick knife. Safi looked closely at Samuel's handle. It had no knife, but there did appear to be some dried blood in the indentations of the engraving.

"Look, what do you think this is? There is a distinct red color to it. It is not just brown dirt."

After careful inspection, Bernard said, "Yep, it looks like dried blood to me. If it is blood, it's too bad we have no way of testing whose blood it is."

That was it for the trunk. They put everything back like they thought it had been, locked it, and retaped the key to the bottom of the door.

On the way to Tree Top, they walked through the dining room and living room, where they noticed that all the usual items on table tops and shelves were gone. Marjorie must store these away someplace.

The furniture was covered with white sheets. They were about to climb the front stairs when Bernard thought that this would be a chance to show Safi Aunt Mamie and Uncle Ed's room on the first floor. Bernard remembered Marjorie saying that each year Aunt Mamie was the last of the great-aunts to return to Chicago. "Now that's strange. Why on earth do you think the door is locked?"

Walking into Tree Top, Safi commented, "What a delightful room this is."

"I knew you would like it. I want you to take the time to enjoy it, but I think we should do this quickly, in case Marjorie comes looking for us." Safi helped Bernard move the cots away from the wall and push the back wall at the top where he knew it was hinged.

"Gee, you would never think this wall would open up like this," Safi said. While Bernard was propping up the wall, Safi glanced out the window. "Look, there're the men ice fishing on the lake."

"Uh oh, that means they can see us if we get too near the window ... Here's the box I was telling you about." He pointed out the inscription: *Rudy Ruggles & Co.* "We'll take this back with us." Safi went to the kitchen to start bringing up the ledgers. She could only carry three at a time. When she put the last one on the shelf of the secret cupboard, she asked Bernard if he had found anything additional of interest. He said he hadn't, but she wanted to be sure that he had looked back in the corners that were hidden from sight.

"I can't see or feel anything." He smiled at her and took her hand. "That's a cold hand."

"It's freezing in here," Safi said.

"I'll just have to warm you up." He held her gently and then brought her to the side of the window so they could look out together. He told her that when he had first come into the room, he thought of it as a place where they could spend their honeymoon.

"So you were thinking of getting married back then?" Safi asked.

"Oh, yes."

How lovely, she thought. Then to their horror, they spotted

Marjorie walking up from the lake towards the house. They sprang into action, took down the props, pushed the wall back down into place, and replaced the cots next to the wall. They started down the first flight. Bernard put the box under his jacket, but it made an obvious bulge. They met Marjorie at the bottom of the front stairs. Safi stood in front of Bernard.

"Hi, Marjorie," Bernard said. "Safi and I were thinking that the front porch would be the obvious place for the wedding if it is raining. If we have to do that, we could store the porch furniture in the garage, couldn't we?"

"Oh sure," she answered.

"I was going to show Safi Aunt Mamie and Uncle Ed's bedroom here, but it's locked."

"Yes, in the fall, your aunt always locks it when she leaves the house for the last time."

"Do the other aunts do that?"

"No ... er ... you must have seen that they were open."

"Oh, yes, of course, stupid question."

"I just love Tree Top," Safi said.

"Yes, everybody does, until they reach the age of 55," Marjorie said smiling.

"How long have you and Freddy been living here?" Safi asked.

"Since 1915," Marjorie answered. "A mere 36 years."

"1915—So you never met CD or his brother Samuel?"

"No, I'm sorry I never met CD, because I loved Mrs. Peacock, Mary Ann, that is. But Samuel, I understand he was a real problem. I'm glad I missed him."

"I bet you're wondering why I'm so interested—it's because I worked on Mrs. Mercer's, or Aunt Let's, book that I really take an interest in the family members. I know CD died in his home in Chicago but where did Samuel die? I thought Samuel was living with CD at the end of his life."

"I don't know where he died, but I have noticed that people never talk about him."

"Really?"

"I'm sorry, but I don't know more about it."

"I don't imagine that there's anyone still living around here that knew the brothers?" Bernard commented smiling.

Marjorie thought and then replied, "Well actually I think maybe Old Man Bixler and his wife, they're getting up there now, but I think they knew both brothers. Old Man used to take them fishing I heard, to make a few bucks, you know."

"I was going to ask you if you'd think that either the Bixlers or Henshaws might be interested in putting up some of our friends during the wedding? I've never been to their farms, so I don't know if you would think that's a good idea or not."

"I go to their farms once or twice a year," Marjorie said. "The Bixler's place is a bit run-down but they are very nice people. They only have one bathroom and lots of dogs. Your friends would have to be dog lovers. The Henshaws are very fond of the Peacocks, at least the older generation was, but this younger group, Earl and Maggie, I'm not sure how they would respond to the request. They have quite a big working farm, you know."

"I thought we would offer to pay $10/person per night. Do you think that's fair?" Bernard asked.

"That sounds more than fair. Of course, Fred and I have friends that would be glad to help, but none are within walking distance. You know we can take two. Oh heck, at that time of year they can sleep on the porch, yes, we can take four ourselves."

"You're always more than generous," Bernard said appreciatively.

"Marjorie, you're terrific. We'd be so grateful if you could do that," said Safi.

The next morning Bernard and Safi drove to see both neighbors. They spent a good hour or two at the Bixlers. The old couple was delighted to have visitors. Old Man talked and talked, while Sarah, his wife, kept offering them things to eat. Safi saw that Bernie enjoyed chewing the fat as much as the oatmeal cookies. Safi, however, found it frustrating trying to keep the old couple on the subject. Yes, they both remembered CD and Samuel, but then they had something pressing to say about last year's pea crop. They were willing to have two or three guests.

The Henshaws were more sophisticated, but less willing to spend time talking with them. They'd never known CD or Samuel, but they would be willing to put up two guests. Bernard made sure he had the phone numbers and addresses of both neighbors so they could contact them nearer the time of the wedding.

They were just leaving the Henshaw's when the phone rang and Mrs. Henshaw came out on the porch to say that Old Man Bixler remembered something to tell them about Samuel. "He wants you to stop by again so he can let you know what it is."

Oh no, another hour's conversation with that guy, Safi thought. He'll probably forget what it was he wanted to tell us by the time we get there.

"Yeah, you know that man was a pyromaniac," Old Man Bixler said, "I think that's what they call them fellows—that like to light fires and watch them burn. I heard they sent him away to California to get rid of him. The story goes that when Samuel was here, they could never light a fire in the fireplace at Sugar Loaf. They couldn't take a chance. As soon as it got cold, my parents said, the family had to return home to Chicago because they couldn't use the fireplace."

When Bernard and Safi were back in their car and alone, Safi asked, "Had you ever heard that Samuel liked fire?"

"Never," Bernard answered.

CHAPTER 38

Neither Safi nor Bernard had ever even thrown a party, never mind a wedding. Some of their married friends said they were lucky in some respects because they could plan the wedding they wanted. "At least your wedding can reflect your values," some said. Of course everybody tried to help. Aunt Let's suggestions for drinks were far too fancy for their liking. They decided on apple cider and champagne. The cake had to be chocolate—both Safi and Bernard loved chocolate. The musicians were a local group from Dartford whose instruments were a hammered dulcimer, two violins, and a guitar. They asked Marjorie to prepare little cucumber, ham, and egg salad sandwiches. Letty advised that the bread be white, the crusts removed, and the sandwiches cut in quarters. It felt wonderful that everybody took such an interest. Bernie and Safi did not see any religious importance to the ceremony. They could easily simply make a vow to each other. The wedding was an excuse to bring family and friends together so they could share their happiness. They were certainly thankful that the aunts were letting them use Sugar Loaf—that would make it so special.

Safi announced she would not wear a traditional wedding dress, instead she hoped to find a simple A-line. That style could be dressy and remain simple. Only Bernard knew that she intended to find her dress in a second-hand shop, even though she knew Bernard could easily afford to buy her an expensive dress. They differed only in the amount of money they had access to, not on what money should be spent on.

When they got back from their week at Dartford Lake, they both became buried in their respective academic work. By the third week in

January, Bernard was finally able to track down the two men who had worked at Rudy Ruggles & Co. ten years before. He told them that he needed to know who ordered the box and when. He didn't explain that it was designed to hold jewels. The men said they would look into it and get back to him. That didn't happen for another month.

The box, they said, was ordered by CD Peacock. It wasn't clear if that meant CD Peacock the man or the store. But the date the order was placed was in the spring of 1893, the same year that the robbery was reported. According to the police report, the jewels had been purchased from the Duke of Hanover in 1888, several years before. Why wait so long to have a box designed to hold them? To Bernard, this was a further indication that the jewels were not purchased as a set.

Why did the family pretend that the jewels were bought together and why fake their robbery? And, as bad as faking a robbery was, it wouldn't warrant keeping the Hanover Collection hidden for almost 60 more years. It's not as though the store tried to collect insurance money for the robbery. Was the family afraid that a more thorough investigation might disclose either CD or Samuel as Leo's killer? Bernard thought that Safi was probably right when she said that the aunts didn't want any negative publicity before the sale of the store went through.

"That's as much as we'll ever know, unless the aunts are willing to tell us more," Bernard told Safi.

Safi agreed but then she said, "Why don't we ask Aunt Ella to lunch at the Pearson Hotel? She may just open up when the other aunts aren't around. In fact, she wanted to tell me something last summer that may have been important, but we were interrupted by someone or other."

"If we take one aunt out to lunch, we'll have to do it for the others," Bernard said. "But you're right, it just may lead to something."

The Pearson Hotel was a residential hotel and was inhabited mainly by wealthy elderly people who could afford to pay for nurses to come in the daylight hours. Some even paid for an additional room in the hotel for a butler who might double as a cook, or for a nurse to live there around-the-clock. Aunt Ella didn't need this help at present, now that Uncle Toby had died. She usually came down to the elegant dining room for her meals. Only when she was at Sugar Loaf did she like to cook. In Chicago, she lived alone. She had no interest in cooking for herself, especially when downstairs in the hotel's dining room she could eat beautifully prepared meals.

Safi and Bernard were to meet Aunt Ella in the lobby. It was an elegant room with walnut-paneled walls. A huge crystal chandelier hung from a center medallion, which complemented the plaster molding around the rim of the ceiling. Below the chandelier was a sizeable oval walnut table holding a vase with a generous bouquet of fresh flowers. Oriental rugs added color to the muted sunlight coming in from the arched windows facing Pearson Street.

Bernard and Safi watched the dial of the elevator as it descended from the sixth floor. Bernard wondered what Safi thought about all this opulence. He knew how observant she was, and often marveled at the details she picked up on that he never noticed. Perhaps even more impressive was her ability to remain emotionally detached. She took in information, but not for the purpose of being judgmental. She liked Aunt Ella as a respected friend and enjoyed her company as an equal. Of course, credit for their frank relationship should also be attributed to his aunt.

During the first two courses, the three of them chatted about the wedding plans. When dessert arrived, Ella wanted to know how Letty was doing. "Is she in any danger doing the work she's doing?"

"I don't think so," Safi explained. "Mainly she identifies someone who is repeatedly doing something suspicious and reports it to the police. The police then follow up and decide whether or not to act upon it. Officer Murphy, whom she's been in contact with for several years, told her recently that petty crime is decreasing at the corner of Clark and Division. Actually the best thing about all of this is that Aunt Let is venturing out, walking and discovering things about her neighborhood."

"But it's such a dangerous neighborhood, from what I hear."

"Well, she's comfortable doing it. The other day, she walked all the way to Newberry Library. She went in, did some research, and then walked home."

"You bet it's great for her," Bernard confirmed. "She's losing weight, too, don't you think, Safi?"

"Yes, I do," Safi answered.

Later on Safi changed the subject, "Do you remember last summer in the kitchen, when we were talking about why Aunt Let was at first reluctant to mention Elijah's second wife's name in her book? I believe you said that you had a theory about that, but then we got interrupted."

"Yes, I do, but it's just a theory." They were now having coffee and tea, and Aunt Ella got back to the topic. "I was told that my grandmother Rebecca died of tuberculosis, and towards the end, she was barely able to get out of bed. Elijah hired Mary Kolze to take care of her and their three children. Grandmother Mary had just recently emigrated from Germany. Of course I never knew Grandmother Rebecca, but she and Grandfather Elijah had three children. My father, CD, was the oldest. He was just 12 when Rebecca died. Caroline was eight, I guess, and Samuel around six. Mary must have had her hands full, and she hardly spoke a word of English. Of the three children, I think it was hardest for Father to lose his mother. Then when Grandfather married Mary two years later, I think Father became resentful that someone was trying to take his mother's place. Around that time it became apparent that Samuel, Father's brother, was difficult. Being the oldest of the three, perhaps Father was expected to keep Samuel in line. Actually Samuel was too much for anybody to deal with. Father may have wanted to blame someone for Samuel's behavior. I don't know the cause for sure, but I think Father blamed Mary for all of it. Then, Caroline died early. She only lived to age 15, as I remember.

"In a wider sense, this is often a problem that the most recent immigrants face. They are blamed. The first to arrive think they own the place and are resentful to have to share it with newcomers. But I'm digressing again.

"Getting back to Father, he was really just a child and didn't understand these things. Elijah and Mary started having children of their own and Father received less of their attention. Four years after they were married, Elijah and Mary moved the family to start a farm. Father was around 19 at that time. He was never interested in the farm. From then on, he devoted himself to the jewelry business, trying to take on more and more of the running of the store, maybe to compensate for the things he couldn't deal with on the farm. Samuel continued to be a problem."

"How was he a problem?" Bernard asked.

"He had what you might call a warped personality. From what I heard, he had no conscience."

"That must have made it even more difficult for Mary to cope," Safi said.

"Yes, indeed, but over the years, my grandparents, Elijah and Mary, were devoted to each other. Father married Mother in 1860, and they started living in Hyde Park. Samuel continued to live on Eijah's farm until he disappeared for several years late in 1871."

"The year of the fire?"

"Eh, yes. After the fire, Father had a new home built on Dearborn Street."

"How does that explain why Mrs. M, I mean Aunt Letty, didn't even mention Mary Kolze's name in the first draft of her book?"

"I think Letitia wasn't interested in the second family because Father ignored them. He felt that people with English backgrounds were superior, had more prestige. Father, I'm sorry to say, passed on that attitude to his children, to my brothers especially. Most of us have grown out of that way of thinking. Letitia would have too, I'm sure, but her husband went bankrupt and died. She lost her status, her money, and her husband all at once. The only thing she could still take pride in was the family. Lineage became unusually important to her."

"And Samuel," Bernard asked, "when did he show up again?

"About 15 years later, he started living with Grandfather and

Grandmother Mary again. He was very difficult, so he came to live with Father until we could take it no longer. Father had him committed to an asylum outside of Baltimore where, after a few years, he died."

They wound up the discussion. Aunt Ella thanked them for the lunch: "I haven't talked so much in years."

After they said good bye to Aunt Ella, they thought of several other things they should have asked her.

That night Safi called Bernard. "How do you feel about being related?" she asked.

"It's a little strange. Of course it used to happen that people married cousins who were much closer genetically than we are, and Aunt Let is right, there is no worry about our offspring," Bernard said.

Safi lowered her voice presumably so Aunt Letty wouldn't hear her: "I'm having a bit of a problem thinking about your great-grandfather possibly murdering my great-grandfather," She giggled.

"Oh my God, you're right. It's both funny and eerie. You don't know who to be loyal to," he chuckled.

"I can't figure out if Aunt Mamie's covering up for the fake jewel robbery or for the murder of Leo," Safi said.

"Or both," answered Bernard. "We ought to do what we can to solve this mystery, for our own piece of mind, if nothing else. I think I'll go down to police headquarters and look at those reports myself. Maybe something will occur to me."

CHAPTER 39

Bernard had only one hour at the police station. A good fifteen minutes was wasted with the forms he had to fill out. Finally he got down in front of Officer Feldman's homicide desk and asked for the Glitz murder case of 1893.

"What's happened? Has this Leo guy risen from the dead or something? Everybody cares now. They didn't in 1893, but now they do."

Bernard thought it might not hurt to solicit this policeman's help. "He's the great-grandfather of my fiancée. She's concerned that the case may not have been pursued adequately."

"It happens."

"May I ask you some questions after I read the report?"

"Sure. I'll do what I can. Of course we have certain constraints too," Feldman answered.

"Of course," Bernard said, as he started reading the report. Everything seemed to be just as Safi had told him. "That's a funny shape to the compressions on his head, you know, where Leo was clubbed. What kind of an instrument would cause that?"

"I have no idea," Feldman answered. "I do have one suggestion, though. Keep in mind that not all the key information was routinely included in the public reports. Often, detectives withhold certain important details or facts so that they can be used to positively identify the true killer. People have been known to falsely confess to crimes, you know, for any number of reasons. If someone is able to verify certain undisclosed facts about the crime during their confession, such as the murder weapon, we can feel more confident that they are the real perpetrator. This is a very old case, though, and I'm afraid some of the information may have been lost over time. The original investigators are no longer around to ask about these things, unfortunately." Bernard understood his point, thanked him for his time, and quickly left homicide to go over to the robberies division, as Safi had suggested.

When Safi read the report, she hadn't known about Leo's letters to CD nor his letter to Samuel. Knowing the contents of those letters, it seemed obvious that Leo's guesses were probably correct, that Samuel initiated faking the robbery and that CD went along with it, but reluctantly. Why was Samuel in a hurry to leave after calling the police, Bernard wondered?

After reading the report of the theft of the Hanover jewels, Bernard only had one question for Officer Waschewsky, who was behind the robbery desk: "What was the police department like in the 1890s?" Little did Bernard realize that Stefan Waschewsky was a man of numerous opinions who loved to talk.

"Oh my God, we only had about 3,000 men on the force then and the system was decentralized. The captain who ran a precinct would have been relatively independent of headquarters and he would have gotten the job from a politician. From what I've heard, there was no real training. You just went through a short apprenticeship, you might say. You'd have about 65 hours a week of patrol duty. Much of it was boring night patrol. We did have a signal service then so the patrolmen could call for an ambulance or patrol wagon.

"Another thing that most people don't realize is that in those days, policemen were concerned with more than just crime and violence. We had to control the traffic at bridges, help pedestrians cross streets, give directions to strangers, return lost children, report broken street lamps, and stop runaway horses—the lot. I bet you didn't know that in those days, thousands of homeless people slept in station houses every year? Now a lot of charities perform that function, like Hull House. Back then, the police force did social service work.

"I know you're wondering about corruption. Most of the city's political bosses were Irish. They tended to look after their own, so people put on the police force were also Irish."

"That's interesting. How likely is it that the police would have followed through in trying to solve a murder case in those days?" Bernard asked.

"To be honest, it all depended on who was murdered."

"If, for example, the victim had been arrested during the Haymarket Riot, you know, if he had been accused of being an anarchist or troublemaker and spent a couple of days in jail, do you think the police would have put much effort into finding his murderer?" asked Bernard.

"Oh boy, that was not our finest hour, but don't tell anyone I said so … ah, chances are, very little would have been done."

"And if he were a Jewish union activist who wrote for the leftist press, would much have been done to find his murderer?"

"Ach, sorry, the police in those days were paid by business people not to help folks like that. This is off the record, now. I will never say these things in court. But my God, in the 1890s—nah—who's going to care what I say about something that happened back then? OK, the truth is the police in those days were probably going to do nothing but write up a report about finding the body."

CHAPTER 40

Bernie's and Safi's wedding was scheduled for July 20, more than a week away, but by this time, most of the regulars had already gathered at Dartford Lake. Blair had brought his soulmate, Tom Hartley, who most of the family members knew was not just a friend. They couldn't sleep in the same room, none of the great-aunts would have allowed that, but in general, everybody was glad to have Tom at Sugar Loaf as he was fun, polite, and always looking to be helpful. Bernard knew that Freddy was probably the only one who might object to Tom's presence, but being an employee of the Peacocks', he had no say.

Cornelia and her five children were already there. Having a place where they could spend their summers and have meals made for them meant a lot to her. It was the perfect place for the children. They could be with their extended and loving family while they were safe to explore and have fun outdoors. It wasn't as perfect for Cornelia, because William had to stay down in Chicago to work in the store for most of the summer. But that is no loss for the rest of us, Bernard thought.

Letty's children, Stewart and Lucy, were due to arrive with their own children. Bernard was so looking forward to seeing them again. It had been at least three years since they last came to Chicago to see Aunt Let. They would be coming two days before the wedding. Bernard wondered how they would react to their mother now that she had changed so much. Stewart and Lucy were not in the habit of coming to Sugar Loaf. While their father had been alive, they went up for their summer holiday to the Mercer home in the apple orchards of Pepin County, Wisconsin. This upcoming reunion meant a lot to his aunt. He hoped it would go well for her.

Safi had four friends coming just the day before the wedding. One was from Loyola College and three from Hull House. Since they were all women, they were going to be put up at Marjorie and Freddy's. Bernard wanted to be sure that Safi had nearby space for her guests since she had so few of them. Easily ten to fifteen of Bernard's friends were coming. They had their own transportation so they were distributed to various nearby farms. Aunt Letty told everybody that there was a surprise guest coming. She refused to say anything more about it than that. All the aunts had been great. They had helped arrange for the food to be made, people to help serve it, and the drinks. Folding chairs were to be set up on the lawn facing the trellis over the path that led to the rose garden.

Aunt Mamie scheduled the jewel hunt a week before the wedding. Bernard and Safi thought that she wanted that business off her chest, once and for all. The last jewel was the ruby. At nine sharp the family gathered in the dining room. The clue was:

What's coming, paralleling Schiller?

When he read the clue, Blair first concentrated on the "paralleling Schiller." He knew Schiller was a German poet. In fact, he thought there was a book of Schiller's poems on a bookshelf in the living room. Maybe the ruby is between that book and another on the shelf. No, no, that would be too much like the hiding place for the emerald. He recalled that Letty lived on Schiller Street. But his thoughts went on to "what's coming." He couldn't get the idea of prediction out of his mind. He returned to "paralleling Schiller," maybe he could get some ideas if he knew what streets paralleled Letty's street. Would it be cheating if he looked at his map of Chicago? He went out to his car and found it in the trunk. The two streets on either side of Schiller were Burton and Goethe Streets. Of course the clue just said "paralleling." There were plenty of other streets that paralleled Schiller, like North Avenue. Hmm, but Goethe...isn't the barometer on the front porch known as a Goethe barometer? He returned to the screened-in porch and saw the barometer hanging on the wall. Attached to its base was the ruby. It was glued onto the blown glass container, but the colored water in the barometer was a deep red so the ruby did not stand out. "Got it. I've found it," he said excitedly.

Being single and the only child of Boots, Blair had no money worries. However he was well-liked, and now each branch of the family had found a jewel, so the others in the family were happy that it was Blair who found the ruby.

"Aunt Mamie," Cornelia asked at lunch, "Are you finally going to tell us the story behind these jewel hunts?"

Aunt Mamie smiled and took a deep breath. "I can do that today, if you would like," she said. "I'd prefer to tell you all at once." Everybody agreed that this was as good a time as any. It was decided that after lunch they would all settle in the living room. Cornelia's kids would be excused to go play. Mamie invited Tom to sit in on the discussion as well, if he wanted.

Once they were all in the sitting room, Aunt Mamie drew her chair in front of the fireplace so she could face everybody and began: "Well, you know CD, your grandfather or great-grandfather to some of you, died in 1903. On his deathbed he told me the following story. Perhaps I should remind you that CD's sister died when she was fifteen, but his brother died only two years before CD. Samuel was his name."

"Well, to get to the story about the jewels: just as the store was closing one evening in 1893, Samuel put in a call to the police and claimed that the store had become aware that a valuable set of jewels was missing. Samuel told the police that the set was known as the Hanover Collection and it was last seen in the viewing room. Now the set was gone. When the police came to the store, CD did his best to down-play the issue."

"You mean, Aunt Mamie, that Grandfather knew right away that there were no jewels stolen?" asked Letty.

"Yes, Samuel had fabricated the entire story, but Father thought it best not to let the police know that Samuel was crazy, as that would bring such bad publicity to the store. With just the robbery reported in newspapers, it wouldn't affect business, but if the Peacock brothers were seen disputing, or if one was revealed as a crazy liar, the store could lose its fine reputation.

"The police left and reported what Samuel had already told them, that CD had purchased the five jewels from the Duke of Hanover in 1888. The jewels were loose gemstones of different types and were known collectively as the Hanover Collection. The police left with the exact description of the gemstones and it was all written up in the newspapers. Father's strategy was just to lay low, and perhaps the public and police would forget about the robbery.

"Well, years later, when Father died, he asked me to take those five jewels and somehow distribute them to his descendents without anybody knowing that they were the Hanover jewels. He suggested that I put off the distribution for as long as possible. And now, decades later, I'm so glad that all the branches of descendents have benefited from his gift."

"Why didn't you just give them out—one to each branch of the family?" Letty asked.

"Because I was afraid people would think I was playing favorites. As you know they aren't all of equal value."

"Did CD say anything to you, Aunt Mamie, about his brother-in-law Leo Glitz?" Bernard asked.

"When Samuel died, I found out that Leo had suspected him of fabricating the robbery. I discovered a letter that Leo wrote to Samuel threatening to take him to the police if he caused any more trouble for Peacock's."

Bernard started to feel uneasy that he and Safi knew things that Aunt Mamie didn't know they knew. He felt it was wrong to be tricking her into admitting things, so he was glad when Safi openly stated: "Aunt Mamie, Bernard and I know that Samuel died in an asylum, but please tell us the circumstances surrounding his commitment?"

"How do you know that?" Cornelia asked looking at Safi with suspicion. Bernard noticed that Aunt Mamie had turned pale. She looked at both Boots and Ella.

Bernard jumped in to answer Corny's question for Safi. He didn't want her to receive the brunt of the criticism, since he and Aunt Let had initiated most of the snooping. "We've found considerable evidence not only that the robbery was faked, but also that CD and Safi's great-grandfather Leo Glitz were communicating at the time Leo mysteriously died."

"We should tell you that we've read the police report about the robbery." Safi added. "You see, there is a mystery concerning Leo Glitz's death. He quite possibly was murdered. Leo thought the robbery was faked and that Samuel had gotten CD into that mess. It is possible that either Samuel or CD killed Leo."

"Not Father! He wouldn't do such a thing. Samuel, on the other hand, we were never sure what Samuel would do. He was a constant worry," Aunt Mamie admitted.

"This has worried me, too," Letty interrupted, "It could appear that a Peacock was in some way responsible for Leo's death."

Aunt Ella spoke for the first time. "You have to understand—the family, Father, Mother, Grandfather, and Grandmother Mary, they all knew quite early on that Samuel was mentally ill. But what could they do about it? That was our problem. Even as late as the 1880s, people with mental illness were treated as lunatics. They were committed and were treated cruelly. They could be chained or kept in cages. Right after Leo was killed, Father finally found an asylum outside of Baltimore where they offered therapeutic treatment. The staff was compassionate. All the patients were guaranteed privacy, sunlight, and fresh air."

Boots verified that their father had committed Samuel soon after Leo died.

Safi asked: "Why didn't you have the police pursue Leo's murderer? After all, he was a relation too. If Samuel were guilty, he should have been brought to justice."

Boots answered, "Well, it was like this—the night Leo died, Father had gone to Bughouse Square to meet him, but when Father arrived, the police were already there trying to figure out the identity of a dead man. Father wasn't able to positively identify the dead body as Leo Glitz. His face was completely distorted. All he could do was tell the police that the dead man may be Leo Glitz, but there was nothing to verfiy that. His wallet was gone."

"Did CD commit Samuel because he thought Samuel had killed Leo?"

"It's possible," Boots said meekly. "He knew Samuel was capable of doing terrible things...."

"But if Samuel had done this awful act, why not let the police go ahead and investigate him as a possible murderer?" Safi asked again. The aunts remained silent.

Bernard broke the silence saying: "What about the other possible explanation of how the man found in Bughouse Square was killed?" All eyes were on Bernard as he told about the newspaper article Safi had found, mentioning the possibility that a runaway horse may have kicked the man's face. "The victim may have tried to catch the horse. In the process, he may have tripped. If he fell down, the horse may have trampled him. When we studied the police report about the man who was found dead, it said that his head wounds were wide and U-shaped. That could have been caused by a horse's shoe," Bernard explained. "But the police must have discounted that possibility, because their final report classified his death as a homicide, for some reason, not an accident."

"You studied the police report about Leo's murder?" Boots asked.

"Yes," Safi said, looking at the aunts unapologetically, "It is an unsolved murder case involving my great-grandfather. I was curious." Again there was silence. "I take it you didn't know anything about the runaway horse story then, did you? So I still don't understand why CD didn't tell the police about Samuel." The aunts looked down.

"Was there another reason?" Bernard asked.

"Could it have to do with the fact that Samuel was a pyromaniac?"

Letty asked. "I remember when I was a very small child—Charles do you remember this? You got into trouble for saying something about how lovely it was that we could have fires again in the fireplace. We were here at Sugar Loaf at the time. Do you remember saying that, Charles?"

"Yes, that's right," Charles confirmed. "Boots, you got so mad at me." The aunts were still quiet.

An idea flashed in Bernard's mind. After a minute of deep thought, he suddenly asked the aunts: "Did Uncle Samuel burn his hand?"

"Yes, his left hand was horribly burned. It was nasty, quite disfigured."

"So when the police came to the store the night Samuel reported the robbery, he wore one glove, carried the other in his hand, and had his coat draped over his arm like he was about to leave for the day and go home." A heavy silence fell over the whole group.

"Oh dear," Aunt Mamie said, "I guess we're finally going to have to tell you, but this is such a disgrace, you can't ever tell other people. We'd hoped that this would remain a secret forever." She looked at the other aunts, then took a deep breath. "We were afraid that Samuel started the fire."

"The fire?" someone asked.

"What fire?" another relative inquired.

"Do you mean the Chicago fire, the one in 1871? Oh, not that—please tell me you're joking—not our family responsible for that! Oh my God!" Charles exclaimed.

"You see, Samuel disappeared the night of the fire. When he came back home, his left hand was severely burned. He knew that Elijah had just bought the fire-proof vault. At least he didn't want CD Peacock's to burn. When he was at home, he had to be watched all the time, but that night he got out." Aunt Mamie started to cry. "Three hundred people died. A third of the city burned. We felt sure that he had something to do with it. Father started to commit him, but before the arrangements were completed, he ran way again. We hired Pinkertons to find him.

They looked for two years, but they never found him."

"Maybe we should start from the very beginning. Samuel had run away before, several times," Ella explained. "At the beginning of the Civil War, he ran away and joined the Union army. Father and Grandfather thought he did it so he could see the fires at the battle front. We know he went on Sherman's March to the Sea, because Father said when he returned home, he talked about it all the time.

"After the Chicago fire he ran away. We never saw or heard from him again until he showed up one day in February in 1885, I think it was. We had to keep watch over him continually. We took turns. We locked him in his room at night so we didn't have to worry about what he did while the family slept.

"The funny thing about Samuel was that he cared about the store," Ella continued. "He wanted the store to do well. Grandfather thought he purposely started the fire after he knew the Peacock's valuables were safe in a fire-proof vault. In a strange way, he wanted to protect the family from the consequences of his insane acts, I think."

Mamie explained that Elijah had originally asked their father to hire Samuel to work in the store. "Grandfather was convinced that Samuel wouldn't harm the store. The plan seemed to work."

"Didn't people want to know about his hand?" Safi asked.

"Yes, the few employees who knew him did want to know," Boots said, "but Samuel was purposely kept in the mailroom where he wasn't on display. He was known as just Samuel. We had one trusted employee down there who always kept an eye on him."

"This seemed to work until the robbery," Mamie said.

"Yes Samuel's reason for reporting a robbery followed the same pattern," Boots added. "When the police left, he tried to convince Father that all the publicity that the store obtained from the robbery would enable Father to sell the gems for a higher price. He thought he was doing Father a favor, you see."

"So let me see if I understand this all correctly," Safi said. "If the man killed in Bughouse Square was Leo Glitz, he was either trampled by a runaway horse or he was murdered. If it was not an accident, and the man who was trampled was not Leo, he could have been killed elsewhere and his body just left in Bughouse Square later. I seemed to remember that, at the time, the newspapers reported a fire at the World's Fair on the same day."

"That's right," said Boots. The other aunts nodded in agreement.

Safi went on: "The fire broke out in the Cold Storage Building, where there was also a skating rink. The article said that Leo Glitz was known to be a volunteer fireman, and had gone to the ice rink there to skate that day."

"Yes, yes, he was a fireman," the aunts said.

Safi continued: "Another fireman who was there claimed to have seen Leo trying to put out the fire. But Leo was not among the firemen who survived, nor was his body found among the seventeen dead firemen recovered afterwards."

"What are you driving at?" asked Boots.

"Is it possible that Samuel also started the Cold Storage fire? If Leo was there, and saw him, maybe Samuel had to kill him to keep him quiet about that, and the fake jewel theft was not the reason for Leo's death at all."

All the aunts gasped in unison. "Oh no," moaned Mamie, "I hope to God that is not what happened.…"

"That makes some sense, in a lot of ways," Letty said. "It is a stronger motive for murder than just threatening to turn Samuel in for faking a jewel heist. In the confusion of the fire, Sam could have carried Leo's body out of the building, like he was rescuing someone, and even transported it down to Bughouse Square, and no one would have thought anything of it. He could have even staged the trampling incident somehow, to make it look like an accident.… But this all happened so long ago, we will probably never know exactly what happened.…"

Bernard was still puzzled, though. "Why," he asked, "would Great-granddad go to the trouble of building a secret cupboard in Tree Top just to hide the ledgers?"

"What?"

"What are you talking about?"

"Secret cupboard!?"

"In Tree Top?!"

"I'm sorry," Bernard apologized, "we should tell all of you about the ledgers that CD kept hidden away because they could be used as proof that the Hanover Collection jewels were not purchased as a set. Each stone was purchased at a different time over the years."

"Secret cupboard? What are you talking about?"

"None of you know about it?" Bernard asked.

"In Tree Top? I've been coming here for 20 years. There's no secret cupboard."

"Yes there is—do you want us to show you?"

"Yes," was the universal answer.

"We should all see this together. We will wait up there until you all can get up the two flights of stairs."

"I could get up there anytime to see this," Mamie said.

Bernard and Safi moved the cots and stacked them one on top of another to allow space for everyone to fit into the room.

"I've always loved this room," said Boots. "This might be the only good thing that Samuel ever did."

"Samuel?" Safi asked.

"Oh yes, Samuel was quite a carpenter and an amateur scientist. He was crazy but intelligent," Boots answered.

"You mean to tell me that Samuel built this room?" Bernard asked.

"Yes, that's right. He adored CD. He would do anything for him," Ella said. "He wouldn't let anybody up here until he'd finished it."

Letty asked: "And when did he finish building the room?"

It was Mamie that practically whispered her answer: "1893."

"When?" shouted Ed.

"1893," someone shouted back.

Bernard pressed at the top and a panel of the wall swung open.

Everybody gasped while he propped it up on the sticks.

"Here are the ledgers." Bernard went through the same explanation that he had given Safi about how the jewels weren't purchased as a set.

"All this to hide the ledgers?" Letty said. "No, there must be more to it." She went to the wall and tapped below the shelves. "I bet this lower part opens, too." She and Bernard pressed and pulled. Their instinct was to press at the top of the lower section, but eventually they found that the inside panel covering the lower section was hinged at the bottom so that the inner panel folded down into the room.

"This is awkward because once opened, you can't get at the shelves very easily. Maybe it was intended not to be opened very often? It appears that there is a tall drawer in this lower section. Look, these small handles are recessed, but can come out. I may need help. No, maybe not," Letty said as she fiddled with the drawer.

"Oh, no, I don't like this," Safi said.

"Make sure the kids don't come up here," Cornelia said.

Letty pulled out the drawer. Inside were a pair of ice skates, a rusty old horseshoe, and a wallet.

"Oh my God!"

"Jesus! The horseshoe has dried blood on it."

"*Oy, gevald!*"

"Oh Safi dear," Aunt Ella said. "I'm so sorry. Those look like Leo's skates."

Safi picked up the wallet, unfolded it, and read the name "Leo Glitz."

"Do you think Samuel built the drawer for this purpose in advance?" Letty asked.

"He must have. The whole room was Sam's doing," Boots said.

Four days later, friends and more relatives started gathering for the wedding. Safi noticed there was considerable whispering going on. When she caught people at it she asked them: "What are you giggling about? OK, what's going on?" They stopped and smiled at her. She knew they were not being critical, so she didn't feel threatened, but she couldn't figure out what they were possibly talking about in such secrecy. Bernard was also involved in it. She had never seen the family so happy. They were bubbling over with enthusiasm, no matter what the task at hand.

It wasn't as if everything was beautifully planned. On the day of the wedding, she and Bernard realized that there were only half the chairs needed to seat everybody outside. Aunt Letty had left her shawl in Chicago by mistake. It went with her dress. She had to wear a hand-crocheted thing that Marjorie offered her. Its white cotton fabric did nothing for her blue brocade dress, but she wasn't complaining. When Boots discovered that the deer had munched on some of her prize pink roses, she simply said: "Oh well."

The day was a little chilly and damp, unusual for July. The ground was soggy enough that the women's heels sank in. It was a good thing that they had planned to have the dancing on the porch. Bernard, Blair, Tom, and Freddy had cleared out all the furniture and put it in the garage the night before.

Aunt Ella had kept the others out of the kitchen while she made the cake, but yesterday she let Safi in so she could talk with her alone.

"You know," Ella said, "Samuel did one thing for me. I was about eleven years old when he showed up again. Wherever we were, at

Elijah's farm, Sugar Loaf, or our home in Chicago, if Samuel was with us, I was the one designated to watch the kitchen. We couldn't take the chance to let Samuel be alone in the kitchen because we always had a fire going in the stove. To pass the time, I started to cook. I was twelve when I cooked my first entire meal for the family. Gradually, cooking became something I enjoyed doing."

That same morning, Safi had the rare opportunity to speak to Boots. She had to admit that Boots was the only relative she still felt uncomfortable talking to. She was as relaxed as a private would be chewing the fat with a major general. Aunt Bertha's straight posture and formidable chest exuded power. But Safi was surprised when Boots told her: "You know, your great-grandfather was quite a man. He didn't mince words. He spoke directly and said exactly what he thought. I admired him for that."

"You mean Leo Glitz?" Safi asked.

"Of course I mean Leo Glitz," Boots said with an edge of impatience.

Boots was right, her question had been superfluous, but no one who knew Leo had ever talked to her about him before.

"And I'll tell you something else—Leo was a brave man. His political views were quite strange, but I have to say he was courageous."

By this time the entire family knew about the secret cupboard and had read Leo's letters to CD. They were flabbergasted that, for all these years, they had never noticed the slight asymmetry of Tree Top.

"Many are the times I stood on the roof of that extension to trim trees," Freddy said. "I never knew what was right under my feet."

Two days later, at the lunch table with everybody present, Aunt Mamie offered to let Aunt Let see the contents of Elijah's trunk. "You might as well see what's there now. You already know everything about Samuel."

Letty was embarrassed and she hesitated a long time before answering. Safi could tell that she was considering her options. She didn't want her aunt to know how sneaky she had been, but on the other hand, if she pretended she had no idea what was in the trunk, she couldn't reveal her cleverness in finding its key. Safi was not surprised when Letty chose to fan her feathers. She told Aunt Mamie in front of everybody just how she had discovered where the key was. In the disclosure she divulged Bernard's assistance with the sleepwalking cover-up. "Yes, I have already seen everything in the trunk."

"What!" At first Aunt Mamie was upset with her niece's slyness. "At 59 years old, you shouldn't be pulling the pranks of a fourteen-year-old," she said. But after a day or two, Aunt Mamie and the others expressed their amazement at Letty's and Bernard's detective work. Both had moved up a notch in their estimation.

"I don't approve of your sneakiness, but to be frank, I am glad this has all come out in the open. You know, I feel that a heavy weight of shame has been lifted," Aunt Mamie said finally.

Safi hated to be ungrateful for all her good fortune. She so loved Bernard and found his extended family charming, but there were still many questions that nagged at her about the "second family." She wouldn't pursue this now, but someday she wanted to know the answers.

Three hours before the wedding was to start, a green sports car drove into the driveway. Bernard spotted it right away: "Oh brother! It's an MG TD—spiffy or what?!" After a moment's hesitation, he called out: "Aunt Let, Aunt Let."

The car was so small it could easily fit on the side of the road without blocking other cars. A tall, overweight man stepped out. He was dressed in what appeared to be suit trousers, but his white shirt with partially rolled-up sleeves and loosened tie gave him a relaxed appearance. He had dark eyes and hair. His nose was large and pointed. "Hello, I am GG Gordon," he said. "Is Letitia Mercer here?"

Safi said: "Hello, sure, I'll go get her." This was exciting! Safi had no idea why he was here but she definitely knew who he was—the senior vice president of the company that was interested in buying CD Peacock's. Was that what all the whispering was about? If so, why didn't they let her in on the secret?

Aunt Letty came out displaying that peculiar smile that indicated to Safi that she wanted to impress someone. "Oh, hello, Mr. Gordon. We are so glad you could come. Safi, I want you to meet GG Gordon."

"How do you do?" Safi replied immediately.

"I am just fine, Sapphira."

Safi gasped. How did he know her name? Why was everybody smiling and looking at her? GG ended her quandary by saying: "I'm your cousin, Safi. Mrs. Mercer here found me and told me that you were getting married. I hope you don't mind if I come to your wedding."

Safi burst out crying. She managed to blubber some question that sounded like: "Cousin, my cousin? How are we related?"

Before he could answer, Aunt Letty ran off saying: "I'll get your wedding present." Safi had never seen her so excited. She disappeared into the house.

"I'm Bernard Peacock, GG, the groom-to-be—'to-be' for three more hours, anyway," Bernie said with a giggle.

By this time all the aunts, Charles, and Gertrude had come out to meet GG. Bernard noticed that Cornelia, Blair, Tom, and William, were also coming. Walter came up from the lake and finally, Marjorie and Freddy came out of their house. Some other friends who had come up to Dartford Lake from Chicago for the wedding came over to where they all were standing on the cement walk that connected the parking area to the house right outside the trunk room. As Aunt Let returned with her wedding present, Bernard asked: "Mr. Gordon, please tell us about your name. Why do they call you GG?"

"Well, my parents wanted to name me after my grandfather, whose first name was Gordon, but my father's last name was also Gordon, so they used my grandfather's last name, which also started with a G, to separate the two Gordons. My initials are actually GGG."

"What's the middle G stand for?" Bernard persisted.

"Oh, I forgot to say—it's Glitz. I'm formally Gordon Glitz Gordon, but everyone has always called me GG Gordon."

"I love the 'Glitz,'" Safi said, smiling at him through a veil of tears. "Are you married? Do you have children?"

"I'm not married yet, but I think I may be by the end of the year," GG answered with a twinkle in his eye.

"But are you the same GG Gordon that wrote us from the Dayton Hudson Company in Minneapolis?" Cornelia asked.

"The very same."

"And you want to buy CD Peacock's?"

"Cornelia!" Aunt Mamie said.

"I do, but I haven't gotten Dayton Hudson to agree yet. I'm just the senior vice president," GG replied quickly.

Safi noticed many in the family started looking quite nervous, but she couldn't help herself, she had to ask: "Why?"

"Safi," Aunt Ella admonished.

"Really, Safi," Boots said. "This is not the time or place for this discussion."

Gordon looked Safi straight in the eye and said: "It's a long story and has to do with a skating contest. Let's just say I'd like to keep the store in the extended family where it belongs," was his cryptic answer. "If Dayton buys it, I think I can get them to keep the store's name as Peacock's."

Safi noticed he didn't say "CD Peacock's."

"So you've known for a long time that you were related to the Peacocks?" Aunt Letty asked.

"Oh yes."

"I wish you'd contacted us before this, ..." Aunt Let stopped short of completing her thought. Safi knew her aunt was feeling the sting from Gordon's cold stare. Her aunt sighed and turned to give her wedding present to Safi and Bernard. "Please open this now." It was elegantly wrapped in CD Peacock's gift paper. Tearing the package open they found inside a framed drawing of the Peacock family tree, hand-lettered in beautiful calligraphy. Safi wondered why it was called a tree, when it appeared more like the root system of a tree. Then she realized if it was inverted, it would indeed look like a tree. She and Bernard looked it over carefully and gave Aunt Let a big hug. Bernard passed it first to GG Gordon, intending to have it passed to everyone there, saying: "Isn't it wonderful to see how we are all connected?"

Several minutes later, the family tree had returned to Safi's hands. She looked up at Letty and said, "I have to learn who my other three great-grandmothers are and their maiden names." She couldn't keep herself from turning to look at Boots. "Only then will I become a lady."

PEACOCK FAMILY TREE

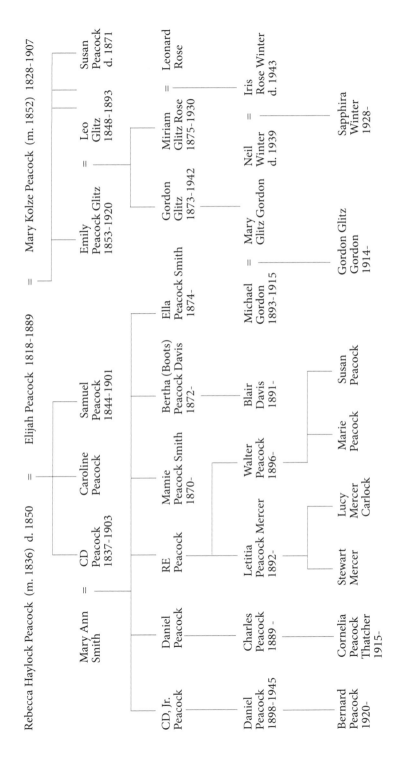

Acknowledgements

Cleaver, Charles; *History of Chicago from 1833 to 1992*; published by the author; 1992

Colton, Dorothy Peacock; *One's Family, (A Family Journal)*; published by the author; 1947

Davis, Bertha Peacock; *Sugar Loaf*; published by the author; circa 1940

Gnewuch, Thomas; editor, *Green Lake Memories: 1847-1997*; published by the author; 1997

Heiple, Robert W. and Emma B.; *A Heritage History of Beautiful Green Lake Wisconsin*; McMillan Printing Company; Ripon, Wisconsin; 1978

Mayer, Harold M. and Wade, Richard C.; *Chicago, Growth of a Metropolis*; The University of Chicago Press; 1969

Miller, Donald L.; *City of the Century, The Epic of Chicago and the Making of America*; Simon & Schuster Paperbacks; New York, NY; 1996

Spinney, Robert G.; *City of Big Shoulders, A history of Chicago*; Northern Illinois University Press; DeKalb, Illinois; 2000

Special thanks to my publishers, Plowshare Media, who have patiently offered advice, corrections, and boundless enthusiasm for my book.

About the Author

The Near North Side of Chicago was home for Pamelia Barratt until 1960. She graduated from the Chicago Latin School and Smith College. Barratt taught high school chemistry before becoming a journalist in San Diego, California. *An Ostentation* is her second novel. She is also the author of *Blood the Color of Cranberries*. Both books are historical mysteries. Her website can be found at http://pameliabarratt.com.

7514789R0

Made in the USA
Charleston, SC
13 March 2011